LIE FOR ME

Mick Bose

For Mum and Dad

CHAPTER 1

I wake up to the sound of police sirens. It's an unusual sound in our quiet and peaceful neighbourhood. There might be an occasional beep from a car horn as one of the mums gets frustrated during school drop-off traffic, but police sirens? In Richmond, West London, they're as alien as snowflakes in the desert.

I lie awake in bed, listening to the sirens wailing as they fade. Where are they headed? The sound persists for a long time, seeping into the walls of houses. I look at Jeremy's sleeping form next to me, his back curved, vertebrae on his spine outlined like beads in a garland. For a moment I think of snuggling up to him, especially as Molly is still in bed.

But the police siren has made me restless. My shoulders are tense, and my heart beats faster. I pad over to the bay window and peek out from the curtain. Empty, apart from Mr Mountbatten who jogs past, back from his early morning run on Wimbledon Common. Cars are parked in driveways, soon to be boarded by raucous children and rushing parents. I look at the red numbers on the digital phone. 6:10 am. Stifling a yawn, I try to get back into bed and close my eyes. Jeremy stirs, but doesn't wake up.

My eyes are closed, but my mind is full of strange thoughts, half-repressed memories. I can't make sense of them, and I don't want to either. This strange state of suspension, half-numb, half-alive, is not one I like. My body still wants to remain in the bed, warmed by Jeremy. If he wakes up, I know I will, too, and one thing will lead to another. But he sleeps with his mouth half-open, almost snoring. So much for that.

Sighing, I lift myself off the bed, and put on my fluffy Peppa Pig slippers, bought by Molly last year for Mother's Day. Well, bought by Jeremy, but apparently it was Molly's wish. I love how snug and warm they feel, especially on this chilly winter's morning. I go to the loo, then pad downstairs and turn the heating on. The kitchen is quite a mess, despite there being only three of us in the house. After Molly came back from school last night, she dumped all her stuff in the hallway by the front door. I look at myself in the mirror as I bend down to pick up her stuff. My coppery-red hair is getting longer, and needs a trim. There are shadows under my eyes, and I look every bit a mother who could do with an extra hour in bed. I would've as well, if it hadn't been for that bloody police car.

As I pick up Molly's gym bag, trainers, hockey stick and scrapbook, I can't help but wonder what the police were in such a rush about. Something must have happened nearby. I hope all of Molly's school friends and their families are safe.

It's 6.45 by the time Jeremy comes down. Jeremy is six-one, rangy, with a thin but muscular build. His dark hair is closely cut, and his hazel eyes twinkle as he hugs me.

"Where were you this morning?" he asks, pecking me on the lips.

"Didn't you hear the police siren?" Unwelcome thoughts rise up like a shadow in my head, and I turn away so he can't see the expression on my face.

He shrugs, and starts to make his coffee. Jeremy is a solicitor at a local law firm. We met four years ago when he moved down here from the South Coast. We met at a bar in Wimbledon, and have been together since. Molly and he hit it off from the start, although she was only four when they met.

I didn't want Molly to meet, or know, her real dad. Ever.

When Jeremy proposed to me last year, it was the biggest moment of my life. After everything I had been through, I never thought I would be this happy ever again. Jeremy is my rock. Steady, dependable, trustworthy. I had no problems saying yes. We had a small registry marriage with a few friends and my dad.

As we get ready, I can't shake the feeling of unease in my veins. The street seems quiet outside the window, trees bending in a slight wind. The police sirens mean something has happened close by. A crime has occurred in our neighbourhood, and it could be serious. There was more than one squad car, I could tell by the sound.

Were they chasing someone? I flip out my phone and scroll through local news. Nothing as yet. An odd premonition of danger has gripped me and I can't shake it off. My breathing is faster, and strange thoughts flutter in my head.

I don't know why, but I feel something awful is about to happen.

CHAPTER 2

Molly is up and dressed soon, and by 8.00, we are out of the door. Jeremy kisses us goodbye as he heads off to work. We get into my Audi A4 Estate and drive off towards school.

Traffic is heavy as we get closer to school, coming to a standstill as we reach the school road.

Eventually, we park and get to the school gates. We have been at this school for four months only. This is a better school than the one closer to our house, with much better Ofsted ratings. Molly was bullied at her last school, and it was painful for both of us.

Crofton High is a grammar school, and bullying is almost non-existent.

Among the gaggle of mothers waiting with their children in the schoolyard, I spot Eva and her daughter, Charlotte. Eva and I have known each other since high school, and we are very close.

"Horrible news at the hospital," Eva says, shaking her head. She scrutinises my face. "That's what the police sirens were about."

"How did you know?" I am amazed.

"Word travels fast around here. Lorna told me." She points to one of the mums in the distance whom I don't know very well.

"So, what happened?" I ask, suddenly curious.

Eva's voice drops a notch and her face darkens. "A baby is missing from the labour ward of the hospital. It's already been on Facebook and Twitter. Someone snatched a baby. Can you imagine?"

I can feel Eva's eyes on my face, but I'm not listening anymore. A cold, numb fear is spreading like ice in my veins. Like a gravestone being pulled aside, malevolent thoughts rear up inside my brain, casting long, toxic shadows. Shadows that grip me mercilessly when I am weak. Like now.

"Emma…Emma…are you OK?"

I become aware that Eva is speaking to me. I snap back into reality, the

4

cold vapours from my mouth suddenly dispelling, clearing the mist from my mind.

For a second there, I lost myself.

"Yes. Yes, I'm good," I try to force a smile on my face, but my best friend can see through it. But she doesn't know the half of it. She never will either. There are things I will take to my grave with me.

"You look like you've seen a ghost," Eva is watching me carefully. "Everything alright?"

I try a non-committal shrug and fail. "It's just awful news, isn't it? Don't expect it to happen around here."

"Hmm." Eva doesn't look convinced. Molly distracts me, barging into me from behind, giggling wildly.

"It's time to go in, Mummy," she says. I give her a hug and peck on the cheek, and watch her go in with the other children.

"Shall we go for coffee?" Eva says, swinging her handbag over her shoulder.

I check my watch. I am an artist, and I sell my paintings on the internet. I have to meet a gallery owner today about an exhibition.

But for some reason, I am loath to be on my own. The grey sky seems to have settled on my shoulders like a heavy but invisible weight. Fingers are reaching inside my eyes, poking out old, bitter memories. I am afraid, and I look around myself at the sea of faces in the schoolyard, spilling out into the road. Mostly mothers, talking to each other, dispersing back to their homes. No one threatening, but I feel lonely and lost in this crowd. I scan the faces, my eyes jerking around, looking for…what?

I don't know. But I don't want to be alone.

Powerful Range Rovers and flashy four by fours are being fired up, the engine sounds erupting like gunshots inside my skull. Quickly, I turn to Eva. She is looking at me with a puzzled expression again, and I know I am acting weird.

"Yes, sure," I say. "Let's go for coffee."

CHAPTER 3

I sit in Starbucks, and curl my fingers around the tall cup of mocha. I insisted we sit upstairs, where it is quieter, and more importantly, I can keep an eye on who is coming up the stairs. There is a bathroom here, and I can hide there if need be. I stop myself. Why am I being like this? Panicked, fingers shaking…I take a deep breath and calm myself.

Eva takes her phone out from her Michael Kors handbag, and puts it on the table. Then she takes a sip of her cappuccino and gazes at me.

"What's going on?"

"Nothing."

She sighs. "Come on, spill."

Eva has known me since we were sixteen. We became friends at senior school, and did our A levels together. Although we went to different universities, we got jobs at the same place in the city, and have been in touch ever since.

Looking at Eva now, I remember the abstract landscape I gave her for her birthday last year, and smile.

"I'm OK, don't worry. Just got shocked hearing that awful news, that's all." I am glad that Eva is here, and I can lean on her for company. The mocha feels hot and nourishing as it slides down my throat.

"How are you?" I change the topic.

"Great. Simon's got a promotion. He's over the moon. It just means longer hours for him." She sighs.

Eva is married to Simon. Like many of the men here, he works in the city as well. One of those faceless, dark-suited men who rush around Canary Wharf looking stressed.

I smile, genuinely happy for her. "That's good news, right? Not the long working hours bit, but I guess he doesn't have a choice in it, does he?"

Eva shakes her head. "Nope. He loves it as well. But he comes back early on Friday, and in the weekends he's always there."

I nod. I have seen Simon doing Friday evening pick-up. I force myself to smile blandly at him. He always stops and tries to make conversation, I am pleasant to him for Eva's sake.

We spend some time talking about the children. But my mind is still on the baby-snatching incident at the hospital.

"Do we know who the mother was?" I ask, keeping my voice casual.

"Yes, a woman called Suzy Elliot. Her elder daughter is in Year 3 so you might not know her. Name's Lisa."

I think for a while but the name doesn't ring a bell.

Eva says, "Hospitals have CCTV everywhere. Surely they will catch the person, won't they?"

"Yes, of course," I say, draining the rest of my coffee. I wonder how Eva will respond to my next question, but I don't know if I don't try. I am thinking about Suzy, and every time I do, a sense of anguish cloaks my heart.

"Shall we go and see Suzy Elliot?"

Eva looks surprised, then her expression softens. "Not sure if she's still in hospital."

"Any sign of the baby yet?"

Eva shakes her head. "Not that I have heard."

I nod. I haven't seen anything in the news or on TV, and I know Eva knows all of the mums in our year at school.

She looks curiously at me. "Why do you want to see her?"

I hide my real reason. "It's a tragedy, isn't it? She needs all the support she can get. I mean, if she doesn't want to see anyone I can understand. But we should try and say hello. The police are involved, aren't they?"

"Yes. I don't know the latest from them. But I guess they're in touch with her."

I ring the hospital and find out that she has been discharged. I ask Eva, "She's gone home, so do you reckon we can ring her?"

Eva shrugs. "Can't see why not. I know her so let me try."

"Only if you think we wouldn't be intruding. I can imagine that she wants to be left alone."

"True. But on the other hand, think how lonely she must be feeling right now. Some company would do her good, especially if her husband's at work."

I nod in agreement. Eva rings her. She talks for a while, and I settle the bill.

Eva hangs up and says, "Her husband's not at home. Poor thing, she sounds so flat. Yes, we can go around this afternoon, before pick-up."

*****

Suzy Elliot lives in a terraced house similar to mine. Two up and two down, in a street of terraced houses, opposite the railway station. The houses are pleasant, several have ivy creeper growing over the front walls. Both of us have driven as we have to go to school after this. I have bought a bouquet of flowers and a card which I carry as Eva knocks on the door. After what seems like a long wait a pale-faced woman opens the door. I don't recognise her. Eva gives her a hug, and she looks me up and down. She is in her early thirties, I guess, with shoulder-length, brown hair. She looks haggard, and her eyes are red-rimmed, sunk in the hollows. I cannot imagine what she is going through.

I go to shake her hand, then end up giving her a hug. She doesn't mind, and I can feel how frail she is. Tears glisten in her eyes as she tries to smile at me, and shuts the door. We walk down the narrow hallway into the living room on the right.

Shafts of light illuminate the darkly carpeted room. There are some photos on the mantelpiece, of Suzy and her husband with their elder daughter, Lisa. Suzy sits down on the sofa, ignoring the curtains that partially cover the bay windows. She has put the flowers I bought for her in the kitchen.

"Shall I open the curtains?" I ask. Suzy looks at me and nods. I reach across an armchair and tug on the heavy drapes. More light spills into the room, brightening the drab atmosphere.

Eva asks, "Any news from the police?"

Suzy shakes her head. "They are still going through all the CCTV images. From the hospital and the surrounding streets. Also knocking on doors and asking people. So far, nothing."

I ask, "Did the police question you and your husband?"

"Paul, yes." Her eyes darkened. "They can be very intrusive. They spoke to our friends, parents, digging deep. Almost as if it was us who stole our child."

Gently, I said, "Just let them do their job. Anything to get her back, right?"

Suzy nodded. I ask her, "What was baby's name?"

The faint trace of a ghostlike smile appears briefly on Suzy's face, then disappears. "It's a baby girl. Her name's Margaret."

Suzy stares at me directly. "Who would do such a thing?"

I feel her pain. "You have to be strong, Suzy. We will find her. Have you got anyone to help you with Lisa?"

She sniffs. "My mum is coming down for a few days."

"I can help with the school travels," I say. I know who Lisa is now. Molly's year is divided into two classes, and Lisa is in the other class.

Suzy nods. "That would be great, thank you."

"How did it happen, Suzy?" I can't help asking. I know she has been through this with the police already, maybe several times. Eva shoots me a glance, but Suzy doesn't seem to mind.

"After she was born, they gave her to me briefly, then put her in the warm cot next to me. She cried a lot later that day." A terrible, dark shadow flits across her face, and my heart aches for her.

"She wouldn't latch on easily. The midwives were really good, they helped a lot. By evening time, she was feeding, and it was a great feeling." Suzy looks down at her hands. Eva reaches out for her, but she moves away. "Don't touch me."

We sit there, very still, dust motes jostling for space in the shafts of watery sunlight. Suzy speaks without lifting her head up. "Paul stayed with us the whole time, and went home to sleep at night. He was knackered, same as me. She woke up three times at night, maybe more. I can't remember. But when I woke up in the morning..." She paused again.

"You don't have to say it," I say.

Suzy stares ahead like she didn't hear me. I wonder if in a strange way, talking about it helps.

"...the cot next to me was empty. I pressed the buzzer for the midwife immediately. They didn't know where she could be. The alarm was raised, and that was it."

Her eyes are fractured, broken. There are some people who wear grief like a shroud. It settles on them, covering their souls, dimming the light in their eyes. Suzy wears that iron cloak on her slight body. It is impossible not to look at her and feel unbearably sad myself.

"I just want her back," she says suddenly. "Whoever did this will be forgiven. You know?"

She looks at us, her face briefly animated. It seems like a strange comment to make, but in her state, maybe it is to be expected.

We leave after a while, promising to come back. I drive to school in a daze, Suzy's lifeless eyes, her sunken cheeks haunting my mind.

After I have parked, and about to get out of the car, my phone beeps. I have received an email, from an undisclosed sender. I frown. I open it and there's no message in the body of the email, only a PDF attachment. I click on it, perplexed. When the document becomes visible, my breath quickens, and a hollow feeling spreads across my stomach, slowly claiming my heart. The panicked feeling is back.

It's a birth certificate. With my daughter's name on it.

CHAPTER 4

I have no idea how to find out who sent it. I look at the document carefully. It's a scanned image of the birth certificate. It says Molly Dixon on it, with her date of birth.

I wonder if Jeremy has found it in his emails and is forwarding it to me. But I have never sent him Molly's birth certificate. There has never been a need. He has always accepted Molly as my daughter, and that has been that.

I look up at the school gates, anxiety bulging inside my heart. The mums are yet to arrive, and I'm alone on the street, inside my parked car. Is Molly OK?

A baby missing at the hospital, and now this…is someone sending me some sort of warped message?

Why?

I put the school pick-up sign on the dashboard and get out of the car. I walk towards the tall, cast-iron gates of the school, and press the buzzer. Security at the school is good, there is no doubt. But I'm not listening to my rational mind. I need to see my daughter. At the reception, I have to explain to a puzzled receptionist that I forgot to give Molly something. No, I cannot hand it over, I need to give it to her in person. The receptionist agrees, looking bemused. I walk across the empty courtyard, and knock on her class door and wait. I know the teacher and she doesn't seem to mind when she hears my request.

Molly comes out, frowning. "What are you doing?" she asks in a mature tone of voice. I cannot help but smile. Partly in relief, partly in pride at my fast-growing little girl. Eight going on eighteen. I hug and then let her go, holding her at arm's length.

"Listen to me carefully, Molly. Has anyone spoken to you outside of school, apart from your friends, or me and Jeremy?"

She purses her lips thinking. "I spoke to Lottie's mum."

"You mean Eva?" I can hear my heart thudding.

"Yes."

"Anyone else?"

"No."

Relief floods through me. I make sure I watch which adult Molly speaks to, but during school time it can be difficult.

I don't let Molly stay over at playdates. I always pick her up on time. She mostly has playdates at home.

I kiss her. "OK, darling. See you soon after school." Molly turns and goes back inside the classroom. I straighten and smile at the teacher, feeling a little foolish. I get back into the car and drive away, thoughts twisting in my head.

I need to tell Jeremy. He deserves to know. Would he think less of me if I told him?

My greatest fear is losing him. I couldn't tolerate that. For the first time in my life I have found a man I can rely on. Jeremy is not flashy or arrogant. He is happy in our small terraced house, although recently he has been grumbling about the rent. I am happy in our small house as well. I don't want a massive mortgage, having to watch the pennies. There was a time when I was different. When I wanted a big, posh car like the other mums in the school. Or wanted to live in a large, five-bedroom house in half an acre of land.

Now I know that doesn't mean happiness. I could live in a mansion full of servants and be unhappy, lonely. Have all the money in the world, but not be able to trust someone. Not have people who were my friends because they enjoyed my company, but because they wanted favours from me.

What sort of a life was that?

Jeremy and I love each other, that much I know. That's all I care about, and the fact that he loves Molly like his own. I know he wants to have another child. And I want to as well, but....

Soon, we have to talk. I know that. If I love him, I need to be honest with him. As I park the car outside our house, I grip the steering wheel and lower my head. I don't want to lose Jeremy. That fear has kept me from telling him all these years. But I cannot go on living like this.

Something is happening, I know that. Who would send me Molly's birth certificate? My mother is dead, and my dad lives alone up in the farm in the Yorkshire Dales. He wouldn't have Molly's certificate either. I can't help thinking someone is trying to send me a message.

As I get inside the house, my phone starts to ring. Caller ID withheld. The numbness is back again, and a cold fear is uncoiling inside me. I answer, trying to control my heart beats.

"Who is this?" My voice is shaky. I am aware of how quiet the house is. No one responds for a while. The silence is total.

Then a male voice speaks, and my mind explodes as I hear the words.

"How safe is Molly, Emma?"

I am clutching the phone so tight it's going to break. My mouth is open and I can't breathe. I need to sit down, but I can't move.

I don't recognise the voice. Eventually I manage to croak. "Who…who is this?"

With a click, the phone goes dead.

CHAPTER 5

The rest of the day passes in a blur. I avoid Jeremy when he comes back from work. I answer in monosyllables, and I can see he knows something is up with me. He's giving me space, but soon he will want some answers. I hate being like this.

The next morning after school drop-off, I can't sit down to read or watch TV. I go into the little studio at the back, and stare at the blank canvas on the easel. I can't sketch or draw. My eyes fall on the little pen of toys and a doll's house that Molly has made.

I can't bear to be inside the studio all of a sudden. The roof is shrinking, the walls are closing in. I get out, lock the main door, and jump in the car. Still an hour left to get Molly – its only 2.30 in the afternoon. But I need to move, do something. Anxiety is gnawing inside my guts. I need to be in front of her school, be the first parent inside those gates.

That's when I see him. A man is standing at the end of the road, staring at me.

Our road curves to the right at the end, joining the main street. This man is standing just where the road curves, and he is not moving. There is no mistaking that he is staring straight at me. Something about him looks familiar, but he is too far away to be sure. I fumble for my keys, and turn the ignition. When I look up, the man is gone. My eyes dart around. Trees and fences. Clusters of houses. No one standing and staring.

I touch my heated forehead. Am I imagining things?

I drive down to the bend in the road. There are no other cars in this quiet street lined with terraced houses. A footpath disappears into a grassy verge at the end, which then enters the park that borders the back of all the houses, including ours.

From here, the man could only have gone into the park. There aren't any cars around that he could have driven off in. I think for a while, then make my mind up. I get out and lock the car. I am still wearing the jogging tights, and I pull the hoodie of the coat over my head. My cold fingers encircle the phone inside the pocket.

The houses around me are quiet. I walk down the path towards the park. My mouth is dry and I can feel my heart fluttering like a tortured bird in a cage. This is where I saw the man, I am sure of it. Not only was he staring at me, he wanted me to know it, too.

He wanted me to know I was being watched.

Turnstiles block the entrance and I go through them easily. The park opens up in front of me. It's a large, green area, with trees surrounding the edges. A kids' playground lies to the left. A patch encircles the whole of it, snaking out in the distance. It's a place I normally like, and come here to run quite often. Molly used to play in the kids' area before she started school.

Today the place fills me with dread. Movement attracts my eyes to the right. A woman running, I can see her blonde hair in a ponytail bobbing up and down. Another woman with a pram appears near the kids' area. There is no sign of the man I saw.

I imagine this place at night. Dark, cold, and overlooking our backyard. Right behind my studio is the fence that forms the boundary of this park.

It would be easy for someone to jump over the fence and come into our house.

I turn away, not wanting to think anymore. None of the houses have been burgled in the four years that we have lived here. But you never know. It's not like I have asked the neighbours specifically. I make up my mind to knock on old Mrs Mountbatten's door and ask her.

I get back in the car and drive off, faster than usual. When I get to school, I am one of the few parents who are there. I go in, and stand in the courtyard, outside Molly's classroom. I am already at the door when the teacher steps out. She looks at me in surprise. I don't blame her. After all, I am making a habit of being the first parent here.

Molly is out soon, and when I see her, the tension goes out of me. There is a weakness in my legs, and a giddy feeling in my head.

I give my Molly her after-school snacks and grab her other hand.

"Ow, Mummy, that hurts," Molly says, pulling her hand away.

"Sorry, sweetheart." I relax my grip, mentally berating myself. I smile at some of the school mums as they walk past.

I hold Molly's hand and give it a little squeeze, and she squeezes back. It's like a game we play.

We drive back home, eat something, then I drop her off at her piano lesson. There is a black Nissan Micra behind me, which drives past when I take the turning to the piano teacher's house.

I have been watching the cars behind me lately. I feel like I'm being watched, and that black Nissan Micra has been two cars behind me for a long time. It's probably nothing, I admonish myself, trying to soothe my frayed nerves. There's always a line of cars on our roads. Lots of houses, each with at least one, or often two cars. I try to think if I've seen that black Nissan Micra before. An odd feeling tells me I have, but I can't be sure.

Louise, the piano teacher, is waiting for us inside her lovely house. Molly is great at the piano, and has completed her grade three exams already. I learnt the piano at her age, but she is miles better than me. I love watching her play, and chat to Louise when I get a chance.

But not today. I feel more stressed than anything else. I go and sit in the car, chewing my nails, watching the cars whizz by at the top of the road. Louise lives in a quiet cul-de-sac, and hardly any cars turn in here. I have half an hour to kill, and normally I would go back to do some yoga at home, but today I want to stay here, close to Molly.

I fiddle with my phone for a while, and find the Facebook appeal for baby Margaret. I share it with my contacts, writing a message of support. I look up at the darkening sky, and the pedestrians crossing the road, about a hundred yards away.

I see a man stop at the mouth of the cul-de-sac. He doesn't cross the road and keep walking. I stare at him, my heartbeat rising, and a pressure growing inside my chest. He looks odd as he just stands there, moving his head like he's looking for something. I see his head slowly turn to the right, and then to the end of the cul-de-sac.

His eyes come to a rest on my car. On me. My hands are white-knuckled fists, pressed into my lap. My breaths are fast and shallow. There's something strangely familiar about his tall, wide-shouldered appearance. His eyes don't move away from my car. I can't see him well enough to recognise him from here, but the fear is rising inside me like a volcano.

He takes a step forward. A croak comes out of my throat, choked with adrenaline. Is he coming into the cul-de-sac? Will he walk up to my car? Then what?

My chest feels fit to burst, and my eyes feel they will pop from their sockets. The man takes another step, and he is crossing the road. He moves over, and walks past the cul-de-sac, disappearing from view.

I stare in the same direction, right hand gripping the door handle. The man doesn't appear again. I debate whether to get out and check, fearful as I am. In the end, I decide to stay inside the car. If he appears again, so help me, I'm stepping out to confront him. It's scary as hell, but I need to deal with him before Molly comes out.

6 pm arrives eventually, and I knock on Louise's door. Molly gets a glowing report as usual, and will have extra lessons for the mid-term music exams. It means more money, but hopefully I will have sold some paintings by then. As we drive back, my phone rings. I pick it up, my heart lurching. It feels like a grenade, throbbing against the car. Thankfully, it's the gallery owner, Steve Ponting.

I apologise for not coming today and set up a meeting with him for tomorrow. Regardless of what else is happening in my life, I cannot mess up this opportunity.

When I get back home, it's the usual blur of dinner, homework, washing, cleaning. Jeremy comes back around 7 pm.

"How's my two princesses?" he says. I smile and give him a hug, feeling bad for the way I've been. I watch as Molly stands on the stairs, shouting at him.

"Catch me, Jeremy."

He puts his briefcase and coat down and balances himself. Molly stands on the third step of the staircase, bends her knees and jumps. She flies through the air, and Jeremy grabs her around the armpits, catching her. Molly squeals in delight. He puts her down, and kisses me lightly on the cheek.

"Good day?"

A simple question, but I wrestle with the answer. I need to be honest with him, or the day will come when he will never forgive me. But now doesn't seem like the right time.

I nod, and duck back into the kitchen. I feel his eyes on my back, watching me as I avoid him.

Jeremy reads to Molly in bed as I pour myself a glass of red wine. I go into the TV room, and have just sat down when Jeremy comes in. He closes the door behind him.

"She's asleep," he says and yawns. "I'm starved. Any dinner?"

"Lamb roast with potatoes. It's in the oven."

"Great," he says, and goes to the kitchen. I follow him, and we chat as he pours himself some wine, and begins to eat.

I leave Jeremy downstairs to finish his dinner and go upstairs. I had a light dinner of a sandwich, I'm not very hungry. The stairs creak under the carpet as I pad upstairs. I pause before Molly's door, listening. It's silent, almost. I opened the door slightly to see the darkness inside. I step in and I can hear her breathing. With the light of my phone I make sure she is tucked in alright, check the curtains and ensure the windows are locked.

I always keep her windows locked.

I come out from her room and go to the loo. The window in the bathroom looks out over the garden and the park beyond it. I lower the blind before I turn on the light. As my hand is on the blind rope, I look out over the dark expanse of the park. Something catches my eyes and I freeze.

Like a giant firefly, a single glow of light flashes in the dark. It bobs up and down, and from side to side. Someone is holding a torch and they are moving. Running or walking?

I can't be sure. Tentacles of fear spread their claws inside me as I watch the blob of light approaching our back garden. It becomes brighter, steadier. Hypnotised, I can't tear my eyes away. The light stops moving just beyond our fence. Beyond my studio.

Then the light raises itself, till the beam is pointed directly at me. The beam is strong and it illuminates the window. The person holding the light can see me. My heart is jackhammering inside my chest, and I feel I will drown in the pounding of blood against my ears.

I scream and fall back.

CHAPTER 6

I am covered in sweat. As I stumble back, my feet slip on the bathroom mat and I fall, jarring my hips on the floor. Pain lances across my lower back and leg, and I wince. I can still see the light through the window, lighting up the bathroom ceiling. Panic grips me. I need to get out of here. Out from where he can see me. I crawl towards the door when it suddenly opens.

Jeremy turns the light on, and I shield my eyes. When I open them, Jeremy is standing there, staring at me.

"Emma, what's wrong?" Jeremy leans over and picks me up. I get up slowly. My left hip is worse, and the whole of my back is now hurting. My elbows got knocked and there is a dull ache in them.

"Are you OK? What happened?"

I swallow, and my throat is dry. "There was someone outside, shining a torchlight on our window."

"Really? Who?" Jeremy looks out the window and then realises he can't see anything with the bright light on. He turns the light off and moves to the window. He peers out, opening the window fully.

He says, "There's no one there, darling."

I join him at the window, limping on my right leg. The inky-black, undisturbed expanse of the park greets my eyes. Nothing is visible.

Jeremy's voice is guarded. "Are you sure you saw something?"

"Yes, I'm positive." I am hurt that he doubts me. He notices my angry tone of voice, and shrugs.

"Just asking, that's all."

He lowers the blind and turns the light on. There is a look of concern on his face, but right now, I don't need it. I don't need my husband to doubt me, instead of backing me up.

"I'm not making this up, Jeremy. I did see someone."

The look on my face makes him relent. "Sure. It's just weird why someone would want to do that, that's all." He thinks for a moment. "Maybe he's looking for something. Shall we call the police?"

"Just leave it for the time being. Let's see if he comes back," I say, not feeling sure of myself at all. I know the police won't be able to do anything about it.

Only I can, and it's time I did it.

*****

At the school all the mums have got together to organise a relief fund for Suzy Elliot. It had been two days and there is no sign of her baby. Suzy is still stuck indoors, and her mother is helping her. Several of the mothers, including myself, were helping with her other daughter, Lisa. When I thought of Suzy, my own troubles paled in comparison.

In the indoor courts inside the school, a few tables had been laid down. T-shirts with the baby's name have been printed. Eva and I pick up a box of the T-shirts and fliers with her face and the police contact details on it. We were teaming up in twos and going to stand on street corners on the main roads, pubs, railway station, handing out the fliers, putting up posters.

As we set off, I ask Eva if we should stop by and see Suzy. She agrees. I am driving, and traffic is heavy. I am looking in the rear-view mirror, and I see a line of cars behind me. My eyes fall on the black Nissan Micra. It's a small car, and one I have seen before. It's probably coincidence, but I keep checking it. It turns left when I do.

As we take another right and then a left, Eva asks, "Which way are you going?"

"The back way, for the traffic," I say. I keep an eye on the rear-view. I cannot see the black Nissan Micra anymore. I breathe a sigh of relief, and soon pull up outside Suzy's house.

When I knock on the door, an older woman opens the door. She wears glasses, and she has dark hair. Looking at her bobbed hair, I wonder if it's a wig. For some reason, she seems familiar.

"Are you Suzy's friends?" the woman asks.

"Yes, school mums." I introduce myself. Eva is behind me carrying a small box with fliers and posters.

"I am Jean, Suzy's mum," the older woman says. She gives us a brief, tight smile, then goes up the stairs, leaving us standing in the doorway. Suzy appears soon, her expression a little harassed. I wonder if all is well between mother and daughter. I give her a warm hug.

"These are for you," I say, pulling out a flier and putting it on the kitchen table. "Hand them out to whoever comes to the house. I know the police have put posters out already, but more, a lot more, will not hurt. The more awareness, the better."

"Thank you so much." Suzy's eyes are glistening.

"Don't be silly," Eva says. "It's the least we can do."

We have a cup of tea, then get going. We decide to tackle Suzy's street first. Eva starts at one end and I at the other. We have the T-shirts on, pink with a white box with baby's name on it, and stop at every lamp-post, sticking on the posters with glue. There aren't that many lamp-posts on the street, and after half an hour, we move to the next street along. The railway station is busier, and we have to see the stationmaster. He is already aware as we rung up ahead. One of the attendants helps us to identify spots with maximum visibility. We rest for a cup of coffee then carry on.

The station is busy work, and I keep glancing at the watch. It's almost midday by the time we finish.

I say to Eva, "Why don't I drop you off at yours, and we can put some posters up around our houses? Then it's almost pick-up time."

Eva agrees. We say goodbye to the helpful railway workers, and get back in my car. I start to drive, and traffic is lesser now as the school and work rush is over. I glance at my rear-view and freeze. I can see the black Nissa Micra again. Its two cars behind, and the black shape of the driver is clearly visible.

CHAPTER 7

Fear coils inside my guts like a serpent. This can't be a random car that I keep seeing. I am loath to mention it to Eva, I don't want her to think I am paranoid. I keep glancing at the mirror as I drive. The Nissan follows. I drive up the hill into the village, the nice part of Richmond where the houses are wide and detached. Eva lives in one of them, one street away from the common.

As I park in front of her house, I realise the car isn't following me anymore. But I am wary. I sense it must be around, hiding from view. I wave goodbye to Eva, and start driving again. I keep checking, but the Nissan isn't there.

I get back to my house without incident. I take an armful of the posters, put them in my backpack, then get out and lock the car. Our house seems fine, and I will go in once I have put all the posters up. I walk to the end of the road. I hear a sound behind me. An engine, a squeal of tyres. In this quiet street it makes a commotion. The roar of the engine gets louder, and, although I am on the pavement, I look back, alarmed. Like a bat out of hell, the black shape of a Nissan Micra streaks past me. It takes the turning on the road at high speed, gears crashing and screeching. I almost scream as the car skids, corrects itself, then races out of sight.

I stare at the empty road, heart pumping fast. I look up and down the street. It's gone back to its usual quiet mode. A couple of net curtains twitch. Composing myself, I keep walking down, to the turning, and then I am at the entrance of the park.

I can't help but stop and stare at it. Through the bar stiles, the green expanse is verdant, dotted with trees. A peaceful place. For me, it spells danger.

For some reason, I am drawn to it like a magnet. Will I see the person who was watching me last night? I wonder if he saw me, he must have. He knows it's me who lives there.

I am being watched. It's a palpable feeling, like someone is touching my skin. I look around me, seeing nothing. Then I head inside the park. I can put some posters up on the trees. Although it's November, families still come to the park. I push the turnstiles and go in.

I expect danger, and my breath fogs in the air around face. My fists are clenched. To the far left, I can see the rear façade of the houses that back into the park. One of them is ours, about halfway down the row. Whoever was here last night knew exactly which one it was. I suppose it's easy to spot the studio.

That makes me wonder. How would the person know I have a studio in the back garden?

I shake off the thought. I am getting more bothered by this now. I take a deep breath. Right, all I need to do is put some posters up, and then leave. Behind the houses, there is only the occasional tree. But to my right, leading up to the soft playground, there is a bank of tall oak trees, and further down as well. I cannot do the whole perimeter of the park on my own, it'll take too long.

I pull my coat against the wind and head for the playground in the mid-distance. I will walk around, and stand in the spot where I had seen the light last night. I will force myself to do it. Maybe I can find something they had dropped.

I shake off my backpack and take the posters out. I walk down, putting them up against the bark of the tree trunks, at eye level. The park is deserted today. The wind is cold and biting, and the sky is clouding overhead. I can't imagine many pre-school children being out in this weather. I am almost up to the playground. I can see the swings, the monkey bars and the sand play area.

The thick branches creak overhead as they move in the wind. It rustles through the skeleton boughs, making a slithering, whispering sound. Then I hear something else. I stop, and listen hard.

It's the sound of a baby crying.

CHAPTER 8

The wind carries the sound away, but it returns. I hear it again, wailing, soft. It's coming from behind me. I shove the posters back in the bag, and run towards the source of the sound. There are bushes by the path, with more trees after them, and then the park fence. The cries are coming from the bush. They are about knee-high for me. I wade in, hearing the cries get louder. My eyes flick from side to side, searching desperately.

And then I see it. A black baby seat, the type you put in a car. The handle is raised, and the seat's covered. Inside, a white bundle. I can already see the red face scrunched up in the bundle, and the wailing is much louder now. I break into a sprint, and crouch before it.

The baby's head is covered in a pink cap, similar to the blankets it's swaddled in. Baby is crying lustily, which is a good sound out here in the cold. A silent baby in this weather, outdoors, is a dangerous sign.

"Shhh," I say, reaching out to her. It must be a her, because the blankets are pink with a white border. I touch her, she feels tepid, but not freezing cold. She couldn't have been here long. I coo at her, feeling her cheeks. She ignores me and carries on crying. I grab the seat handle; it doesn't give way.

I put the backpack on my shoulder and grab the seat handle tightly. I walk as fast as I can to the entrance of the park. What I am doing seems surreal, like I am living someone else's life. I put baby in the back seat of my car, strapping her in. I make sure the car seat is secure, then I start driving. I head straight for the hospital. Thoughts are racing through my mind. Memories are loosened, raining on me like the stray leaves of winter. Memories I keep locked up tight.

Whose baby is this? I hope and pray the answer is the one all of us have been looking for. It's Suzy's baby. Only time will tell. First things first. I need to get to the hospital and make sure she is checked over. Then I call the police. No, I call the police now.

I ring the 101 number for non-urgent police calls. I have put my phone on hands-free, and I speak as I drive, telling the woman on the other end everything.

When I hang up, I look in the rear-view mirror. Some traffic behind me, but I can't see a black Nissan Micra.

I can't believe this is happening. At the back of my mind, I can't shake the feeling that what I saw last night in the park, and now the baby, are somehow linked. Someone is trying to tie up…a dreadful thought rears up inside me.

What if the police think I am responsible? My knuckles are white on the steering wheel. I try to rationalise. I wouldn't bring the baby back if I had stolen it, would I?

I try not to think too much. My brain is on overdrive, and I should just focus on getting the baby to hospital, and report to the police.

Accident and Emergency is heaving when we arrive. I park in the visitors' bay, and barge past the queue of people, ignoring the looks and comments. I lift the seat with baby in it on the reception counter, in front of the astonished nurse.

"Baby left abandoned in Cottenham Park. I don't know for how long. She could have hypothermia. Please help."

The nurse moves quickly. She presses a buzzer and waves me in through a double door. She takes baby off me, and soon there is a swarm of white and blue vests around the little body.

The nurse comes back and stands in front of me. "Are you the mother?" she asks.

I am surprised as I have already told her where I found baby. "No, but you know about the missing baby, don't you?"

Her eyes widen.

I say, "I have already called the police."

She rushes off and speaks to the group of carers milling around. I get up, feeling restless. The police will be here soon. But there is something else I have to do first.

I dial Suzy's home number. She answers after five rings. Her voice is low, tired. "Hello?"

"Suzy, this is Emma. I need to know something. Before baby went missing, did you wrap her in a white fleece blanket with a pink border?"

The tone of my voice, and the question must have stunned Suzy. I listen to the hiss of static for a few seconds. Then she speaks, urgent and fast. "Yes, yes. On the top-left border, the letters MLE are sewn in gold letters. Margaret Louise Elliot. Why—"

I cut her off. "Hang on." I put the phone in my pocket and approach the group around the cot she has been placed in now. The car seat is on the floor. I look inside the cot, baby is still wrapped in the white fleece. One of the nurses is slowly removing it, while another supports the tiny body.

"I need to see that fleece." I point at it. "I am the person who found her."

The nurse hands it to me, and it strikes me that all this handling has wasted valuable evidence the police might have wanted. It's too late for it now. I look at the top-left border, and my heart soars.

The initials MLE are right there. I pick up the phone. Suzy is still holding.

Without telling her what I have found, I ask, "Does baby have any birthmarks?"

"Yes. She has a brown mole on the back of her neck. Quite big, you can't miss it. Emma, what's going on?"

"Let me call you back."

I ask one of the doctors who checked for me. I join him as he leans over, and with one gloved hand, lifts baby's neck up gently. I duck down peering at the back of her head, and then the neck comes into view. There is a pea-sized brown mole in the centre of the neck part of her spine, and it is unmistakable.

Baby is more comfortable now with a bottle of formula milk at her lips. She is chugging away, content. The doctor has seen the mole now as well and we exchange a glance.

My breathing is fast and jerky, and surging blood is clogging my throat. I ring Suzy back.

"Get to the hospital. Paediatric A/E. Come fast, I think we found her."

I can't speak anymore. Suzy gives out a shriek that's between a mortal wound and wild panic, and the phone goes silent.

I slump on the chair just as the doors burst open and uniformed police walk in.

CHAPTER 9

A man wearing a black suit is standing in front of me. A woman hovers behind him, also suited. They arrived with the police, so I guess they must be detectives. Uniforms now stand in front of the double doors of the entrance, and several more are strolling around the rest of A/E. Nobody wants to see baby go missing for a second time.

"My name is Detective Chief Inspector Charles Rockford," the man says and shows me his badge. It's a raised gold relief of the London Met Police Force symbol, on a leather base. Rockford is in his forties, I guess, but he could be older. He is tall, Afro-Caribbean, with more than a passing resemblance to Idris Elba. His chestnut brown eyes focus on me and I don't look away.

"Are you the lady who found the baby in the park?"

It sounds like my new name. Lady who found park baby. I nod. He pulls up a chair, but the woman behind him remains standing. She is blonde, slim, with sunken cheeks and a frazzled expression like she's drunk too much coffee or smoked too many cigarettes.

Rockford introduces his colleague. "This is Detective Inspector Shelly Ingram." Ingram gives me the briefest of nods, and a slight twitch of her lips.

Rockford says, "What were you doing in the park, Mrs..." He looks at the paper in his hands. "...Emma Mansell?"

I clear my throat. "Yes that's me. I was putting up some posters for baby Margaret, as it happens."

"And?" Rockford speaks slow, measured. The hectic atmosphere in the place doesn't seem to affect him.

"I heard a baby crying. I ran over, then brought her here."

"Hmm." Rockford is silent, and Shelly stares at me with her arms folded.

"Where do you live, Mrs Mansell?"

I tell him. He knows the area well. "That's on the same road as the park, right?"

"Yes, my house backs onto the park." As I say it, I realise how odd it sounds. I feel hairs prickle at the back of my neck.

"Was there anyone else in the park, Mrs Mansell? When you found the baby, I mean."

"No."

He taps the pen on the piece of paper he's holding, staring down. Then he looks up and purses his lips. "Would you mind coming down to the station to give a statement?"

"No. I mean yes, I can come."

"Good." Rockford's eyes are friendly but watchful. He stares at me like he has a lot of time on his hands. "Detective Ingram will take some more details from you, and bring you back to the station, if that's OK?"

"I have a school pick-up in an hour and a half."

Rockford stands up and exchanges a glance with Ingram.

"That should be fine, Mrs Mansell," Ingram says, her tone brisk. "If you're not driving then we can also drop you off at the school."

"I will be driving, but thanks for the offer."

Ingram opens her mouth to speak but the doors burst open for the second time. Suzy, her mother and Eva burst in, eyes wild.

"Where is she?!" Suzy screams at the top of her voice. All heads swivel in her direction. I point her towards the cot, and without a second look in my direction, she flings herself at it. Two nurses and a female doctor hold her as she strains for the cot. All of a sudden, it's pandemonium.

"My baby…"

"Miss Elliot, please calm down. Margaret is fine…"

Eva hurries over to me. She hugs me, then looks at me with a puzzled expression. "Did this really happen? I mean, you just found her?"

"Yes, I did." I tell her what happened, and Eva listens with eyes wide.

My heart sinks as I consider the implications. If my best friend finds it weird, what do the police think?

Then I realise it's Eva who can vouch for me. I was with her most of the day till I went to the park. Rockford and Ingram are watching us, and I introduce Eva to them. One of the doctor's ambles over.

"The DNA swab has been taken, from both baby and mother. Miss Elliot has identified baby, but we have to wait till tomorrow for the swab results to come back."

In the crowd, I can't see Suzy anymore. Other children have been moved away from this corner, and the uniformed police have now formed a human cordon around us. Two senior doctors with badges that say Accident and Emergency Consultants have appeared, and they're in intense conversation with Rockford and Ingram.

Ingram peels away from them and turns to where Eva and I are standing. "Mrs Mansell, do you mind if I ask you a few questions?" She glances at me. "In private."

I walk away and watch as they talk. In front of me the tangle of paediatric nurses and doctors is unravelling, and I catch a glimpse of Suzy. Her cheeks are streaked with tears and she is clutching the precious bundle tight to her chest. A lump arrives at my throat and I find it hard to swallow. Our eyes meet and my heart melts a little when Suzy's lips quiver, and she beckons me over. She doesn't move Margaret from her chest but manages to give me a hug anyway.

"Thank you. How can I ever thank you?" she cries.

It's making me well over, and I bite my lower lip and disengage from her. "I'm so glad we found her." And I am. The relief is washing over me in waves.

And so are the pangs of doubt. It's too much of a coincidence. The light in the park last night, beamed right at our house. At me. And this morning the baby left in the same park. Then I remember the black Nissan Micra. How it followed me around, then streaked around the corner of the street...

I didn't take the number of the car, and I feel stupid. All of it now seems a rush, a blur. One surreal event has merged into another, like clouds fusing in a stormy sky.

Is it my fault that Suzy and her baby were targeted? I can't help the feeling that someone is sending me a message, after all these years.

"Emma."

I turn to see Suzy staring at me. "What are you thinking?"

"Nothing," I lie. "Just glad I was there at the right time."

She shakes her head, her nose tip red. "I know, what are the chances, right? God knows how long she had been there for."

I notice Suzy's mother isn't around. I am about to ask her if she needs help getting back when I feel Detective Ingram come and stand at the entrance of the open cubicle.

I nod and turn to Suzy. "I have to give the police a statement."

"Of course." Suzy stands up and puts Margaret carefully in the cot, then hugs me. "I really can't thank you enough."

I say goodbye, and follow DI Ingram out of the door. I don't see Eva anywhere. I would like to see her before I leave but the police are waiting to give me a lift. She might be in the loo. I will text her later.

CHAPTER 10

There isn't a police station nearby, so Ingram gives me directions to Wimbledon. She arrives before I do, and is there to buzz open the electric barrier to the car park. She checks me into the front reception of the station. The place is cold and stark. A few hard faces turn to look at me, all of them men. A sergeant is leaning over the counter, resting his meaty hands on it. He looks at me with interest. The green plastic seats are scuffed and worn, the blue lino on the floor has scratch marks on it. This place is alien, strange, and it makes me shiver.

I follow Ingram through the doors. She has her ear on a mobile phone now, and is talking to someone in a low voice that I can't pick up. We come to a room with a green door that says Interview Room 4, and we go in. I notice the rectangular glass window on the wall opposite as I enter. There is a table with two chairs on either side, and a camera on the wall above it, with a red light that blinks.

"Have a seat. Would you like a glass of water?" Ingram says. I nod.

A side door opens and Rockford steps in. The low ceiling is not far off the top of his head. His curly, black hair is glossed down, and it gleams. He greets me, then sits down.

Ingram presses a button on a black machine that sits on the side of the table. She introduces herself and us and notes the time and date.

Both of them look at me. Rockford asks, "How long have you known Suzy Elliot for, Mrs Mansell?"

"She's one of the school mums, and I heard that her baby was missing. I didn't actually know her before that."

"So you only met her after the baby had disappeared?"

"Yes."

"And you are sure that you have not met her anywhere else before that? I mean outside the school. Socially maybe, in a pub." Rockford is relaxed, friendly even, but his eyes are fixed on me.

I don't know where they are going with these questions. Of course I haven't seen Suzy before this. Didn't they hear me the first time?

"No," I say firmly.

"What about her husband, Paul?"

"Nope, never seen him either."

Rockford says slowly, "And yet Suzy's missing baby appears in the park behind your house, just when you happen to be there."

"I…" I try to swallow and find my throat is parched. I drink hastily from the cup. The water feels cold going down my throat. I put the cup down slowly and it shakes. Damn it.

"I was putting posters up there. For the missing baby. I told you that already."

"And you had no idea that the baby was going to be there?"

My throat constricts despite the water. "What are you trying to say?"

Neither of them reply. I look at each of them in turn. "What is this? You suspect me of abducting the baby? That's ridiculous."

Still they keep looking at me, and below the table, my thumb is scratching against my index finger, and my feet keep shaking. I feel nervous. My rational brain tells me they are cops. This is what they do to freak people out, gauge their reactions. But I don't like the way they suspect me already. What did Eva tell them?

I clear my throat. "If you ask my friend Eva, she'll tell you I only met Suzy a couple of days ago."

"Yes, I spoke to her." Ingram speaks for the first time since Rockford came in.

"Then you must know that I'm telling the truth."

Rockford says, "Please think carefully, Mrs Mansell. What you say in this room is an official statement."

I don't like the tone of his voice. His face is so neutral I can't make anything out of it. He seems to have all the time in the world. I sense he is giving me space…to trip me up?

"Do I need a lawyer?"

He shrugs. "It's up to you. There's one available if you want to."

"Am I under arrest?" Even as I say the words cold sweat trickles down my spine. The thought is nauseating.

Rockford shakes his head. "No. But you are a suspect. As soon as you turn up, so does the missing baby, and in a location that is very convenient to you. There are no witnesses to verify what happened at the park, either."

"But you can ask…" I stop myself. I was going to mention Jeremy's name, but that's the wrong thing to do. I don't want to drag him into this.

"Who?"

"The rest of the mums at school," I say.

Ingram asks me, "You have a child, don't you?"

"Yes. Molly, aged eight." Panic prickles inside me, but I meet their gazes full on.

"You never had another?" Ingram asks.

Her remark annoys me. What business it of hers? "No," I say coldly.

"Did you want one?" Ingram is very still, focused on me. I meet her head on, angry.

"No, I did not. Not that it's any business of yours, DI Ingram."

She sits back in her chair, and I give myself a mental high-five. I look to Rockford. "Can I go now?"

He nods. He fishes out a card from his pocket and slides it over to me. "Please call us if you think of anything new. Anything at all. Child abduction is taken very seriously, as you know."

I take the card, thank them and leave the room.

CHAPTER 11

Ten years ago

I couldn't take my eyes off him.

Neither could most of the women at the party. Clive Connery had a crisply pressed dinner jacket on, white shirt open two buttons down, showing sparse curls of black chest hair. As I watched, he shrugged off his jacket and draped it over the back of the chair. His muscular shoulders and biceps rippled under the tight cotton shirt.

"Who's he?" Eva whispered in my ear.

"My boss," I whispered back.

"I can see why you took the job." Eva giggled. I stuck an elbow in her ribs playfully. Clive did interview me, in fact, but he was one in a panel of three. Every time he turned those dark, glittering eyes on me, I stumbled my well-rehearsed answers. To this day, I didn't know how I got the job.

But I was doing it well. I had become one of the better sales agents, trusted by customers for my laid-back and non-pushy style. Most sales agents did the reverse, they tried to shove a property down a buyer's throat. I didn't, and buyers respected me for that.

It was a far cry from waking up at five in the morning, to get the loaded train to the city.

I enjoyed my new job more, but I had to say my heart wasn't in it. More than anything else, I would like to get back to my easel and canvas, like I did in my teenage years. Sitting by the window of our Yorkshire farmhouse, putting brushstrokes on the rough white paper. Watching sunset colours claim the sky, and my canvas.

But I couldn't complain. Painting wouldn't pay my bills, and being an estate agent meant I could pretty much choose what hours I worked. I went running and did yoga the rest of the time, trying to stay in some sort of shape.

Eva leaned towards me again, her voice dry. "He's coming over!"

I shifted my eyes away towards the other tables. This was a black-tie dinner event for the National Independent Estate Agents Association, or NIEAA for short. I tried to act interested in the rest of the people, all the while aware that Clive was walking deliberately towards Eva and myself.

"Hi, Emma," Clive said. His voice was warm and baritone, with an undertone like logs crackling in a fireplace.

I turned my head, feigning surprise. "Oh, hi, Clive, didn't see you there. May I introduce my friend Eva Harris?"

Clive faced Eva and actually did a half-bow. "Enchanted, I'm sure." He shook her hand lightly, and Eva made a funny noise in her throat. Then he turned to me with a gleam in his eye, and a big smile.

"So glad to see you here tonight."

I cleared my throat before replying. "Lovely to see you, too."

"You look ravishing." His eyes swept up and down my little black evening dress slowly. I failed to keep the heat off my cheeks. I heaved a breath, I needed to say something or I would turn into a statue like one of those ice maidens.

"Thank you, Clive. You look nice yourself."

He fixed his eyes on mine. When Clive Connery stared at you with intensity, you had no choice but to look back, hypnotised. His blond hair was wavy and combed back straight. His square jaw framed a sharp nose, strong lips, and eyes that were designed to devour.

He leaned closer, and I could smell his cool aftershave. "Guess what a little bird told me," he said in a lower voice.

"What?" I asked, intrigued.

"The best new sales agent award is coming to our firm." He raised his eyebrows, and gave me a knowing smile. "And guess who's on the board of the judging panel?"

"Who?" It was a silly question, as it was becoming obvious.

"Yours truly." He spread his arms slightly and winked. "It's going to be an entertaining evening." He nodded at Eva, and walked back to his table.

"What was that all about?" Eva asked.

"Not sure," I said, feeling butterflies in my stomach.

We sat down to wine and starters soon, and the stage was taken by the MC of the awards ceremony. I almost spilled my white wine when I heard my name being announced.

"The award of best new sales agent in the independent sector goes to…Emma Dixon!"

I hastily swallowed the wine, and put the wine glass on my table. Shakily I stood up, encouraged by Eva. My colleagues at Connery's, sitting around me, were all smiles and clapping. Feeling acutely self-conscious, I walked down the tables to the stage, hearing the applause grow. All I could think of was my dress, and feeling mortified I hadn't worn something more suitable. Heck, what did I know what suitable was in these conditions?

Thankfully, I didn't have to deliver a speech. I clutched the round disc on a pedestal in my hands, and walked back to my table.

"Congratulations," Eva said, and others around the table followed. I beamed, feeling happy and bubbly, and reached for the wine.

When the music started, Eva dragged me to the dance floor. From the corner of my eye, I saw Clive approaching. Suddenly I was dancing with him, swept up in the rhythm, losing my inhibitions. He was a fantastic dancer, his taut, jerking body gyrating to every beat. He put his hands on my waist like it was the most natural thing to do, and we started moving as one.

When the music came to an end, he followed me back to my table. I could feel everyone's eyes on me. Every woman in that place wanted to be with Clive Connery. I couldn't believe my luck.

CHAPTER 12

Present day

I park near the school gates, and walk Molly up, joining the parents taking their kids to school.

"Do you have to come up to my classroom?" Molly asks me.

"Yes, why not?"

She shrugs. "Nothing. It's just that not all the mums do it. You didn't used to do it either. Did you?"

She can understand everything. Still, I don't let go of her hand, and keep an eye on her till she goes inside the classroom. When she is in, I walk back to the car quickly. I will see Eva for coffee and pastries later, but first I have to go and see Steve Ponting, the gallery owner.

The gallery is in the old-town section of the high street. Its cobblestone paths, and arched passages are from the medieval time, and the modern vies for space with the ancient, giving the place a timeless vibe. Shoppers stroll in and out of fashionable boutiques. I walk into the gallery and spot Steve at the counter, showing someone where to hang a canvas.

Steve first saw my work hanging in the walls of a local café. He took down my details from the café owner and called me. I did two exhibitions with a group of artists, but this was my first solo venture. Steve seems surprised to see me.

"How are you?" he said. Steve is medium-height, only slightly taller than me. He is in his fifties, and has a paunch that is the result of his fondness for food and fine wine.

I become aware there is something in his stance that seems off. "Is everything OK?" I ask with some trepidation.

He spreads his hands. "Yes, fine. It's such a shame we had to cancel the show with such short notice."

I feel like I have been hit by a sledgehammer. After a stunned silence, I say, "What? I didn't cancel anything."

Steve frowns. "But your husband came around. He said that you had to go abroad because your father was unwell."

I am struggling to catch my breath. "My husband? Steve, my husband would never..." My voice trails off. "Hang on. This man, who called himself my husband. What did he look like?"

"Tall, blond hair, dark eyes. Square-jawed, handsome guy." Steve's eyes twinkled. He's never made a secret of the fact that he's gay. "Shame I haven't seen him around before."

There is a pain in my chest, and lights are flashing in my eyes. I need to sit down, before my knees fold. Somehow, I remain standing.

"What did he say his name was?"

"Jeremy. Gave me his card. Jeremy Mansell."

"When did he come?"

"Two days ago, in the afternoon."

I know for a fact Jeremy was at work then. And the man's description? This man is nothing like Jeremy. He's dark-haired for starters. He doesn't have that square-jawed, broad face that Steve is describing.

I know who Steve is describing, and the knowledge turns my insides to ashes and ice.

Steve doesn't have CCTV on the premises so we can't check images. He looks at me with a strange expression in his eyes.

"Are you saying someone was impersonating your husband?"

I know this sounds crazy and can't blame him for being puzzled.

"What was this person like, Steve?" I ask.

"He was very nice, actually. Charming, in fact. Showed me his card, and it did have your partner's name on it. The way he explained, it seemed he knew about your dad, too. Does he own a farm in the Yorkshire Dales?"

My hands and feet are getting numb, despite the heating in the art gallery. I look at a giant canvas in front of me and it seems the oils are dripping down, forming a puddle on the floor. Decomposing.

"Emma?" Steve prompts.

I touch my forehead and clear my throat. "Sorry, Steve. Yes, my dad does live on a farm."

I catch the look in his eyes. "But no, that person wasn't my husband." Something strikes me, and I ignore the expression on Steve's face. "Can I please see the card he left you with?"

"Sure."

The card is a typical business one, black embossed letters on a white background. The words 'Jeremy Mansell and Family Law Solicitor at Burnham and Drexel' are printed in raised letters. I turn it over. Nothing.

I ask Steve, "Can I keep this?"

He shrugged. "If you want."

I look at him hopefully. "Steve, I can't explain everything right now, but that man who came was pretending to be my husband. If you ever see him again, please call me." Even as I say the words I know I sound paranoid and elusive. Nothing cloak-and-dagger happens in this town. There is the odd scandal, but no criminal activity. Well, not until recently, that is. I think about Suzy Elliot with her missing baby and another flutter of panic hits me.

"Please, Steve." My voice is steady, not betraying the anxiety I feel inside. He nods. I wonder if I should just call the police. If the cops do get involved, then they will question me. Once they start picking on a thread of my past, how far will that spool unravel?

Apart from involving me, they will question Jeremy as well, and he knows nothing about this as yet. I need to resolve the situation with Jeremy quickly. I realise now that I should have come clean with him four years ago when we first met. Secrets are like skeletons in the grave. Getting them out is as traumatic as having them in the first place.

I say to Steve, "Now that you know, can we hold the exhibition?"

To my dismay, he moves his head from side to side. "I'm sorry, Emma. Gallery space is scarce as you know. The same day your husband, I mean this guy, came in, another two artists wanted to book the place."

I clamped my jaw shut. These artists would be paying, whereas my deal with Steve was that sales from the exhibition would make money for the gallery hire. We had an arrangement, and that's now blown.

Steve says, "I can't keep changing my mind either. You know it's bad for business. Maybe we can do this later. Sorry."

I can't be angry with him. It's not his fault. But this was my big chance to get my name known locally. My paintings sell, and there are plenty of people around here who would buy reasonably priced work. I could have slowly raised my prices, and progressed towards my dream of making a living from my work.

I say goodbye to Steve and walk out of the gallery, furious and frustrated. In my coat pocket, I am clutching that miserable business card. Disturbing thoughts rise up in my mind.

The person who did this has been spying on Jeremy as well. He knows where Jeremy works, down to the fact that he is a family lawyer specialist. That does not bode well at all.

My phone chirps, and it's Eva. I long to see her, as she is the only person I can talk to right now. We meet up for coffee, and I tell her that my solo exhibition has been cancelled.

Eva is surprised. "What? Why?"

Right now, I don't want to tell anyone what I think. "Got rescheduled," I say. "I'll see you at the pick-up."

CHAPTER 13

We arrive at the school gates on time. Eva is good friends with a lot of the mothers. She is talking to them, while I stand to one side. I have one or two friends here, that's it. Eva is my main connection to this crowd. She beckons me over, and reluctantly, I walk up to the group. The mums are wearing jeans and casual clothes, but from the Prada and LV handbags I can tell they are wealthy. My River Island fifty quid shoulder bag pales in comparison.

"This is Emma, everybody. She just joined the school. Molly is her little girl in Year 4."

They give me vacant smiles then go back to their chatting. I stand awkwardly, and only join in when Eva drags me into a conversation.

The girls come out in a queue, and their parents take them away. Molly takes her time, and I stiffen slightly when I see the form teacher, Miss Laker, approaching with Molly walking next to her. Molly seems OK, her face blank. But Molly has always been good at hiding her emotions. I stride forward quickly, as Miss Laker is definitely staring at me.

I grab hold of Molly's hand as soon as they get closer. She stands close to me.

"We had a small incident at playtime today," Miss Laker says. She is young, in her twenties. I doubt she has children of her own. I'm judging her, I know, but she doesn't strike me as being very maternal.

"What incident?"

"A girl was pushed to the ground, and then kicked in the head."

I frown. "And what does that have to do with Molly?"

"Well, she said that Molly did it."

I look down at Molly and give her hand a squeeze. She looks to the ground. I bend down on my knees and make her look at me.

"Darling, don't be scared of anything. Nothing will happen. Just tell me the truth. Did you hit that girl?"

"No, Mum, I didn't." She holds my eyes. Every child is different, and I know mine well. She doesn't believe in lying. She shakes her head again, staring at me. "I didn't, Mummy. I swear."

I give her a hug and stand up. My voice has steel in it. "You heard her. She didn't do it. Did anyone actually see her doing it?"

"No."

Anger bubbles inside me. "Then how can you accuse her?"

"She is not being accused, Miss Dixon, please remain calm."

"I am calm. I just want to know on what basis my child is being accused of hitting this girl."

"She was pointed out by the girl who was hit."

"And who is she?"

Miss Laker is normally a nice person, and I get on well with her. In the past, she has commented on how well Molly does her homework, and how attentive she is. Another quality is her competitiveness, Miss Laker told me last week. While it's lovely hearing all this, I hate what she is saying now.

She says, "Why don't you come to my office, where the child and her parents are waiting?"

I take a breath and square my shoulders. Before I walk off, I sense Eva hovering nearby. She catches my eyes and strides over quickly. Miss Laker has already moved up ahead, heading for the reception office.

"What's going on?" Eva asked.

"They're saying Molly pushed another child and then kicked her when she fell."

Eva's mouth falls open. She looks like I feel.

"I don't believe that for a second. Molly is gentlest child. Did anyone see her?"

"That's what I asked. Apparently not. But the child is accusing Molly." My gaze wafts down to Lottie. Eva gets my drift. She asks Lottie, "Honey, did you see the girl who was pushed in the playground today?"

Lottie is shy. She steps back behind Eva's skirt, but she is already shaking her head. Lottie and Molly are good friends. They look out for each other. I have no reason to doubt what she says.

"I better go and see who this child is. The parents are waiting apparently."

"OK. I'm going to wait here for you," Eva says.

"What? No, you don't have to do that." I am touched by her attitude.

"No, don't be silly. I would be furious if they said that about my daughter. I have a sandwich with me, and we'll sit in the canteen, then come back here in ten minutes."

"Really, Eva, you don't have to."

"Well, I will, and you can't stop me." She lifts her chin and gives me one of her cheeky smiles. I know that look. Eva has always been a tough cookie. Once she gets her mind set on something she sticks to it.

"OK, I'll text you."

"Cool," she says cheerfully and heads down to the canteen with Lottie.

CHAPTER 14

Ten years ago

I smoothed down the navy blue skirt of my business suit, holding the black folder with the property details. I was showing Mr and Mrs Smith around the spacious five-bedroom property on the hill, with great views of the Wimbledon Golf Club, and the distant skyscrapers on the horizon. The couple clutched hands as they entered the upstairs bedroom and looked out the windows. The view was stunning, I knew that. They stood in front and put their arms around each other. It was sweet, and a little wind blew around the lonely corridors of my heart, banging and closing doors of empty rooms. My life was empty. I was in my early twenties, and still had not met the man of my dreams. I was beginning to wonder if it would ever happen.

To add to the heartache, my mother had passed away last year. Eva and I had travelled up for the funeral. Dad now lived alone in the Yorkshire farm, and he would find it hard to cope. I was their only daughter. Mum never got to see me in a wedding dress. I would take that regret to my grave.

The couple turned, and I stood to one side, giving them space. This property came with vacant possession, but the interior decoration was done nicely. I could tell from their faces they liked it.

When we stood in the hallway, I waited for them to speak. This was their second visit, and I had developed a sixth sense about these things. I knew they liked it. I also knew that if I gave a client long enough, they told me what they wanted. They appreciated that.

Mr Smith, slightly older, in his mid- to late-thirties, looked at me and beamed. "We have decided to go for it. I would like to make an offer of two million pounds, the asking price."

I smiled at their expectant faces. Theirs was the highest offer so far, and I was sure it would be accepted. But I couldn't tell them that yet. "Thank you very much. I will pass it on, and be in touch with you tomorrow."

Mrs Smith looked apprehensive. "Do you think it will be accepted?"

"I can't tell you…"

"It's just that we have sold our house already, and are living with the children in rented premises. Our contract ends soon, and we just need to know as soon as possible."

I hesitated.

"Please," Mrs Smith said, her face earnest. I relented.

"Your offer is excellent, and I think it has every chance of being accepted." I had no doubt the seller would be over the moon with this offer. He was getting a lot less before.

"Great," she smiled. "Shall we inform our lawyer?"

"Please wait for my email."

They went out of the door, chatting to each other happily, making plans for their home. It was a nice summer day, and as I locked the doors behind them, the sunshine made a radiant glow around us. I drove back to the office, wondering if I would bump into Clive again. That night at the awards had only been two days ago, and I knew something had happened between Clive and me. We had danced with passion, soaked in sweat. He kept up with me, and bought me drinks after. He was easy to talk to, and I was getting to know the man behind the image.

My heart skipped a beat as I approached my desk. Clive was standing next to it. His face brightened when he saw me.

"Aha. How are you, Emma?"

We exchanged pleasantries, then he asked me into his office. He closed the door when I stepped inside. He brushed close to me as he did so, and the musky, fresh odour of his cologne assaulted my nostrils. He stood a few feet away from me, without sitting down. Those dark eyes were fixed on me again. I could feel my throat going dry.

Clive sighed and shifted on his feet. "Ever since you started here, this place has got a new lease of life. It's not just the sales, you just make things look nicer." He smiled. I turned crimson, wishing I could hide my face.

"Have a seat," he said. I sat down opposite him.

He said, "I need to ask you a favour." I waited. He opened his drawer and took out an envelope.

"These are two tickets for a stall at the Royal Albert Hall, to watch *Les Misérables*. Would you like to come with me?"

If my throat was parched before, now I could barely breathe. Clive Connery was made of money. Apart from this agency, he owned a number of properties in London, not counting his holiday villa in Marbella, Spain, and a cottage in Antibes, South of France. He was handsome, sexy, but also open, down to earth. Was he really asking me out on a date?

I closed my open mouth quickly and tucked a stray strand behind my ear. There was a hint of a smile on his lips when I looked up. He leaned forward.

"Can I take that as a yes?"

I nodded. He smiled broadly. "Good, that's a date then."

I stood to go. At the door, I became aware I was still holding the property folder to my chest.

"By the way," I said, "24 Home Park Road should be under offer soon."

He looked up, his face blank. "Why?"

I told him about the Smiths. I thought he would be happy, but a shadow passed over his face. He beckoned for me to sit down again.

"Tell me more about the Smiths." He leaned back in his chair. I told him what I knew, and he tapped his lips lightly.

"So they want it, huh?"

"Badly," I grinned. He grinned back.

"Tell them there is a higher offer. 2.2 million."

I stopped smiling. "What?"

"See if they can match it."

"But..."

"Emma." He leaned forward again. "Do you know you are both beautiful and intelligent?"

I thought my heart would stop beating. Keeping my face calm, I waited for him to continue.

"Therefore you will understand the basics of our business. The market is fluid. So is the price. The selling price is what people are willing to fork out.

It could be three million. Who knows?"

"Is there really a higher offer?"

He didn't bat an eyelid. "For properties in that location, there is always a higher offer. Remember that."

He stared at me, his eyes probing. "Are we on the same wavelength?"

I nodded, hiding the conflict I felt inside. He relaxed and flopped back, the tension going out of his shoulders. He seemed like the Clive Connery I knew again.

"Are we OK for tonight?"

"Sure," I said.

As I went back to my table, I tried to gauge what he had said. I made the call to the Smiths, and relayed the bad news. They were unhappy but called back later in the afternoon. They agreed to match the higher offer.

*****

I was ready and waiting at eight pm when I heard the doorbell. Clive was dressed in a blue suit without a tie, and he handed me a bouquet of red roses. They looked gorgeous. I was wearing my long, red dress, and I couldn't help noticing how he stared at me.

He held out a hand. "Shall we go? The night is young." I gripped his fingers, feeling the warm strength in them. The velvety blue evening was suffused with the light heat of summer. There was a promise in the air, laden with the smell of roses as I walked down with him to the waiting car.

We held hands and turned the corner. I was expecting a car, but what I saw made me gasp. A silver and white stretch limo was parked on the road, lights blinking.

"Like our ride?" Clive said. His eyes were dancing with mirth.

"Looks great. Is it just us?" I asked, trying to act normal.

He gave a short laugh. "Of course, it's just us!"

A liveried driver got out, and opened the door for us. I went in first. I had never been inside a limousine before and it blew my mind. The space inside was thrice the size of the living room in my small flat. Light dazzled the ornate glass in the corner bar, and shone off the chrome handles. The red leather was deep enough to sink into and wrapped around the corners. The driver shut the door. A flat-screen TV was on, and light music was floating from speakers. On a table in front of us, a bottle of Dom Pérignon was being chilled on ice.

"Clive, this must be expensive?"

He was sitting next to me, leaning forward. "Company expenses. All of it is tax-deductible. Don't worry." He smiled engagingly, and I caught my breath.

As the limo took off with a purring sound, Clive uncorked the bottle. He handed me a flute and smiled.

"To new beginnings."

"New beginnings," I echoed, feeling warm and fuzzy inside.

CHAPTER 15

Present day

I walk into an office opposite the teacher's common room. A man and a woman wearing business suits are already sitting there. It seems they have come straight from work. They both glare at me as I walk in. Their eyes fall on Molly and I instinctively step in front of her. I notice their daughter sits behind the mum, her eyes to the floor. She doesn't look up as we walk in.

"Is this the girl who hit my Henrietta?" the woman demands in an angry tone.

"Please Mrs Burton-Smyth, let's not make any hasty judgements," Miss Laker says.

Mrs Burton-Smyth – I don't know her first name as yet – turns to her daughter. "Hen, darling, is this the girl who did this to you?"

Henrietta has blonde curls and speckles on her nose. She looks at Molly quickly then lowers her head again. "Yes, Mummy," she says in a small voice.

The woman glares at me. "That's unbelievable."

The couple look angry. They are older than me, in their mid to late forties, I would say. The man has a beard, looks fit and tanned like his wife, and wears an expensively cut suit. The woman is wearing a blue and black skirt suit with nice shoes.

"Hang on a minute," I snap. "This is your daughter's word against mine. Molly has denied this already. There are no witnesses." I look at Miss Laker. "Are there?"

She purses her lips. "No, there aren't."

Mrs Burton-Smyth is not having any of it. "Look at this," she says. She turns Henrietta's face and I see the ugly bruise on her temple. Its looks tender and painful, and I feel sorry for the girl. I notice that Mr Burton-Smyth is sitting very still, watching me.

Mrs Burton-Smyth says, "How can someone do this to a little girl? How?" She points daggers at Miss Laker. "I thought this was a grammar school. How can these things happen here?"

Miss Laker voice is smooth. "We take pride in our pastoral care, Mrs Burton-Smyth. I can assure you, we will get to the bottom of this."

The woman glares at me again, but speaks to the teacher. "You better do. I will be telling all the other parents to keep a very close eye on my daughter from now on. If anyone as much as touches her…"

"It's OK, darling." Mr Burton-Smyth speaks for the first time. Behind his well-trimmed beard there are a pair of shapely lips, and his eyes have a ferocity in them that I like. But he is gentle, softly spoken. "Children can get hurt sometimes in the playground. As long as this is not repeated, it should all be fine."

"It's not fine, Rob," his wife seethes. "Hen was pushed to the ground and then this…this child kicked her. I mean, that is vicious!" She looks at me again, and I am getting more and more angry. If she looks at me like she's scraped me off the bottom of her shoe one more time…

Miss Laker says, "For now, let's just rest on the understanding that Molly didn't do this. Did you, Molly?" she asks Molly directly.

My daughter is fearless, and she squares her shoulders. She looks her teacher in the eyes and says, "No, Miss. I didn't."

I ask her, "And did you see anyone push Henrietta? Not just today, but at anytime?"

She shakes her head. "No, Mummy, I didn't."

I walk out of the office in the cold air with my head held high. I have already texted Eva and she is standing outside with Lottie.

"Who was the child?" Eva asks me. When I say the name, she groans.

"Not Joanne Burton-Smyth!"

"Why?"

"Let me guess. She was dressed for a board meeting, spoke like her tongue's on fire, and accused Molly from the second you walked in."

"Pretty much."

We sit down outside the canteen and I give Molly a packet of crisps. "Who is she?"

"She's a director of some insurance company in the city. Board-level executive. Her family are loaded, so is her husband. Not like she needs her million-pound job, but she loves it. The nanny raises the children, I swear to you. She's only seen at school if there's a crisis."

That explained a lot of what I have seen of her. I often think women who rely excessively on nannies become overprotective of the children. I tell this to Eva and she nods.

"They also donate money to the school."

I arch an eyebrow. "They do?"

"Yes. The school is a charity, so they call it a charitable donation." Eva drops her voice. "Between you and me, Henrietta isn't clever enough to be here. She got in at reception, but apparently her teachers have said she might not progress to senior school."

I am aware that this can happen at Crofton High, where academic standards are high. The penny drops about the donations.

"How can this be allowed?" I ask.

Eva has opened a packet of Maltesers and offers me one. Some chocolate is just what I need now. As I chew, she says, "It happens all the time. We just don't get to hear it."

We say goodbye and head back home. It's almost five o'clock and Molly is hungry. I look closely at her, wondering if she is upset by the whole thing. She seems OK.

"Would you like some hot chocolate?" It's her favourite drink. She beams and grabs me around the waist. I hug her back, feeling how tightly she holds me. Then I hold her at arm's length.

"Did anything happen today at the playground today, Molly?"

She shakes her head slowly. "I didn't see anything, Mummy. I don't know what Henrietta's mother was saying."

She has no reason to lie. I hug her again, wishing the uncomfortable feeling inside me would go away.

I boil the milk and add the chocolate power, then stir it and bring it to the table where Molly is sitting expectantly.

I put the glass down before her, warning that it's hot. I lift up the blind over the sink, slowly. The garden is empty, strewn with lifeless winter leaves. Beyond the fence, the park is barely visible. But it's there, and so might be the person I saw the other day. I lower the blind quickly and check the kitchen door to the garden is locked.

I hear a sound at the front door. A quick glance at my wristwatch says it's half past five, too early for Jeremy to come back home.

Fear blossoms inside me. "Stay here, Molly," I say, and run to the front door. As I feared, I forgot to lock it. These days, I have made it a point not to leave the door on the latch. Today I had other things on my mind. Damn it.

The key is turning still and any second now the door will open. Panic surges through my body like electricity. I fling myself at the door to close it. I hear a muffled exclamation from the other side.

"Jesus, who's that?" It's Jeremy's voice. I put my hand to my forehead, trying to control my breathing, my racing heart.

I reach out and open the door, feeling silly. Jeremy is in his work suit, tie undone, staring at me quizzically.

"Sorry, I thought you were someone else."

"Who?" he asks, coming in with his briefcase. He doesn't kiss me. I step back and let him close the door.

"One of these people who knock on doors trying to sell things. They can be burglars sometimes."

Jeremy turns around, a half-smile on his lips. "Darling, you're watching too much Crimewatch." He comes to hug me, but I move away and into the kitchen. I am tense, nervous. With shaking hands I get myself a glass of water. Is it my nerves, or is it guilt?

Jeremy says hi to Molly when he comes into the kitchen and I can feel him standing behind me. I turn around.

"I'm sorry. Just got a bit scared, that's all."

"This is a safe neighbourhood. Don't worry."

I know that, but right now my heart is telling me something else.

CHAPTER 16

Eight years ago

It had been two years since I had moved in with Clive. We had a two-bed ground-floor apartment in a lovely Victorian conversion just outside Wimbledon. It had been a whirlwind romance, and I knew we were meant for each other. We had travelled around the world, stayed in his villa in Marbella, and he had met my father. I still hadn't met the rest of his family, but his mother lived in Slough, outside London, and I would be seeing her soon, he had promised.

When we went up north to see Dad at the farmhouse, it was great to see how well Clive got on with my dad. Despite being a city slicker, he helped Dad tend to the pigs and chickens, and woke up at the crack of dawn to take the buggy out to the hills, where Dad and Pixie, our German Collie, herded the sheep. Dad had never had a son, and I felt a lump in my throat at seeing how well the two of them bonded.

Back in London, reality had hit. There was a crisis of funding in the banks, and the sub-prime mortgage disaster was just unfolding in the USA. Apparently, so-called wizard bankers had given million-dollar mortgages to convicts and drug dealers, thereby creating a boom in the real estate market. Now the boom had turned to bust, and the ripples had spread all over the world.

Our sales had sunk to almost nothing in the last eight months. Clive had become stressed and frustrated and spent a lot of time outside the office. Before the financial crisis hit, he had been in talks to open branches in Richmond and Putney, two important markets for us. Now the loans had been withdrawn, and Clive had meetings with new fundraisers every day. I hardly saw him. When he came home, I was often asleep.

One summer evening, I was waiting for Clive while he finished up a business meeting in the city. I comforted myself with a tub of Ben & Jerry's chocolate chip ice cream and a chick flick. I was curled up on the sofa with my feet tucked beneath me when the phone rang. It was Eva. We spoke for a while, swapping stories. She was in London, but her work meant long hours, and she was calling me from the office. She had a new bloke in her life, too, a guy called Richard, who worked for a securities firm.

I hung up when I heard Clive come in the door. He looked exhausted. I got up and gave him a kiss. He responded slowly, like he did when he was tired.

"Gin and tonic?" I asked.

"Please," he said, sitting wearily down on the sofa. I made the drink and brought it back to him.

"How did it go?" I asked him. He took a long sip of the drink.

He stared at the glass as he spoke. "Not good, Emma. There's just no money around anymore. The banks don't want to lend. It's not just mortgages. It's business loans, everything."

I hated seeing him like this. His shoulders were slumped, and his eyes had lost their glint. Suddenly, he kicked out with his right foot, and his shoe caught the coffee table, turning it over. The smashing sound rattled the TV. The table fell within inches of the screen.

"Clive! What are you doing?"

He didn't answer. He ran a hand over his face. I stared at him with a stricken face. I knew he was under stress, but I hadn't realised the effect it was having on him. This wasn't the Clive I knew.

"What I wish I could do to these bloody lenders," he said vehemently. "Blood-sucking arseholes, sit there and talk about return on their investment. Fucking ROI. What they need is a good kicking."

He was in a dark, moody place, and I watched his nostrils flare, his face redden. He looked up, caught my eyes, and his face softened. He got up and put the table back up.

"I'm sorry," he said. "It's going to be OK. Just going to need some time."

I moved closer to him. "Remember you said all business cycles go through ups and downs." I ran a hand through his hair, and it felt soft to the touch. His head fell back on the sofa.

"Yes," he breathed. I leaned over and kissed him on the lips. This time, he kissed me back with more urgency. Soon, all talk was forgotten, and we were entangled in each other, my fingers unbuttoning his shirt.

*****

We arrived at work together the next morning. For the last two years, we'd had this routine where I went in, sat down at my table, and he came in with a cup of coffee a few minutes later. He didn't want others at the office to know, and I didn't mind. I was reasonable friends with the other girls in the place, and we met up for office socials, but I didn't know them well enough to hang out. Things could get awkward if they found out about me and their boss.

Jim, our mortgage broker, answered the phone on his desk and rose up. He hovered in front of my desk and said, "Clive wants to speak to us." Another one of the agents joined us and we went to the office at the back. Clive was finishing a call as I knocked and went in.

"Jim," Clive said without delay, "what's happening with the mortgage on 345 Hill Walk?"

"They want more documents from the buyers. Latest payslips and bank statements. It's all progressing."

"No, it's not!" Clive raised his voice. "I've just come off the phone with Mr Jones, the buyer. He said that a mortgage advisor from the bank has contacted him directly. They have told him he can't have the funds."

Jim looked astonished. "But they can't do that."

Clive clenched his jaws tight. "They can and they are. You told me this mortgage deal was in the bag, Jim. We really need this deal to go through."

Jim said, "And it will. I just need to speak to them again."

Clive stood up, picked up a file from his desk and threw it across the room at Jim. It missed him narrowly, hit the wall behind him, and fell to the floor, papers swaying down slowly. Everyone was shocked. Jim had an open mouth, and he took a step backwards as Clive got out from behind his desk. Clive was a compact, powerful man, and he moved menacingly.

"Those are the files for the Smith account, Jim," Clive snarled. "You have been working on this for the last four weeks, and you have nothing to show me."

I came forward. "I think we all need to calm down. Jim's doing his best, Clive."

He turned on me, and the sheer rage on his face left me breathless for a minute. His face was carved in stone, the colour of lava, a deadly coldness radiating from him. I stepped back, afraid.

"And what do you know about his best, Emma? Have you been keeping tabs on him? No, it's all down to me."

Clive reached out and slapped a stack of files on his desk, near the edge. They smacked down to the floor, scattering invoices and papers.

"It's all going to hell," he thundered. Jim was cowering against the wall.

"I'll do my best. I'm going to call the bank right now."

Clive sat down at his desk and lowered his head in his hands. "You do that, Jim. And remember I want good news. Got it?" He looked up at him. Jim nodded, and left the room. Clive's eyes flickered to me. "Leave me alone," he said. I was more than happy to. His behaviour had no excuse. I slammed the door shut on my way out.

CHAPTER 17

Jeremy reaches up into one of the kitchen cabinets and pulls down a bottle of red wine. He doesn't open the bottle. I catch him watching me with a half-smile on his lips. He seems to have got over me slamming the door shut in his face. I still feel silly about it. Who else would have keys to our front door apart from Jeremy? And myself obviously.

His parents live in Hampshire, miles away, and I know he hasn't given them a key. I remember thinking about giving Eva a key once, but I didn't.

"Are you going to open that bottle?" I ask as I sit down next to Molly. Our kitchen isn't big. Its ten square metres of space with kitchen counter, oven and hob, and dining table all cramped into one. I keep an eye on the garden as I sit down. Light is fading fast, strangled by dark, threatening clouds. It might rain tonight. A wind picks up, bending the trees in the park. I hope the clouds blow over.

Jeremy asks, "Do you guys have anything planned now?"

"No," I say, wondering why. Then I realise Jeremy has come back home early from work. "Is everything OK at work?"

"Yes, it is," he says easily. "I had a half-day due, so decided to use it." There's a twinkle in his eyes that I don't quite understand.

"Well, if you two aren't doing anything shall we go for a ride?"

"Where to?" I ask, even as Molly claps her hands and slides off the chair.

"You shall soon find out," Jeremy says mysteriously.

I lock up the door of our two-bed terraced house, after I've set the alarm. Molly is standing next to me, and I take her hand, walking to Jeremy's car. He doesn't say anything, and looks straight out of the windscreen.

"Am I OK dressed like this?" I ask, before he sets off.

"You'd look good no matter what you wore, darling," he says, melting my heart a little.

"Lying will get you anywhere," I say, suppressing a smile.

"Who's lying?"

"Then tell us where we're going." I don't mind surprises. But it's been a long day, and I still haven't told Jeremy about what happened at school. I want to wait till Molly is in bed. Which reminds me of what I need to tell Jeremy about: everything. My good mood starts to evaporate.

We drive out towards the A3, and head down towards New Malden, a nice, leafy suburb with semi- and detached houses on either side. It's a far cry from the narrow street that we live on. Our area is nice, very residential, but space fetches a stonking premium in London. New Malden is a little out of the way, but easily commutable by car and train. It takes us half an hour to get from Wimbledon to here. Jeremy parks outside a semi-detached house on the corner, which is easily three times the size of where we live. I can see from the large bay windows that the lounge and bedrooms must be spacious. I can't help wondering whose house this is, and why Jeremy has brought us here.

"What are we doing here?" I ask him. He covers my hand with his and leans forward to kiss me. Our lips meet and he murmurs, "Let's get out and see."

I open the door for Molly and she hops out, still in her school uniform. The front lawn needs tending, and the conifers that shade the house from the street are tall and lovely. We open the gate and step inside a path that leads up to the house. When the door opens and a man in a suit steps out, I suddenly have a funny feeling. The man waves at us and Jeremy waves back. He is obviously expected.

"Mr Mansell, how do you do?"

They shake hands. I see the property brochure in the man's hands and there is no doubt in my mind now. We have come to view this property. The estate agent hands me a piece of paper with all the property details on it. I feel a little delirious, this used to be my job way before meeting Jeremy. Seems like another lifetime ago.

The carpets have a paisley pattern and are old-fashioned. The furniture is also dated, but there is no mistaking the space inside. The house is structurally sound, I cannot see any damp patches or any leaks anywhere. The walls are painted and there aren't any wide cracks visible. Molly is excited, pulling me out of the back door to see the broad, wide garden. Again, easily three times the size of our tiny garden now. And the rooms are huge as well. Five bedrooms. A kitchen where we can entertain more than ten guests with ease.

When we get back to the car, I turn on Jeremy. "What on earth?" I am excited and scared at the same time. I know how much these places cost, and I know Jeremy doesn't have that sort of money. He is a nice, sweet, dependable guy. That's why I am now engaged to him.

"Do you like it?" Jeremy asks.

I shake my head. "Like it? Listen to yourself, Jeremy. How on earth can we afford anything like this?"

"Trust me, we can." There's a grin on his face.

"You always complain about how much rent we have to pay. The mortgage on this place will be more."

"That depends on how much deposit we put down."

"Yes," I say slowly. "And where is the deposit coming from?" I am perplexed because Jeremy's parents aren't wealthy. His dad used to work in the council and his mother is a housewife.

Jeremy's eyes are shining. "Our firm completed a long and complex divorce case last month. I was the lead solicitor." Jeremy specialises in family law so this isn't surprising. He is fond of saying that 50% of marriages in England end in divorce. I find that number incredibly high. That's every other marriage, basically.

He continues. "It was a Russian businessman who had loads of money. He was sleeping around and his wife found out. She filed for divorce and his lawyers fought back. We won, and got her a great deal. She's very happy, and we got a windfall from it." He pauses, and looks at me with smiling eyes. "So I got a big bonus."

"How much?"

"Enough to put down a 25% deposit on this house and have some left over."

I breathe in sharply. That is a lot of money. For a while I am so happy I can't speak. But then visions from the past come rolling in. Like a high tide, drawn by the eye of an evil moon, submerging all my hopes.

I look down at my hands, suddenly worried.

Jeremy's voice changes. "What is it?"

I say nothing. Molly has been very good, she is quiet and is observing us with interest from the back seat.

"Let's go back home and talk," I say.

Jeremy says nothing for the rest of the trip. I reach over and give his thigh a squeeze, and he rubs my hand. He holds my hand as long as he can.

*****

When Molly is upstairs to get changed and brush her teeth, Jeremy opens the bottle of red and pours himself a glass. I prefer a white and have a Pinot Grigio chilled. We sit down with our glasses, facing each other.

"I don't want us to struggle," I say, taking a sip of wine. It's cold, citrus, refreshing.

"I just told you about my bonus," he says.

"I know. But we don't need a five-bedroom mansion. To be honest, I am happy where we are. Why don't you save the money?"

"For what? The rent we pay is just wasted money."

I know he's right. But I know what happens when the costs start to mount, and…maybe I am just too scared to dream. My dreams have been broken once, and like a broken heart, dreams aren't easy to fix. I would rather hold onto the happiness I have, for as long as I can.

As if he can read my thoughts, Jeremy asks softly, "What are you afraid of?"

CHAPTER 18

His question jolts me back to the moment. I am staring at him, a hundred emotions running through me. I need to tell Jeremy the truth about me. More than anyone else, he needs to know.

Once the past is out of the way, we can talk about the future. No, that's not true. We *are* talking about the future. The fear is back again, clawing at my throat, suffocating me. If I do tell him, will he think less of me?

Will I be able to give him everything he wants? Even as I ask myself the question I know the answer. It's not an answer I like, and never will. I look down at my hands, and the ring flashes like a thousand suns beaming light into my eyes. My heart wrenches inside.

What am I supposed to do?

I never thought my heart would be so full as it is now, not after what happened. But even as my life begins to flower and bloom, I can feel the cold hand of the past, heavy on my shoulder.

I look up at Jeremy. He is watching me with a frown. I open my mouth to speak, to tell all, but the moment has passed. I don't have the strength to do it now.

"I don't want you to become stressed," I say, and I mean it. "There's only three of us, and we could easily live in a smaller house, or even a flat."

"I don't want a flat. I want somewhere Molly can play outside."

I nod, my shoulders dropping. Of course I want that for Molly.

Jeremy is speaking again. "And if we have new arrivals..." He leaves the sentence unfinished.

I don't look at him. "You know I've had problems in the past..."

"I know, Em. But you're still young. We can see the best doctors. We can try."

A sob catches at my throat. Every time we speak about this an invisible barrier appears between us. Jeremy is 36 and I am 34. He's being generous when he says I am still young. I know the clock is ticking. Loudly.

I grip the glass and take a long sip. Jeremy reaches out across the table and I let him hold my hand. His touch is warm and strong, a touch I have learned to trust. Jeremy has always been stout, resilient without being flashy. He is just what I need. We are happy. Now this new house will uproot us, and make changes when none were necessary.

Am I being unreasonable? Wouldn't most women be ecstatic at the chance of living in a nice, big house with a garden the size of a football field?

But I have lived in a large farmhouse at our farm, and I know how much it costs to maintain it. Dad did most of the work when he was younger, but Jeremy wouldn't be able to do it now, not with his demanding job. Which would mean spending loads of money.

I tell him this. He considers it. Jeremy is reasonable. He says, "I know, but the place will also go up in value. That's good for the long run. And you don't want to move again, do you?"

"Why can't we look for something smaller?"

From the look in his eyes, I can tell he has his heart set on this place. "OK," I admit defeat. "I'll think about it."

His eyes brighten. "You will?"

"Yes, I promise." I smile, and he walks around the table. I move into his embrace and we hold each other for a while.

"How was Molly's school today?" he asks.

Memories of our stressful day at school come flowing back. "Not great. Molly's doing well, but this girl has accused her of bullying."

"What? Our Molly?" Jeremy leans back, disbelief in his eyes.

I nod. "Crazy, I know. This girl was shoved, and then kicked. Poor child had a bruise. But fancy accusing Molly. I asked Molly and she denies it totally."

"Does Molly know who did it?"

I shake my head. "No, none of the children saw anything. Which makes it worse, because there's no one to back Molly up."

"Stuff like this doesn't normally happen at the school, does it?"

I shake my head, finishing my glass of wine. "No. And you should have seen the parents. Pompous gits. Mother seems to have made her mind up about Molly already. Bloody cheek." I am seething again, remembering that woman's attitude.

"Who are they?"

"Woman's called Joanne Burton-Smyth. Does some big job in an insurance firm. Thinks that gives her the right to talk down to me."

Jeremy is giving me a funny look. After a few seconds he says, "Is the husband called Tim Burton-Smyth?"

I widen my eyes. "You know them?"

"Not sure if it's the same family, but I know Tim's daughter goes to the same school as our Molly."

I think fast. As far as I know, there isn't anyone else with that last name. Maybe Eva will know more.

"How do you know this guy?"

Jeremy has a troubled look on his face, and his eyebrows are knit together. "He is the senior partner in our law firm. He decides who gets paid what."

It takes a little while to settle in my mind. Molly has my last name. Dixon. So Henrietta's parents wouldn't be able to identify Molly on that basis, and in any case, there could be a number of Mansells.

"How well do you know them?" I ask.

Jeremy shrugs. "Not that well. Played golf with him a couple of times. Nice guy. We spoke about the girls but only briefly. Talked about work mostly."

It occurs to me this man could be behind Jeremy's promotion and bonus at work. I slump back into the chair.

"Great."

Jeremy massages my shoulders. "Don't worry. I'm sure they're going to find the boy or girl who did this. These things happen at school."

I shake Jeremy's hands off my shoulder. "Before they find out, they're busy accusing my daughter!"

Immediately I feel bad. It's just bad luck that he is now involved in this. "I'm sorry," I say, standing up.

"Don't worry. I can see how it can be stressful. Like I said, I think this will blow over."

"I hope so," I sigh.

CHAPTER 19

Eight years ago

Days passed into weeks. The summer of 2008 was hot and flustered. The banking crisis was sending quakes all across the world, cracks appearing in the safe and secure grounds everyone took for granted.

Sales in the estate agency had dwindled to almost nothing. We had fallen back on what agents relied on during a housing crisis – the rental market. My new role was to show as many people the flats we had for rent. Occasionally, we had problems getting people in and out of flats as well.

In a smart apartment complex in Putney, we had the misfortune of having a young man who was falling in arrears over his rent. It had only been a month, but our finances were tight as they were. And I had found someone new who was interested in the flat. A professional couple who, unlike many, still had their jobs intact.

I arrived at the flat and rang the doorbell. I knew the guy was inside as his car was there in the parking lot, and the newspapers and bottle of milk had been removed from his door. I waited but he wouldn't answer. I could hear someone moving inside as well.

Exasperated, I rang Clive. He said he was coming over. I didn't want him to in fact, because although he had apologised over the way he had treated Jim, his stress levels weren't doing him any favours. But it was too late. He was in charge of the business, and I didn't have any option but to call him.

Within minutes, it seemed, I saw his black BMW had pulled up downstairs. He came up in the lift, his face calm.

"Pretty sure he's in there," I said. Clive put his ears to the door. He looked at me and nodded. He banged heavily on the door.

"Mr Dobson. Please open the door. We have to call the police if you don't."

There was no answer. Clive tried a couple more times, and with each effort, I could see he was getting more worked up. I caught the sleeve of his jacket.

"Let's leave this, Clive. You are right, call the police."

Clive's face was slowly turning purple again, the colour I had learnt to be wary of.

"And what will they do?" He sneered. "Take four weeks to get a warrant, during which time this moron will have missed another month's rent." He looked at me with hooded eyes. "We need to take matters into our own hands."

Fear caught in my chest. What was he going to do?

"No, Clive," I said quickly. "Just leave it. It's not worth it."

He came close to me, his face calm again, the scent of his aftershave cool and fresh. He stroked my left cheek. "Hey, don't worry. Problem with guys like these is that they need to be taught a lesson. Once it's done, he won't bother us again."

Before I could say anything, Clive had turned, and fished out a jangle of keys from his pocket. He tried several in turn. I watched, mystified. I had no idea all these keys existed in the office. We had a well-organised keyboard which was kept in his office. I had never seen this assortment before.

Clive tried several, till one clicked. He smiled at me, but the smile faded on his lips as the rattle of the chain lock sounded. He stood up wearily. He shot me a look.

"This never happened, alright? And I have to do this because there's no choice."

Clive took three steps back. I watched in disbelief as he rushed forward, and kicked the door with all his strength. The chain snapped off, and the door banged against the back of the frame. Clive barged in. I didn't know what to do. I waited outside, heart beating rapidly, as I heard sounds of crashing and breaking inside. After a while, Clive emerged, holding a straggly, thin young man with long hair and tattoos. He pushed Mr Dobson against the door, fist on his collar.

"Tomorrow, did you hear me? Either that, or you clear out from here. If

I come back here and see you here, you know what's going to happen."

"I'll report you to the police," Mr Dobson gasped. "This is assault. You can't get away with it."

"Oh yeah? Who's going to believe you? I haven't left a mark on your body. You kicked in the door when you were drunk. And there are no witnesses."

Mr Dobson's eyes flickered over to mine, and I looked away, embarrassed. Without saying another word, I went down the stairs as fast as I could.

I was lighting up a cigarette when Clive joined me. I stood well away from him. I didn't know this person he was turning into. Everything about him was suddenly alien, strange.

He brushed a hand through his hair and sighed. "I'm sorry you had to see that. But now he knows. He won't try to mess with us again."

I gave him a withering look. "Is this what you're going to do to everyone who goes into arrears? Go round their flat and beat them up?"

His expression was pained. "Darling, be reasonable. I didn't beat this guy up. It was just…"

"Just a friendly kicking down his door and gripping him by the throat, was it?" I threw the cigarette on the floor and stamped on it with my heel. "Jesus, Clive, will you look at yourself? What is happening to you? You have changed. You're not the man I…"

The sudden hurt in his eyes made me look away. I was angry, and I had to let him know. I heard him sigh.

"You're right," he said. I glanced at him, and his face was pointed downwards. "I built this business up from scratch, Em. It's all the work I did. And now it's falling apart." He looked at me intensely, and my heart skipped a beat. His devilish good looks still took my breath away.

"I am good at my job, you know?"

"You are, Clive. But there are things beyond your control." I softened my voice. "When bad things happen we have to compromise. There's always a deal around the corner. Who told me that?"

He looked at me with a rueful smile on his face. "I know. And you are right. I cannot do what I just did. I think I should go back and apologise to him."

That made me happy. "I think that's a really good idea. I'll see you back at the office."

He turned around. "Why don't we go for a drink after? Just at the local pub, The Pig and Whistle. A couple of my old friends are coming down."

I stopped. "What friends? You never told me."

"Oh, just some of my friends from school. They called this morning and said they would be in the area. We'll have a couple of drinks and then be on our way. Nothing special."

Despite feeling slightly uncomfortable, I thought I would sound rude if I refused the offer. After all, I hadn't been out with Clive for weeks now. This didn't sound like a romantic night out, but it would still be social. I nodded. He beamed back at me.

*****

Clive and myself were the last ones to leave the office. I left first and walked over to the pub which was five minutes away on foot. There were some people at the bar and sitting around, but no one I recognised. I breathed a sigh of relief. I didn't like coming to this place because I didn't want our co-workers finding out about us. I would tell them in due course.

I felt someone at my back and turned to see Clive. He gave me a peck on the cheek, and pointed to a table.

"My friends are sitting there. Why don't you take a seat with them and I'll bring the drinks over. Double gin and tonic?"

I nodded, looking at the table. The two men who sat there wore suits, but they looked nothing like Clive. They were both bald, and there was a hardness in the angles of their faces, and in the way they looked around the pub. Their eyes alighted on us, and one of them gave a grin. For some reason, it made me shiver. The guy had a gold tooth.

"Who are they?" I asked without leaving his side.

"We go way back. Schooldays."

"Where from?"

"Dagenham. You know I grew up there."

I did. Clive did his best to hide the East End twang in his accent now,

68

rounding it out with the mellow South London suburban vowels, but I could see through it. I stared at the two men, and noticed the gold chains that hung from both their necks. They looked like cockney gangsters.

CHAPTER 20

Present day

The next morning I have a nice surprise. I have come back home having dropped Molly off and make myself a coffee. I plan to have a morning at the easel and canvas, doing some abstracts. With what has been happening in my life at the moment, I have gone off figures and landscapes. I shut the door of the studio, and turn on the wireless doorbell for the front door in case someone knocks.

I take out my paints, and spread them in front of me like a fan. The sky is the colour of gunmetal grey, low-bellied clouds grazing it like dark thoughts. My mood is also dark, and I am in a closed, reclusive place. I mix brown with red, and black with dark blue. I start with bold lines, framing them out like the bars of a jail cell. Inside I flow softer colours, the morsels of my mind that evade expression. I pour in the anxiety and pain I have been living with the last few days.

It is strangely therapeutic. Painting gets me relaxed. I am in full flow when the bell rings. I look through the eyepiece to find a woman who looks familiar, with a baby. I open the door immediately to find Suzy Elliot standing there, with a grin on her face, and holding baby Margaret to her chest.

"She wanted to say hello," Suzy said.

It's really nice to see them. I hold little Margaret, and she is sound asleep. Only ten days old now, and strange to think that I found her the other day, abandoned in the park. I brush the thought away. She is safe now, and always will be.

Suzy goes to her car, and comes back with a bouquet of flowers, a box of chocolates and a thank-you card.

"You shouldn't have done that, Suzy," I say, and she shushes me.

"Nonsense. I owe you everything." She gives me a meaningful look. "I just came from the council house."

I waited for her to elaborate. Suzy said, "We made a change in her birth certificate and changed her name. From now on her middle name is not Louise. It will be Emma."

It takes a while to sink in. Then I am overcome. "No, Suzy. You really don't have to do that."

"I have already spoken to Paul. He agrees, too. Both of us really wanted to do this. Without you, I wouldn't have a daughter today."

Her eyes are burning brightly, and I feel a strange emotion wash over me. A week ago, I didn't know this woman. Now life finds us bound together inextricably, like links in a silver necklace.

Suzy says, "Her full name now is Margaret Emma Elliot. The initials will be MEE."

"Hope she doesn't grow up obsessed with herself," I say, and we both laugh.

"Tell me what happened at the police station," Suzy asks.

My face falls. I tell her the best I can. "They think it's all too convenient, the way I found her. As if I could have planned all this."

Suzy shakes her head. "Unbelievable. You would think the cops would be thanking you for making their job easier. They don't have to keep looking now. The massive search operation got called off only due to you."

I want to tell her about the man in the park, but I hold back. I don't want to cause her undue stress. This is my problem, and not hers. "Is your mother still here?"

"No, she's gone back."

I indicate the sleeping Margaret. "How is she?"

"All intact, nothing missing." Suzy grins. The freckles on her nose are so profuse they almost make the skin brown. Her red hair is tied back in a ponytail, and she has no make-up on, but she still looks pretty.

"Nice house you have here," she says, looking around our messy living room. Although there's only three of us, this room gathers a lot of junk. I have some of my paintings on the wall, the TV hangs next to them, and with the L-shaped sofa the room can look small. Molly also uses this place to dump her stuff after school. It's polite of Suzy to pay the compliment.

"Jeremy wants a bigger place," I confide in her. "But I'm not sure."

She nodded. "So does Paul. But I don't think we can afford anything around here unless we move further out." Her eyes become hard, and she looks away from me. "To be honest, not sure I want to live here anymore. Don't feel safe."

I nod, not knowing what to say. She has a point. If that had been me...I get up and smooth my jeans down, feeling restless all of a sudden.

"Do forgive me," I said, "haven't offered you tea or coffee. What would you like?"

"Some coffee please."

We move to the kitchen and I brew some coffee for both of us. Suzy says, "Who would do something like that?"

I stir the milk in her coffee, head bent. "Someone who's twisted and depraved," I say, handing the cup to her. Margaret is now in her travelling cot on the living room floor, fast asleep.

"Have the police got in touch again?" I ask Suzy.

"Not yet. They said they will only if new evidence comes to light."

I sip my coffee, wondering what that new evidence might be. It's hard to forget the interrogation Rockford and Ingram subjected me to. I hope they don't cross my path again. At the same time, I cannot help thinking if *I* will need their help one day. Will they see me as more of a suspect then?

"How is Molly doing at school?" Suzy asks, interrupting my thoughts, which I am grateful for. These morbid daydreams are becoming more frequent for me, and I don't like it.

"She's doing great, she loves it." I debate whether to tell her about the bullying allegation, then decide there's no harm. Her daughter is not in the same year as Molly anyway. I know that during playtime all the children run around in the same ground, but that is most of the contact they have. More importantly perhaps, the parents don't mix, unless they have daughters in different years. In addition, Suzy will now be busy with little Margaret to socialise too much. I know how the rumour mill works, and I think I can trust Suzy.

"A child said Molly had bullied her," I say. Then I tell her the whole story.

Suzy thinks for a moment, then her eyes light up.

"Oh yes, the Burton-Smyths. I have seen her a few times. She organised the summer ball last year. You know, the one at the All England Lawn Tennis Club."

I wasn't in the school at the time, but I heard it was a big party. "Do you know Joanne Burton-Smyth?"

"Briefly chatted to her once, at the ball. Don't know her well."

"Well, she seems very cocksure my Molly beat up her Hen. But Molly didn't. Problem is, there aren't any witnesses."

My mood darkens as I recount the story. No child should be blamed like this, not without concrete proof. I despise Joanne for doing this.

"She is one of the school governors, I know that," Suzy said. "It's a panel of parents and teachers that deal with school issues."

The more I hear about this woman, the more I realise why Miss Laker, Molly's teacher, was trying to smooth things over at the meeting. It doesn't matter. As long as she stays away from Molly I don't care what she does. The fact that her husband is Jeremy's senior colleague just adds a toxic twist to the mix, one I'm trying hard to ignore.

Suzy says goodbye, promising to make some discreet enquiries about Joanne's daughter, and the family situation. I tell her not to. I don't want my daughter's name bandied about, and in all honesty, I don't care about what's happening inside the Burton-Smyth household.

CHAPTER 21

It's getting to pick-up time, so I leave my painting unfinished and get ready. It's a pity as after almost a week of upheavals, I was getting into the flow of it. It also made me realise how much I have missed it. Painting allows me to give expression to feelings that are buried deep inside. I guess we all have them. The really important stuff, the things that make us who we are, often find no expression unless it's through painting, music, words. That's what I believe anyway. Putting colour to canvas helped me get through the worst patch of my life. Sounds weird, but it all makes sense when I look at the paintings. My art is more important than the little money I make from it. I really enjoy it.

As I get into the car and start driving, I habitually look into the windscreen. I am going up Copse Hill, a leafy road with large, detached houses on either side. There are cars behind me, and my eyes flicker from the road to the windscreen.

I see it.

It's like a bucket of ice just got poured over my head.

The small, black shape of the Nissan Micra. Once again, it's about three or four cars behind, so I can't read the number plate, and I can't see the driver well. From the shape, I can tell it's a man. I watch for a while, driving carefully. Then abruptly, it disappears from view. I strain my eyes at the rear-view and other mirrors, but it's gone.

Did I imagine it? I exhale and lower the window, letting cold air blast on my face. I am looking for odd things, and I keep finding them. My nerves feel shredded.

The phone beeps, and I stiffen again. I don't like that my hands shake as I pick it up. It's not a text. Instead, a familiar name has popped up on the screen. It's Steve Ponting. I answer immediately.

"Emma, can you talk?"

"Yes, hold on," I say and put him on the hands-free. His voice comes on the loudspeakers.

"Go ahead Steve. How are things?"

"Not very good, Emma. Pretty awful in fact." His voice has an edge to it.

"What's the matter?"

"My gallery was burned down last night. Police are calling it an act of vandalism. Someone broke in, and set a fire. The alarm went off, but by the time the neighbours called the police the fire had been going for an hour."

"Oh my God." I am shocked. "You had paintings stored inside, didn't you?"

"Yes." Sorrow creeps into his voice. "It's all been burnt."

I indicate and pull over. This is horrible news. I am glad that I got my paintings out of there once the exhibition was cancelled. If I had left them there, it would all be destroyed now. I really feel for Steve, he must be going through hell.

"I am so sorry, Steve. What will you do?"

"I am calling up all the artists and letting them know what happened."

"Thanks for letting me know, Steve. Was the gallery insured?"

"Yes, it was, and so were the paintings inside. But that is not the point."

"No, of course not." I check my watch. I am planning on getting to the school a bit early to check on Molly and speak to the sports teachers. Molly is a keen gymnast, and the school squad trials are coming up soon.

"Look, Emma, I need to ask you something." There is a hesitant tone in Steve's voice. For some reason it puts me on guard.

"What is it?"

There's a pause, the Steve says, "The police are here, and they want to speak to all the artists who were connected to the gallery. They want to speak to you, if that's OK."

My heart races and my head feels light. I really don't want to speak to the cops again, but given my recent history with them, what does it look like if I refuse? Besides, Steve sounds like he could use some moral support.

"No problem," I say, keeping my voice steady with an effort. "Where are you now?"

"At the gallery."

"I'll come down there, Steve. In about ten minutes?"

He pauses for a while, then replies in a quiet voice. "I would like that Emma, yes."

"Fine, I'll drop by."

Steve thanks me and I hang up. I change direction, going back the way I came and head for the High Street. I park in the Sainsbury's where it's free for two hours. Steve's gallery is a short walk away. As I approach I see the traffic due to the police vans. A barricade has been created, and blue and white police tape has cordoned off the area in front of the gallery. I see Steve talking to some onlookers, and I saunter over.

He looks at me, and I can see his wilting posture, shoulders sagged. His eyes are blank, hollow. My heart goes out to him, and I give him a hug. Without speaking, we stare at the smoke-blackened frontage of the shop that Steve had renovated five years ago to make the gallery. The glass on either side has collapsed, and rotting, smouldering furniture is visible inside. Some paintings are still on the wall, and they look charred, dirty, a ghastly sight. I look away, horrified.

Steve shakes his head. "Who would do such a thing to works of art?" he says in a low voice. His eyes are downcast.

"Ridiculous," I mutter, feeling a wave of nausea surge inside me. A flicker of movement catches my eyes, and I see a woman walking towards me. It's Detective Inspector Ingram. I can see from her face that she has recognised me.

"Afternoon, Mrs Mansell," she says without a smile on her face. "How are you?"

"Fine, thanks," I say, on my guard. "Terrible business, this."

"Yes, indeed." She takes out a notebook. "Do you mind if I ask you a few questions?"

I want to tell her that I have nothing to say, but then think better of it. I excuse myself from Steve and walk over to near the police van. Ingram leans against it and I keep standing. Curious onlookers walk around us.

Ingram says, "It might be better if we step inside the van." She holds open the passenger seat for me.

"I need to collect my daughter," I say.

"This won't take long, Mrs Mansell."

I hunch my shoulders and step inside the van. It's only me and her inside. When we shut the doors it's warmer than outside. The upholstery smells of old leather and diesel. I watch Ingram as she opens her notebook to a page and smooths it over. She holds a pen in her hand. Her blonde hair is free today, and it falls in waves around her shoulders.

She looks at me with flat, expressionless eyes. I return her stare.

"We meet again, Mrs Mansell."

I shrug. "Coincidence."

"Do you believe in coincidences?" Her tone is light, blank like her eyes.

"They can happen. No point in looking for connections where they don't exist."

I can see she is thoughtful at my remark. I suddenly realise I shouldn't have said it. She is a detective, and it's her job to look for connections. I need to be more careful with her. I am not used to this. I want to get out of this bloody van, and go back to living my life.

"Where were you last night?" Ingram asks.

"At my house, with my daughter and husband."

"So your husband can verify that?"

"Yes, of course."

She makes a note, and taps the pen against the page a few times. She asks, "You have a business relationship with Steve Ponting, don't you?"

"I have exhibited a few of my paintings in the gallery, yes."

"And you had a solo exhibition planned, which I understand had to be cancelled at short notice."

"I...yes." My answer is hesitant, and she picks up on it.

"Were you going to say something else?"

"No." She stares at me for a while. I am aware of cars passing on the road, their sounds muted to whispers inside the van. The silence between us grows, amplifies, filling the space. I am the first to look away.

"Mrs Mansell..."

"Call me Emma, please."

"OK, Emma. Is it true that your husband came to tell Steve that your first solo exhibition would have to be cancelled? Because of your father's ill health."

My heart constricts, and I tighten my fists inside my jacket pockets. "Yes."

Ingram taps the pen again, a thoughtful look on her face. "But apparently, you came two days after that, and denied it. You said that your husband had never been to see Steve. Is that correct?"

I would like to deny it, but doing so would be contradicting Steve's statement, which Ingram obviously has taken with some detail. I wonder why Steve had mentioned my exhibition, and I begin to feel uneasy.

"Yes," I say with a straight face. "I don't know who this person was, and why he said what he did. My father was not unwell, and I didn't have to cancel the exhibition."

"Isn't that strange?"

"Yes, it is."

"Do you know who was impersonating your husband?"

"No."

"Have you asked your husband?"

The three seconds it takes me to answer causes her grey pupils to constrict, and I feel my pulse beat a little faster.

"Yes, I have," I lie. "He doesn't know who it might be."

Ingram raises an eyebrow. A drizzle has started. Drops fall silently on the windscreen and course down without a sound. I can hear my heart beating.

"Are you sure it wasn't him?" Ingram asks.

I don't like the angle she is trying. "I trust my husband," I say with what I hope is conviction in my voice. "He wouldn't lie to me."

"So someone pretended to be your husband, and cancelled your show. And you have no idea who that person might be?"

Her eyes are boring into me now, and the air inside the cabin is suddenly heavy and oppressive. The gaseous smell of diesel is cloying, itchy at the throat. I want to inhale the rain outside the windows.

"No, I don't."

She changes tack again. "You came back and removed your paintings three nights ago. Is that correct?"

"Yes."

"Your paintings weren't damaged in the fire."

"What's your point?" I meet her gaze, and tilt my chin slightly upwards.

"Lucky you, I guess," she says with a little shrug.

I break off eye contact and glance down at my watch. "Look, Inspector Ingram, if that will be all, I have a school pick-up in ten minutes. Don't want to be late." I reach for the handle and open the door a fraction. The sound of traffic seeps inside, with spatters of rain.

"You are sure there's nothing else to add, Emma?" she asks.

I turn back to face her. "No. I really don't."

"Call me if you remember anything. I will be in touch."

I thank her and step out of the vehicle. The gutted remains of the gallery face me. So many of my dreams were tied to this place. It's the first gallery where I exhibited. It was also going to be the place of my first solo. Those dreams were now destroyed.

Worse than that, the police now suspected me. I could see it in Ingram's face. Could I blame them? No.

The cat is now out of the bag. The cops know about this man, and that he is connected to me. My thoughts return to Jeremy. I have to tell him, I don't want him to find out from the police. There just doesn't seem to be a good time to do it. I need to bite this poisoned bullet and get it over and done with. If he hates me as a result, then so be it. He deserves my honesty, more than anything else.

Steve is nowhere to be seen, so I head for my car. I slam the door shut and start the engine when I hear my phone beep again. I pick it up, and freeze. Fear blooms inside me, and my mouth feels sandpaper-dry.

Shame about the art gallery. Your house is next.

CHAPTER 22

Eight years ago

After one drink, I left the pub, making some excuse about being tired. It wasn't a lie, I was feeling washed out. Liam and Gary, Clive's two mates, not only looked like the Kray Brothers, they sounded like them as well. Liam, the younger one, kept smiling at me in a suggestive way, and it was giving me the creeps.

I was watching TV when I heard a crash in the doorway. Clive appeared soon after, and stood swaying in front of me. His breath stank of alcohol, and something else. Some sort of perfume.

He grinned at me, his dark eyes dull and flat. His face had a lecherous, rabid look. It frightened me. I had never seen him like this before. He crashed on the sofa next to me, and reached for me. His hands were rough.

"Stop it!" I shouted, and got up. I left the room and went to bed, leaving him on the sofa.

When I woke up the next morning, Clive had left already. I wasn't feeling well. My body felt bloated, and I was nauseous. I tried to heave, but nothing came out, save a trickle of bile. I called up the office and told them I wasn't coming in. When I pulled my jeans on, the buttons felt tighter.

As I made coffee, I checked the calendar. It felt like the time for my periods and I was right. Only, it wasn't right. Something felt off. I didn't feel like this normally when I came on. I got dressed and walked to the pharmacy in the corner.

Half an hour, and three tests later, there was no doubt. I sat in the loo, my back straight, staring at the double bars on the pregnancy test kit. I was filled with a nervous elation. I tried calling Clive, then sent him a text to call me back. This was news he had to hear in person.

He would be excited. We had talked about a family in the past. Maybe this was what we needed to get our lives back into gear. I waited all day for Clive to get back to me. I left messages at the office, on his email and phone. I didn't break the news to anyone. The father of my future child had to hear it first.

I stayed up again, waiting for him to return. I must have dozed off on the couch, because I awoke with a start to find another body on me. It was Clive, and he was trying to take my bathrobe off. He smelt of booze again, and his eyes were defocused, hazy.

"Clive!" I shouted, brushing him off.

He smiled and slurred his words. "What's the matter, princess? Playing hard to get?"

I shook my head, anger filling every pore of my body. "Did you get the messages I sent you?"

He put his feet up with a thump on the table, and leaned his head back on the sofa. I repeated my question. He waved a hand.

"Yeah, what is it?"

"I'm pregnant."

He went very still for a while. Then he put his legs down, got up, and trudged up the stairs. His silence, the complete lack of response, was like a slap in my face. Inadvertently, my hand went to my belly. Tears came to my eyes, and I brushed them off furiously.

Was his excuse just being drunk? But my words had penetrated his drunken stupor, I knew that. Hurt and angry, I took myself to bed, curling myself into a ball, as far away as possible from him. If the business went under, then I wouldn't have a job. If I lost Clive as well, then so be it. I had a little nest egg that Dad had prepared for me. A fifty grand trust fund. I could have used it after I turned twenty-one, but I hadn't. I had saved it for a rainy day. I was glad I had.

When I woke up next morning, Clive was still in the house. I could hear him pottering around downstairs. I heard him coming upstairs. He came into the bedroom with a tray. He put the tray on the bed. He had made breakfast for me, bacon, eggs, croissant, coffee and orange juice.

"I'm sorry," he said, his eyes bleary and red from last night. "I've been working too much these last few days, and my behaviour last night wasn't right."

The clouds of bad mood lifted from my shoulders. Maybe there was hope for us after all. I sipped the coffee, and nibbled on the croissant. I still wasn't hungry.

I asked, "Do you remember what I said last night?"

He rubbed his forehead. "Yes. Yes, I do." Silence. My heart sank again. This was not the reaction I had been expecting. He might have been drunk last night, but now it was the clear light of day.

"What is it?" I asked in a trembling voice.

He spread his hands, standing up. "Nothing, Emma. It's just that things are really hard right now. The offices in Putney and Richmond are not going to open. I have more or less been told that. Without those branches, we can't win new business." He looked at me and attempted a smile.

"We can have a baby, that's fine. I just wish the timing was different."

Hope fluttered inside me. "So you want to have the baby?"

He looked vague, non-committal. I could see he was struggling, but he hid it with a smile on his face. "Yes, I do." I locked eyes with him. He looked away.

"I do," he repeated. "We just have to accept that things will be difficult. We need to pinch and save."

Clive stood up and walked over to the window, looking at our postage stamp-sized garden. He swung around suddenly, a gleam in his eyes.

"I wouldn't normally ask this."

"Go on," I said, watching him carefully. My mind was trying to loop around his thoughts.

"And I don't want to come across as being rude." He looked at me hopefully. I wondered what he wanted to say. It wasn't like Clive to be indecisive.

"Just say it, darling."

He pulled out the chair and sat down. "Do you think your dad could help us out with something? I mean with the baby coming and all..."

I couldn't believe what he was saying. He wanted a handout from my dad?

Really? He saw the expression on my face and held his hands up. "Now before you say anything, I am going to ask my mother as well." He softened his features. "You know she has never seen you. I think it's high time."

"That might be the case, Clive, and I'm happy to see her," I said with a deep breath. I didn't want an argument. God knew I had a lot on my mind. I wanted to say it without being rude, and it had to be said.

"Clive," I said slowly. "I will never ask my dad for money, OK? I just can't do that."

He narrowed his eyes. "You have a trust fund, right?" His words knocked the air out of my lungs. I leaned forward, my lips slightly apart, trying to catch my breath.

I closed my mouth with an effort. "How did you know that?"

He smiled innocently. "Your dad told me when we were up there. He didn't tell me anything about how much there's in it, mind you."

I fumed inside, wondering why on earth dad had told him that. It made no sense. I needed to speak to him.

"I don't want to talk about this right now, Clive, OK?"

He nodded. "I understand. It's your money. All I'm saying is with the new baby and our jobs now being what they, we are in for a rocky period."

He got dressed and left, leaving me to ponder his words. The breakfast lay uneaten on the tray. I threw most of it away.

CHAPTER 23

Eight years ago

Four weeks had passed, and things remained tense between me and Clive.

When Clive came home one evening, he had a defeated look on his face. He sat down heavily, shoulders hunched. I asked him what the matter was. When he looked up his eyes were red-rimmed.

"My mother's dying," he said, and burst into tears. His body heaved up and down. Suddenly, a few things made sense. The business going downhill, and now his mother's illness. Maybe he has been using alcohol to numb the pain of it all. A wave of guilt flooded inside me. I had been judging him, while he was seeing his life fall apart.

He dried his tears and then looked up. "She wants to see you. Her cancer is terminal, and it has spread all over her body." He stood up and walked to the kitchen. I followed him. He poured himself a glass of red wine. "She knows we are having a baby. She wants to see you before she dies."

That touched me deep inside. Finally, I had a connection to Clive's family and his past. It was sad that my child would never have a grandmother. My mum was gone, and now Clive's mother was terminally ill. But it also meant I would be closer to Clive's family this way. It gave me hope for the future.

The next morning, we drove to her flat. She lived in Putney, in a nice block of flats with a lawn in front. Clive pressed the doorbell, and we waited. Eventually she buzzed us in and we took the lift to the fourth floor.

His mother, Rita Connery, was on the sofa, a shrivelled and sunken old lady. Two pipes from her nose were attached to a black cylinder. *Must be oxygen*, I thought. She tried to stand up, and failed. She lifted yellow eyes towards me. It was shocking to see how ill she looked.

"You must be Emma," she wheezed. "Come and sit next to me."

I did. I felt a passing sense of guilt at not having come to see her before.

In a way, I wished Clive wasn't here at all, and I could just speak to Rita. I could find out more about his past that way, too.

"I'm sorry I haven't met you sooner," she said. "Clive talks about you a lot."

"Good things, I hope," I said. She smiled at that.

Rita looked at my belly. "How many weeks are you now?" I exchanged a glance with Clive. So he had told his mother. I hadn't asked him about it. This was turning out better than I had hoped. Maybe there was hope for us still, hope to start a family.

"Eight weeks," I said. Rita reached out a hand and held mine in her fragile, bony grasp.

"I won't see the little one," Rita said, her voice tinged with sadness.

"Surely you have…"

Clive said, "The doctor's given her one month to live."

I was shocked. Rita looked down into her lap, and her lips trembled. Her grip on my hand tightened briefly, then she let go. She didn't have tears, just the sad, lost look of someone who had given up hope. I felt a lump forming in my throat, blinking back the emotion.

We talked for a long time, while Clive made us tea. I caught him watching us once, and he seemed on the verge of tears. His mother had a lot of stories about Clive's father, who had passed away many years ago. I saw the photos in an album.

"My Barry, he was such a handsome man," Rita said, a tinge of sadness in her voice. She gazed at the photo fondly, evoking memories. I watched as, with a gnarled, shaking finger, she traced the outlines of his face.

"Life passes you by quickly, you know," Rita said to me. "Make the most of it while you have time."

It was getting to mid-afternoon when we left Rita. I promised to come again. We sat in the car in silence for a while.

I shook my head. "One month? That's it?"

"You saw the oxygen. She will die without it. There are also ten pills that she has every day." Clive paused and looked out of the window. I had never seen him look so sad.

"There is one anti-cancer drug," Clive said. "But it's not available on the NHS. It could buy her two more years of her life. It costs twenty-five grand a year." He fell silent.

I said nothing. We drove back to the apartment. Clive got ready for work, and came in to say goodbye. His face was sad, drawn. It reminded me of how my father had looked when my mum died. I couldn't save her. No one could. And now Rita would pass away soon. I had been thinking, and now I made up my mind.

"I need to ask you something," I said to Clive.

"Yes?"

"I can give you the fifty grand you need for Rita's treatment."

Something lit up in his eyes. "What? No, I can't ask you to do that."

"It's a loan that I will make to you. We can put it against the agency business. You have to pay me back. If you default, then I get fifty grand's worth of the agency business."

He was interested, I could tell. He churned it over in his mind. "I need to write you into the contract of the agency," he said. "Once I do that, will you put the fifty grand in my account?"

I didn't have anything to lose. I nodded. "Yes."

CHAPTER 24

Present day

I'm not sure if I can drive. With shaking, clammy hands, I drive off towards school. I have fifteen minutes, with the traffic it's going to be tight. My mind is a blur. I feel like I'm in a blizzard, heavy snowdrifts blinding my eyes.

My life is spiralling out of control. I need to get a grip, but there's not much I can do. I need to speak to someone. Jeremy is the most important person, but before that, I need to confide in someone else. Eva is the only person I can think of.

Who is after me? It has to be him, I can't think of anyone else. I need to contact him, but I am so scared. I circle around the school till I find a parking spot. It's tight but somehow I manage to park.

I am hoping Eva will be there today. She is the only one who knew him. She is the only one who can help me.

When I spot Eva, I make a beeline for her.

"I need to speak to you," I whisper.

She studies my face. "Everything alright?"

"Yes, fine. Why don't we go back to mine after this?"

She nods. I head up to the indoor sports hall, where the gym squad trials are held. I hate the fact that I am late. Molly loves her gymnastics, and she's good at it. These trials are important, and girls from different years are competing for a spot. I have been told twelve girls have been selected for five spots, which means there will be seven disappointed girls there today.

I can't help feeling like a bad mother as I open the doors and see the mothers standing there. They turn towards me, and I catch a glimpse of the blonde locks of Joanne. She hooks eyes with me then looks away. There is anger in her face but I ignore her.

The girls come streaming out, still in their leotards. Molly is one of the first, and she has a big grin on her face, and she is jumping up and down. "I made it, Mummy, I made it."

I give her a massive hug, holding her so tight she might melt into me. I don't want to hurt her, but she hugs my neck back even tighter. My eyes are moist. I know how much this means to her. Many of the girls who competed for a space have private gymnastic lessons. Molly didn't.

Some of the girls are crying. I notice Henrietta is one of the last ones out. I didn't know that she had been selected for the trials. There are tears in her eyes, and Joanne gives her a cuddle then marches up to the teachers for a word. I can't hear, but from the moving heads and pointed fingers I can tell there is a heated discussion going on.

Lottie, Eva's daughter, and Lisa, Suzy's older child, were also in the trial, and neither of them have been selected either. They are sad and being comforted by their mothers. Baby Margaret is in a pram.

Suze walks over to me and congratulates Molly, who can't stop smiling. The girls go off to get changed. The changing rooms are one flight of stairs below. When the girls come back up, Joanne storms past the rest of us, and stalks out, dragging Henrietta.

We are coming out when I spot Miss Laker standing outside the sports hall. Joanne is standing next to her, and a sense of foreboding rises up inside me as I see them. Joanne's face is livid, and she give me daggers. She remains where she is but Miss Laker walks up to me. She looks harassed.

"Emma, can I please have a word?"

"Can it wait? I have a busy afternoon." I need to get back home, give Molly some food and have a chat with Eva.

Miss Laker says, "I'm sorry but this can't wait. Can we please step into my office?"

I am aware the other mums are looking over as they walk past slowly. Eva is right behind me, and I glance over to see Suzy next to her, holding the pram, Lisa and Lottie playing around them.

"What's this about?" I ask.

"Please. It would be much better if we could discuss this in my office."

Eva steps forward. "I hope this is not about bullying again." She indicates where Joanne is standing with her daughter, glaring at us. "Molly has already said she had nothing to do with this."

Miss Laker looks at me with pleading eyes, and I give in. I nod at her, and with a relieved face, she walks towards the reception area, followed by Joanne.

"I'll call you when I'm done here," I tell Eva. "We need to talk."

Eva nods. "I've got the evening free."

I wave goodbye to Suzy and head for Miss Laker's office. The door is open when I walk in with Molly. I am surprised to see Joanne's husband there as well. Tim Burton-Smyth looks at me with interest this time, and I wonder if he is aware that I am Jeremy's wife.

Miss Laker says, "Henrietta has been hurt again. Once again, there were no witnesses, and we don't know when it's happening."

I can't believe it. "I am sorry that she is going through this, but what does this have to do with us?"

Joanne speaks up. "Because she says it's your daughter again!"

I turn to Molly. "Did you hurt Hen, darling?"

Molly shakes her head. "No, Mummy. I am friends with her."

I glare back at Joanne. "How dare you accuse my daughter? This is going beyond ridiculous now. How many times does she have to deny it?"

"Look at this!" Joanne unbuttons the top of Henrietta's dress and shows me the ugly bruise on the back of her left shoulder. "Someone punched her. How would you feel if this was your daughter?"

"Terrible. But I wouldn't go around accusing another child without proof."

Joanne holds Hen and asks her. "Darling, who did this to you? Tell me."

Henrietta looks to the ground, and sucks her thumb. I glance at Miss Laker, who is observing Hen with interest. Hen doesn't say anything, and her mother has to repeat the question. Still, the child keeps her mouth shut.

"See," I say, feeling vindicated, and also angry. "I want an apology."

Joanne turns to me, her mouth open in surprise. "You want *me* to apologise? To you?" She snaps her mouth shut and grabs her daughter by the shoulders.

"Hen!" She raises her voice in frustration. "Just tell me what you said last night! Or point, at least."

Tim Burton-Smyth intervenes. "Honey, please. You're scaring her."

Joanne glares at her husband. "We need to know what's going on here." She speaks to her daughter in a lower voice again. Still Hen stares at the floor and shakes her head.

I get up, holding Molly. "I want an apology from you, Joanne."

She stands up as well, facing me. "You know why my daughter won't say anything? Because she is scared of Molly, that's why. Because that's what bullying is, isn't it? The victim is scared to point them out because then they get hurt more!"

I lose my temper. "The only person your daughter is afraid of is you, Joanne. Didn't you just hear Molly say they are friends?"

Tim stands up and steps between us. I stand back, holding Joanne's eyes. I don't care who she is. My daughter's done nothing wrong, I know that.

Tim says, "Let's break this up, please." He turns to look at me. "Look, we just want to find out who could be doing this. Will you keep your eyes open? Just to make sure that you don't miss anything. It could be any child in the school."

I am slightly mollified. "OK, I will. But it's not my daughter who is responsible for this." I give Miss Laker a look, and she holds her hands up.

"I think Mrs Mansell is right. Henrietta is not accusing Molly anymore. I think we can draw a line under this, and all of us can keep watch on the matter."

Without saying anything, I walk out of there. I feel flushed and angry. My earlier euphoria at Molly getting into the gym squad has gone somewhat. I flash back to thinking how disappointed Joanne must be that Hen didn't get in. Bet you she had private lessons. On top of that, she's still being bullied.

My anger starts to abate. If I was Joanne, I would be clutching at straws as well. Still, that doesn't excuse her behaviour. She is rude and arrogant. But my heart melts for Henrietta. She seems a docile girl. This school is full of confident, loud girls, and they are prized. I watch the girls and know for a fact that some of them are bossy. It wouldn't surprise me to find out there was a group of them who bullied poor Hen.

CHAPTER 25

Eight years ago

Once I had wired the money into Clive's bank account, he went from being sorry and crestfallen to rude and drunk again. I found excuses for his behaviour all the time. He was under stress, and for the first time in his life, he had found out he was going to be a dad. Maybe the best I could do was cut him some slack, and put up with his behaviour for now. I was sure that when baby arrived, everything would change. I couldn't wait for the day.

Six weeks passed by quickly. When we did talk, all he mentioned was how badly he wanted to expand the business. It made no sense to me, because the entire property market was cratering. Trying to borrow money and open more offices now didn't seem like the right idea. For all his talk about the business, most of the workers at the agency, myself included, hardly saw him at the office. Half the sales force had been laid off. Only two girls now worked in the back office. We had shrunk from twenty-four employees to seven.

I had come back from the doctor's office one evening, two weeks away from my first scan. I was fourteen weeks, and my bump wasn't easily visible as yet. But I could feel the little life growing inside me. I saw Clive park his BMW, open the boot, and take out two large suitcases. I met him downstairs.

"What's in the suitcases?" I asked. I hadn't seen him leave with luggage, and he didn't have anyone with him.

"Stuff," he said, heaving them inside. He took them into the lounge at the back. He knelt on the floor and opened them. I came and stood behind him. Over his shoulder, I could see black parcels stacked inside one of the suitcases. They had a red stamp on them, some letters in a foreign language I couldn't read. Clive picked one up and sniffed it. It was flat, slightly larger than an A4 envelope. Hundreds of them were arranged neatly. Clive shut the suitcase and stood up.

I faced him. "Tell me what they are."

There was a flushed, irritated look on his face. "If I told you, you wouldn't understand. Now get out of my way."

"No. I need to know."

He tried to push me aside but I barred his way. He stepped back, rage turning his eyes red, blood rushing to his face.

"What are you doing?" he said in a raised voice.

"Tell me what you have in those suitcases."

He ground his teeth, flexing his square jaws, handsome face working. Eventually he grit the word out. "Merchandise."

I folded my arms, frowning. "What sort of merchandise?"

"Just stuff I need to sell. You want me to keep a roof over our heads, and raise this," he pointed to my belly, "this thing, don't you? So, shut the fuck up and listen to what I have to say."

I felt like he had slapped me. Apart from the vile language, he was referring to our baby as "the thing". I fought back the tears that were threatening to pool in my eyes.

"*The child* belongs to you as well!" Maybe it was the hormones, or just plain frustration with him, but my fists were balled, and I was angry enough to hit him. "And I don't want you selling dodgy stuff to make ends meet."

He lowered his face to mine. His lips were turned up with hate. "Oh yeah? Precious princess with Daddy's trust fund, aren't you? Money grows on trees for you, does it?"

Before I could do anything, he had gripped my arms tightly. His fingers were like claws, digging into my flesh.

"Let go of me!" I cried, struggling. He shoved me back against the wall, hard. I hit the back of my head, and pain exploded in my skull, radiating down my spine.

I held my head, and looked at him with crazed eyes. "You bastard!" I raised my arm to strike him. He parried my blow easily and kicked me hard in the stomach. The sudden spear of pain was like a deep tear inside me, like I had been stabbed with a knife.

My eyes shook, and I sank to my knees.

He stormed out, banging the door shut. I held my belly, and knelt on the floor, sorrow and rage fighting a terrible battle inside my heart. For a while, I stayed there, gasping, trying to fight the waves of pain. As they faded, I fell back on trying to piece my life together. What was happening to me?

My eyes fell on the suitcases. I went over to then, and tried to open one. He had locked them. Try as I might, they wouldn't budge open.

I gave up after a while, and sat in the chair. The suitcases sat there, taking up a corner of the lounge. Discomfort prickled my skin every time I looked at them.

I got up and decided to go into the office. Make some phone calls, see if any new properties had come onto the market.

I was in the shower when a pain suddenly gripped my lower abdomen. It wasn't a normal tummy cramp, this was deep, visceral, clutching my guts in an iron grip. I went down on my knees, crying out. The shower kept splattering water on my face. The pain became cramping, vicious, moving further lower. Like it was trying to come out.

I looked down, face twisted with pain, and that's when I saw it. On the wet shower floor there was a trickle of blood. It was coming from me. The water washed it away but more came.

"No," I whispered. The pain came in waves, making me double over with its intensity. With it came the bleeding, spasming out of me. It stopped eventually, to a trickle. I got up, feeling sick and dizzy, taste of bile in my mouth.

I rummaged in the bathroom cabinet till I found a pad, and somehow got dressed. The belly pains came again in waves, this time much worse than before. I was doubled over, clutching myself, mouth open. Saliva trickled out onto the carpet. I wouldn't make it out of the door, and I suddenly realised something was seriously wrong with me. My eyes fell on my hanging coat. I crawled over to it, and pulled it off the peg. I found my phone, and dialled 999.

"Ambulance, please, I'm bleeding…pregnant."

The woman on the other side was asking me questions, but her voice was far away, at the end of a long tunnel. My eyes glazed over again, and the wall, mirror, corridor wobbled and went out of focus.

"Hello? Hello? Can you hear me...?" I could hear the woman's voice still. I wanted to answer, but the light darkened in my eyes. Then I didn't remember anything else.

CHAPTER 26

Present day

When we get back home, I offer Molly a treat for getting into the gym squad. She wants pancakes with maple syrup. I have some ready-made pancakes, and I start frying them while she watches TV.

My mind remains on the sickening vandalism at Steve's gallery. That fire burnt many of my hopes as well. Despite having online sales, like every artist I wanted people to see my physical work, too.

And then the warning on the text message. I flip a pancake over quickly as it sizzles, slightly burnt. Once four pancakes are done, I call Molly to the table. She doesn't have more than two normally.

I look out from the front room window as Eva parks. I open the door for her. She's on her own, having left Lottie with the au pair. She waves at Molly, who's busy going through her pancakes. Molly gives her a thumbs-up.

"Coffee?" I ask.

"And cake, I hope," Eva laughs. As it happens, I have some lemon drizzle slices leftover from last week. I put them out on a plate and put some beans into the coffee-maker.

Eva takes a bite of the lemon cake and closes her eyes. "Mmmm, this is lovely. You are such a good baker."

"Thanks," I say, putting a steaming mug in front of her.

"What did you want to talk about?"

I put Molly in front of the TV, and she is very happy, being allowed to eat her pancakes and watch TV in the living room. I come back to the kitchen where Eva is sipping her coffee.

I take a minute to compose myself. "This is going way back, alright?"

Eva nods, her face looking comical with a slice of cake puffing out the left cheek.

"Do you remember Clive Connery?"

She is blank for a few seconds then her eyebrows clear. She swallows hastily. "Oh yes. What about him?"

I don't know where to start. It all sounds silly, till Steve Ponting described the man who came to see him. I tell Eva about the birth certificate sent to me, the text about Molly, the problems with Steve, and the man in the park. I go on to mention the torchlight in the park the night before we found Suzy's baby. When I tell her about the art gallery and the last text message I received my voice breaks. I compose myself, and drink the coffee.

Eva is digesting all of this in silence and I pause to let her consider it.

"So," she says, "the only reason for you to think this might be Clive is the description that Steve gave you? Have you actually seen him?"

"That's a pretty good reason. Unless he was describing his body double, which I doubt. And I did see a man by the park, watching me, but he was too far away to identify."

"Besides," I continue, "who else would have Molly's birth certificate?"

Eva nods. "But why would he be sending it to you now? What does he want?"

I have my thoughts, but I keep them to myself.

"I don't know," I say, and then shiver.

Eva says softly, "Maybe what he wanted the last time."

"But I don't have anything..." I begin to say, and then stop. He impersonated Jeremy. Does he know about Jeremy doing well in his work? I think back to the card he left with Steve. He knew enough about Jeremy to print a card with the right job title. What else does he know about my husband?

I have wondered how he found me, but these days that's easy. All he has to do is a Google search on my name or look in the electoral register to track me down.

"Has he ever tried to get in touch with you?" I ask.

Eva looks surprised. "No. Why do you ask?"

"Just wondering if he asked you about me, and so on. But I know you'd tell me if he did."

"Exactly," Emma nods rapidly. "I saw him a couple of times, with you, in the beginning. Before it all happened."

I purse my lips.

Eva says, "After that, I never clapped eyes on him. Has he tried to contact you?"

"Not yet, no. Not directly, I mean. It can't be anyone else who's behind these calls."

We let the silence hang between us for a while. Then Eva says softly, "Have you got in touch with him?"

Even the thought makes me shiver. Like there's a snake at my feet, ready to sink its sharp fangs into my leg. I draw my feet up under me and wrap my arms around my legs.

Eva is watching me, and our eyes meet. She says, "I take that as a no."

"That's right. But I know I have to now. This is going beyond a joke."

Speaking to Eva is making me feel better. I hardly slept last night, listening to the leaky radiator pipe dripping somewhere in the house. The creak of rafters in the ceiling. The wind speaking, whispering outside the window like a restless soul. Endless sounds of the night.

This morning I barely brushed my hair and tied it into a ponytail. Couldn't be bothered to put any make-up on. I must have looked like a hobo when I arrived at the art gallery. I wonder if my dishevelled appearance made Ingram more suspicious.

I didn't care. I need to sort my life out first.

Softly, Eva says, "Do you want me to speak to him?"

Jolted, I stare at her. She has been my friend since God knows when. I guess she can see how disturbed I am by this. But as generous as her offer is, I can't let her go through with it. She can't fight my battles for me.

"Thanks, Eva. But I think I need to speak to him myself."

"Have you got his number?"

"No, but I will find him."

After Eva leaves, promising to make me call her after I had seen Clive, I delve into my handbag. I have put the business card I got from Steve into my purse. I look at the phone numbers carefully. Like I thought, the mobile number is not the same as Jeremy's. I punch the digits in, and wait with bated breath while it rings.

"Hello, cupcake," the baritone voice drawls. A tremor shakes me from the core of my being, spreading outwards, growing like a growling tsunami, and goose bumps prickle my flesh. I feel hollow, my stomach full of acid, making me nauseous. Memories slide free from the closet I keep them enclosed in, and I shudder, trying to get rid of them.

"I wondered when you would ring," he says, in that same deep voice.

"What do you want?" I say, trying to keep the quake away from my voice. I don't want to say his name.

"What, no hello or hi? How have you been?" His voice becomes taunting.

I grit my teeth. Although I'm scared, I can't let the bastard hear it in my voice. "I'll give you five seconds. Then I'm hanging up."

"Tough cookie now, are we?"

After what he did to me, I had to become tougher. It's only now that I realise how naïve I had been back then.

"I'm counting. One, two…"

"Meet me today and I'll tell you all about it. How about…"

I cut him off. Firmly, I say, "No. I choose where we meet."

He chuckles. "Sounds good to me. Where, cupcake?"

I hate it when he says that, it feels like a rake running over my skin.

CHAPTER 27

It's the next day, and I have done my school drop-off and some food shopping.

I go back home, pack the food in the fridge, doing things like an automaton. I am going through the motions, my mind on what is to come today. It has been ten years. I promised never to see him again. He destroyed me. He even broke my mother, who made me promise on her deathbed I would never see him again.

Today I have to break that promise. And I'm not doing it lightly. If I don't see him, if I don't deal with him, he will destroy me once again. And this time, I don't think I will have the strength to rise up.

I finish stacking the fridge, put stuff out for dinner, then take one look around the kitchen. My lips tremble, and my heart squeezes painfully against the ribs. My hands shake. But I am also angry. He is a bully, a bastard, and I will not give him the satisfaction of thinking he can run roughshod all over me again.

I am tougher than who I was.

After half an hour's driving, I pull into a car park off Purley Way in Croydon. There is a complex of department stores in this retail park, mixed with a cinema, bowling alley and restaurant. I head for the TGI Fridays in the right corner, next to the cinema. I know this place has CCTV, and it's public. He can't do anything to me here, and I am far enough from Wimbledon not to know anyone. Not that Clive will do anything obvious to harm me physically. He's far too clever for that.

I take the table by the window as agreed. I order a cappuccino and wait. The coffee steams into my nostrils, but I am too distracted to drink. I watch the cars as they park. After ten minutes of waiting, I check my watch. Its 11 am. He should have been here by now.

"Hi, Emma," a voice says behind me.

I turn around so fast I almost spill the coffee. Good job it's not in my hand. The seat behind me is occupied and a shape lifts from it and comes around to my table. He has been sitting behind me all this time, observing me.

He is wearing a hat that tips down over his forehead, obscuring his face. He takes it off as he sits down. He smells nice. I can't help but stare at him. He still has a pull on me, I realise, as I look into his intense, dark eyes. The familiar glint in them is mocking me. He is clean-shaven, and the square-jawed handsome face is still the same.

The face I see in my nightmares.

He studies me intensely, and I drop my eyes. I look away, then lift my chin and stare back at him. Anger, frustration and regret scythe their way through my heart. I want to scream and shout, wish him away in a puff of dust. But it doesn't happen. It's the cold light of day, and like a spirit risen from the night, he sits there, staring at me. The angles of his face are the same. I wish he didn't have the power to affect me so much still, and it's definitely not something I want him to know.

"What do you want?" I asked.

"You owe me, Emma."

"What?" Despite everything, I snort derisively. "How did you figure that one out? It's the opposite, if anything."

He shakes his head slowly. "You know what for."

A spike of fear jabs inside me. I say nothing, just look at him impassively. Finally, he utters the one word I didn't want to hear. "Molly."

"Leave her out of this," I say brusquely. "She's nothing to do with you."

"On the contrary, she is everything to do with me." He grins at me now, an evil, lopsided crook of his lips that I want to reach out and rip right off his face. He says, "You want Molly to be safe, don't you?"

Rage bubbles inside me. It evaporates off my skull like smoke off a volcano. I jab a finger at him. "You try to get anywhere near her, and you'll be sorry," I hiss.

"What will you do, Emma? Call the police?"

He smiles as I cringe inside. A heavy weight is pressing down on my chest.

I can't breathe, my lungs are blocks of cement. Clive knows very well that for Molly's sake, and mine, I cannot go to the police. Doing that would let the mistakes of my past destroy my present life. It would kill off Molly's future, too, and I can't sit around and watch that happening.

Clive smiles again, and I want to be physically sick. "I thought not. Now, listen to me carefully."

He pauses for a few seconds. He lowers his voice. "Your husband is going to meet with a fatal accident. After he's dead, you get all his money, including his pension. I might need your help in how the accident occurs, or do it myself. I will let you know."

I am listening to him with wide eyes, but my brain can't believe what I'm hearing.

Clive continues. "When you get his money, you hand me half. You keep half for yourself. Then we are done."

He sits back in his chair, observing me intently. My tongue won't move. It's become a block of ice. I lick my lips with an effort and clear my throat. "What do you mean by accident?"

He leans forward again and clasps his hands on the table. "I will let you know. It won't be anything difficult."

I shake my head. "You're mad. I can't do this."

"Can you do it for Molly?"

I feel my eyes bulging, veins standing on my forehead. To infuriate me even further, he smiles again. Revolted, I look away. Outside, its cold yet sunny. People are laughing and chatting as they come inside the restaurant. A flock of teenagers come out of the cinema. Normal people, enjoying their normal lives.

What had happened to my life?

Just when I was getting back on my feet again. Anger burns inside again, and I clench my teeth.

Clive says, "You do this, and we're even. I'll never bother you again. But if you don't..." He leaves the threat hanging. I want to cover my ears. I don't want him to say my daughter's name again.

"And don't bother trying to run. I will find you. When I catch up, it's going to be worse. No more Mr Nice Guy," he sneers and I feel like hitting him.

"I'll be in touch." He knocks on the wood of the table, then gets up. Hat on head and head bent, he goes out of the double doors. I look out and catch a flash of him running to the left. Then he disappears from view.

I want to pinch myself. Did that just happen or was it a bad dream?

My world is imploding around me, the sunshine turning into sickly yellow, poisoned rays. Essentially, Clive is giving me a choice.

Who am I willing to sacrifice?

My daughter, or my husband?

CHAPTER 28

My fingers are shaking and I drop the car keys on the ground. I swear and pick them up. Somehow, I get in the car, and slam the door shut. I sink down in the seat and close my eyes.

I wrap my arms around me, hugging myself. What shall I do? There is an immediate solution. I leave Jeremy. Pack my bags, and head off, without leaving him any forwarding info. That will break his heart, but it will save his life.

But will it save mine? More importantly, will it save Molly's? Clive can still come after us, purely for revenge if nothing else. The thought of him makes me sick. Maybe he's been watching me all these years. Waiting to pounce on me when I got some money.

If I run, he will come after me. And what if I collude with him? Go along with his plan, do whatever he wants me to do? I can't bear thinking about it, but a voice inside my head tells me that if I do what he wants me to, it won't be the last time he expects something of me. He will keep coming back, holding what I did as a cross over my head. That talk of leaving me alone if I did his bidding was just that – talk. Now that he had found me again, he would never leave me alone.

I am damned if I do, and damned if I don't.

I think seriously of going to the police. But then…thoughts twist in my head till I can't think anymore.

The car is freezing inside. My breath creates fumes in the air, shaped like question marks. Shivering, I turn the engine on, turning the heating up full blast. It's past midday. I need to pick up Molly from school. In a daze, I drive back home.

As I open the door and disable the alarm, I step on a pile of papers put in through the letter box. I bend down and pick them up. They are interior decoration and lifestyle magazines that I have subscribed to. I stare at the

103

happy, smiling faces on the glossy covers and a bitterness stabs at my heart. I clutch the magazines and sink to the floor, a heavy weight at the back of my throat.

A red mist cascades over me like the waves of a storming river, drowning me in its crimson deluge. For a while, any action is impossible, and I can just about breathe and feel. Then the waves recede, leaving me like a wreck.

I bare my teeth. It was a simple desire, wasn't it? To have a happy married life? But for me, it was too much to ask for. Because of one man. One man who had hounded me for the last decade, turned my life into a living hell, and now come back for me again.

Well, I wasn't going to give him the satisfaction.

I open my purse and take out the ring. I put it back where it should be, and then stare at it in wonder. I think of the love that had made Jeremy buy it for me. Damn thing was still loose. I wiped tears away and smiled. I needed to get to the jewellers soon to get the width corrected. To be honest, part of me was worried about getting it back. I hadn't asked Jeremy if he had insured it.

Is love like that not worth fighting for?

Deep down in my bones I feel the answer reverberate, filling me with a conviction.

*****

I am in a daze when I pick Molly up. I barely say hello to anyone, and I can't see Eva. After I have picked up Molly, and given her a snack of jam biscuits, I hear a voice calling my name. I want to ignore it, but I feel a presence behind me and I stand up. It's Suzy, with the pram and Lisa in tow.

"Are you OK?" she asks in a concerned tone. Guess my washed-out appearance is obvious for all to see.

I try a smile. "Just tired, that's all. Have you seen Eva around?"

"Yes, she was here, but left early. Heard you guys are going out tomorrow night."

This is news to me. Then I remember Eva mentioning Simon and Jeremy wanted to go out, and I mentally smack my forehead. She has been sending me texts, which I have ignored as I have been so caught up with everything else. Is that what she meant when she said see you later? I flip my phone out. Damn it, the message even has an emoji of two champagne bottles. I groan. I really don't feel like going out.

I tell Suzy. She says, "You should make an effort. Maybe a night out is just what you need."

I haven't even called a babysitter. How can I go out? Jeremy left early this morning, and last night he came in very late. Haven't seen much of him the last couple of days as he has been so busy with work.

Instead of going out, I need to tell him about my meeting with Clive. That is now more important than anything else. I have to do it tonight.

"There's something else I had to tell you." Suzy's voice is lower and she is leaning forward.

"What?"

"Joanne Burton-Smyth is speaking to the sports teachers to stop Molly from taking her place in the gym squad. She is claiming that Henrietta couldn't perform to her optimal level because she was scared of being bullied by Molly. So, she wants Molly's name withdrawn from the squad, and a retrial."

Colour is rising to my face and my breath comes in short, spasmodic jerks. "What?" is all I can say. I am speechless with anger.

Suzy's eyes widen at my change in expression and she touches my arm. "Calm down. I'm sure the teachers will see sense. What Joanne's doing is silly."

"Silly? It's downright pathetic and vile. I have a good mind to go around her house and give her a piece of my mind."

Suzy closes her eyes. "I shouldn't have told you. I'm sorry. Look, it's just something one of the mums in my year overheard. The teachers will have to think long and hard about this. Molly got into the squad on merit."

"Yes." I am seething with anger. "How dare she! She has is it in for Molly, anyone can see that. But to go this low, well, I..." words fail me again. I glance to where Molly and Lisa are playing with each other.

"Thanks, Suzy," I say. "I will check with the teachers tomorrow, that's for sure." My mind is made up. If that Joanne tries to take Molly off the gym squad, I will personally make her life a living hell.

I speak to her for a bit longer, then leave. My mind is in turmoil. I can't figure out women like Joanne. She has everything in her life – money, family, security. It's unfair that her daughter is being bullied, but pointing fingers in the wrong direction is not the right way to deal with it.

How would she like it if the roles were reversed, and I was blaming her child? What if I was taking her to the teacher's office every week, complaining about Hen being a bully?

Something tells me she would raise merry hell if that happened. Probably would call Buckingham Palace and get The Queen in.

I am still festering when we pull up at home. We do Molly's homework, and I keep glancing at the clock.

What Clive said is playing on my mind like on a feedback loop. I cannot leave this any longer. Whatever happens, Jeremy must know about it. There is simply too much going on inside my head, in my life, and I am struggling to keep so many plates dancing in the air. Something has to give.

At 7 pm I hear the key turn in the lock and I am at the door swiftly. It's Jeremy and he looks exhausted. I give him a hug and he kisses me back.

"Is everything OK?" he asks.

"Yes. Can we talk after dinner?" I am bubbling away inside.

"Yes, sure. Is everything OK?" Jeremy's eyes are watchful.

"It's fine," I smile the best I can. "Why don't you have dinner?"

I have made a chicken curry and rice, one of his favourites. It's out of a jar but he won't know the difference. There's a nice bottle of red as well, and my wine is chilling in the fridge. I've had a glass already, just to cool my nerves. OK, two glasses.

"Smells nice," he says as he takes his shoes off.

"Made a chicken curry," I say and he gives me a wan smile. He goes upstairs to get changed. I am washing dishes in the kitchen while Molly is doing her homework on the kitchen table. It's very dark outside, and the yellow halogen glow of the street lamps only serve to emphasise the darkness.

I look up to dry my hands and my breath freezes. I stare as if hypnotised.

On the opposite side of the road, under the lamp-post, a man is standing. He has a hat pulled over his head, just the type of hat that Clive was wearing this morning. I can't tell if it's Clive from here. He is smoking a cigarette, and the red tip glows as he pulls on it.

We do have pedestrians walking past our house, like in any residential street. But this man is clearly watching our house. He is not looking in any other direction but at us. His face is turned at the kitchen. At me.

Fear spikes inside me. My heart hammers inside as I quickly lower the blinds. Molly is oblivious, she is still doing her homework. I rub my cold hands. What shall I do? I have to go outside and face him. There is no other way. Unless he leaves of his own accord, which is the best scenario.

I hear hurried footsteps coming down the stairs. I go out into the hallway to see Jeremy with a frown upon his face.

"Have you seen that guy opposite our house?"

My heart sinks. He has noticed it as well. Breath rasps in my throat. "Just leave it, darling. Probably a homeless man, he'll go soon."

"He doesn't look like a homeless man. Seems quite intent on checking out our house." He sits down to put his shoes back on.

"What are you doing?" I ask apprehensively.

"I need to go out there and ask him who the hell he is."

"No! There's no need, Jeremy."

He looks up at the tone of my voice. He stands up and gets close to me.

"Don't worry. He won't do anything to me. There might be an explanation. He might think our house is for sale or something and he's just having a look."

"Jeremy, please. Just leave it." I catch his sleeve, and pull him towards me.

He frowns, and passes his hand over my cheek. "Darling, what's the matter? You look like you've seen a ghost."

His expression changes and I can see he remembers something.

"The other night, when you said there was someone in the park, behind our house..."

I don't let him finish. "It doesn't matter. Just leave it be. Like you said, he might just be here to look at the house."

Jeremy gives me a strange look, and it wounds me deeply to see the scepticism in his eyes. He doesn't believe me.

He pulls out of my reach, and opens the door. I shout his name, and rush after him. If he's going out there, then so am I.

Jeremy is standing outside the porch, on our front garden. The pavement opposite is empty. The yellow haze from the light shows an empty space underneath it. There's no one there. I look around, and the whole street is empty.

CHAPTER 29

Jeremy follows me back inside the house. He shuts the door and then locks it. I don't look at him, I walk down to the kitchen. Molly is doing her homework. I take her upstairs, and put her to bed.

When I get downstairs, I reach for the drinks cabinet and pull down a bottle of gin. I pour myself two fingers and mix it with tonic water. I am aware that Jeremy is standing opposite, leaning against the kitchen counter.

He shifts closer to me, and we look at each other.

"What's going on, Em?" he asks, his tone neutral. I can see from the way his arms are folded and the stiffness in his posture he is not happy.

I take a gulp of the G and T. After the glasses of wine it's making my head swim a bit, but in a nice way. Things are getting hazier, a bit softer around the edges.

"I used to have this boyfriend. From a long time, ten years ago. He was…" I close my eyes as the creaky doors in the hidden recesses of my mind open. Like oozing black liquid the visions come out. Once I open these doors there's no going back.

"…He was dangerous. A crook who cheated me out of my trust fund money. I broke up with him and left. For some reason, he's now come back."

I pause. Jeremy is looking at me intensely. "So that was him out there just now? And the other night, behind our house, in the park?"

"I don't know. Maybe him or one of his friends."

Jeremy looks confused. "Then how can you be so sure it's him?"

"Because someone sent me Molly's birth certificate, and then threatening texts about her."

"He threatened his own child?"

I put my drink down and cover my face with my hands. This is worse than I thought it would be. For Molly's sake, there are things I can't share with anyone.

Jeremy gives me time, to his credit. I look up and say, "Sorry. Can we sit down?"

He gets himself a glass of red wine and sits opposite me.

"A man came to Steve Ponting's art gallery, pretending to be you."

He looks aghast. "Me? Whatever for?"

I tell him about the gallery, including its destruction in the fire. I leave nothing out, telling him about the police, and how he might be interrogated as well, to be my alibi. He listens with mounting disbelief, I can tell by his frown.

He shakes his head when I pause. "This sounds crazy. So what does this guy actually want?"

"What he took from me last time. Money."

Actually, what he took from me was far important than the money. But for the time being, I keep that to myself. Jeremy will know one day, but not now.

I look at him and know what he's thinking. "Your money," I say.

He knots his eyebrows together. "But how can he..." Then his puzzled expression clears. His eyes take on a startled look as realisation hits. "He wants you to..."

I nod, feeling miserable. "He wants me to, I don't know, harm or kill you, something bizarre like that." I hold my hands up. "I know this sounds strange. But believe me, this guy is crazy. I think he's a psychopath."

Jeremy is looking at me with a strange light in his eyes. "Have you ever done anything like that...?"

I am stunned. I close my mouth eventually. "How could you even think that, Jeremy? No, for the record, I have not done anything like that to anyone, ever," I continue. "And if you think this is some sort of a plan, then you are very wrong. I am telling you all this, aren't I?"

"I know." His voice is warm, strong. The usual voice that I know and depend on. My fingers shake on the ice-cooled glass as I pick it up. I don't want this voice to go away. Ever.

I gulp down some gin. "Then why are you asking me?"

"How do you know? He must have told you something."

I tell him about my meeting with him. It still gives me shivers. Jeremy listens attentively.

"Do you still have the texts he sent you?"

"Yes."

"Did you take any photos when you went to see him?"

"No."

"But you did meet him at a public place, right? So, there will be CCTV images."

"Maybe. But I don't want to go the police, Jeremy."

"That doesn't make any sense. Why not?"

Because he's blackmailing me. I want to scream the words out, but somehow, I keep them in.

Aloud I say, "I don't think you understand what kind of person we are dealing with here. He will hit first, ask questions later. At the same time, he's very clever and manipulative."

"Can I see the texts he sent you?"

I get up and get him my phone.

Jeremy spends some time going through the texts. "We need to tell the police," he says.

"And tell them what? That this guy is out to get me?"

"You have the texts to show them. I agree it's not much and of course you can't go to court with this, but it's something."

I grip my forehead. "But what will the police do, Jeremy? They can't guard us 24/7."

He gets up and looks out the window at the darkened garden outside. It's an inky-black, amniotic evening. He scratches the back of his head.

"I don't know what to make of this. It's all very strange."

I hate to think I have brought this upon him. He has a right to be upset. It's a lot to take in. His next question throws me a bit. He is still facing the unlit garden, a granite darkness, with his back to me. I can see from the tautness of his broad shoulders he is tense.

"How long have you known about this?" The tone has an undercurrent of steel in it, like he is bracing himself for the answer. I know Jeremy. The question he really wants to ask is: How long have you been hiding this from me? But he doesn't ask that, because he suspects he won't like the answer.

"Since I started getting the odd messages. About a week."

"Why didn't you tell me about it, then?"

"There was never the right time. You've been busy with work, and I've been busy…"

"Keeping secrets from me," he says, turning around. His eyes are dark, deep, unfathomable. "What else are you hiding from me, Em?"

I can't look at him for long. I seek refuge in the glass, only to find it's empty. Jeremy is standing, watching me, and I have to answer him. "Nothing. This was a long time ago. Look, I never thought it would be like this, OK?" Almost to myself, I whisper, "It's not my fault."

CHAPTER 30

Jeremy is still not happy, and I can see it in his eyes. He grips the top of the chair he's standing behind, holding it like a shield in front of him. Afraid of my lies. I can't blame him, and I feel the fear myself. The fear of unravelling, of sliding down that slippery road of destruction.

"Is this the reason why you don't want to buy the house?"

"What? No! I don't want to buy the house because I don't want you to become stressed. A large house will need a lot of upkeep, not to mention the bigger mortgage." I can't escape the attention he's focusing on me, and in the end, I just stare back at him. "That's the real reason. I promise you."

He scrapes the chair back and sits down, running his hands through his hair. He looks up and grins cynically. "So what has this ex-boyfriend of yours have in store for me? Some nasty surprise. A car crash maybe?" His lips bend downwards and a muscle twitches in his jaw.

I close my eyes. "I don't know, Jeremy. Please don't ask me."

"Then who do I ask?"

I slam the palm of hand down on the table. It makes our glasses jump, and I regret it instantly, as I don't want the sound to wake up Molly.

Jeremy has a right to ask me questions, but he can also be pedantic at times. He likes things to be plotted out in advance, like neat lines on a map, tracing a destination. He hates uncertainty, and I have just dumped a whole cauldron of that mess on his head.

"I am not a part of his sick game, Jeremy. Can you get that, please?"

I push off the table and shove my empty glass in the sink. I have good mind to have another glass of G and T, but I don't want to lose it. I turn the tap on and start scrubbing dishes aimlessly.

Jeremy comes and stands next to me. "You have been out of sorts recently. I was wondering why."

I say nothing. My fingernails feel they are holding tightly to the edge of a precipice, my legs dangling free, whipped about in a wild wind. This is not a fall I want to, or am prepared to, take. Yet, with every passing moment, every heated comment, I am dragged closer and closer to the edge.

I don't want to feel like this again. That black hole of helplessness. That horrible, restless anxiety that eats away inside like a malignant termite. I went through that once, and I came out on the other side. Rebuilt my life from scratch. And now, that bastard is back. I realise with a sick sensation that maybe he has been watching me all this time. See where I get to. Then turn the screws on when he needs something.

I would like to say I am different now. Stronger, leaner, harder. In many ways, I am. But I am also vulnerable, and Clive knows about it.

I turn the tap off, clutch the sides of the sink, and hunch my shoulders over it. On any other day Jeremy would engulf me in a hug by now. But tonight he is cold and distant. When he speaks, he looks ahead, at the ground, as if his words are meant for someone else.

"We need to call the police. This is crazy."

I nod in resignation. Given my brief encounters with them, I'm not looking forward to it, but at least it will put things into perspective for them. It might even make it believable. They might stop thinking I am this weird, evil woman around whom strange things keep happening.

Jeremy is still not looking at me, but he's speaking to me. "I have a dinner tomorrow night at the golf club. It's for everyone at work, to celebrate the recent success we have."

Now he does look at me, and I don't miss the reproach in his eyes. "I'd like you to come with me. All the partners and their wives, husbands, are coming. So is Timothy Burton-Smyth, with his wife."

The implication hits me like a spear. Not only am I unleashing a murderous ex-boyfriend on him, I could also screw up his career by fighting with the wife of his senior partner at the law firm.

I'm starting to resent Jeremy's attitude. I am going through a lot more stress than he is over this, and part of me thinks he is just not getting that. When it comes to Molly, I know I am not going to give an inch of ground to that supercilious woman. The thought actually strengthens me, fortifying my defences.

"You know that his wife is trying to get Molly out of the gym squad of school?"

Jeremy is aware of how passionate Molly is about her gymnastics, and he takes her to training sessions at the weekends. His eyes widen.

"She's doing what?"

He is aware of the bullying allegations as well so I bring him up to date. The frown on his face deepens as he hears.

"That is ridiculous. How can she think our Molly is a bully? You haven't seen any signs, have you?"

"Nope. Molly is behaving her usual way."

Jeremy is deep in thought. He sighs at the end, giving up on whatever mental dead end he has reached. "Whatever. She can't do that, but tomorrow night is not about any of this."

He looks up at me, and his reproachful look has changed. I recognise the expression on his face. It's when he wants to say sorry, but there's too much in the way, stopping him. An obstacle course of worries. I hate to say it, but it's come between us. I feel the same way, too.

"Will you come?" he asks, his face betraying the feeling that he's not sure about my response.

"If you need me to, yes. We don't have to spend too much time there, right?"

"Right."

CHAPTER 31

I spend most of the morning getting a hair appointment at short notice with Paul Rogers, my regular hairstylist, where I will also get my eyebrows done. I have told Eva and Suzy, and Eva has been able to get hold of a babysitter for me. Luckily, my black evening dress that I want to wear came back from the dry-cleaner a fortnight ago.

I am borrowing black heels from Suzy and I am over at her house to pick them up. When she opens the door I see more lights on inside, and a floral pattern has been pasted across the wall, something for baby Margaret, I think. A smell of fresh flowers mingled with coffee wafts out, and Suzy has Maggie, as she calls her, on her shoulder, being burped after a feed. The place has lost the dreary drabness I saw last time and seems like a new house almost.

"It's at the private function room of Mandarin Oriental." I say, taking the box of shoes from her.

"The big hotel in Knightsbridge?" Suzy says, agape.

"Yes," I say, trying to smile, wishing I felt more upbeat about this. Whatever I try, I'm not relishing the prospect of sitting opposite Joanne, wearing a fake smile on my face. I'm doing it for Jeremy, and he appreciates that, which makes the whole charade tolerable.

"Sure you're going to have a great time. Take photos."

"Guess who's on the guest list."

"Who?"

"Joanne Burton-Smyth."

I explain her husband's relationship to Jeremy. Suzy asks, "And what does Jeremy think about it?"

"Well, he's stressed about…" I stop, not knowing whether to tell Suzy about Clive. But she is fast becoming the only other person apart from Eva in whom I can confide.

"About what?" Suzy asks. "Is everything OK with you guys?"

116

"Yes," I sigh. "It's just my ex-boyfriend. He's a psycho." I tell her in brief about my recent troubles. Suzy's expression becomes more and more shocked.

"My God. This guy sounds like a total psycho, like you said. Have you told the cops?"

"I'm thinking about it. But that won't stop him. You know how the cops have been with me. If I tell them, they'll probably think I'm making it up again."

"But you have to do something. Do you have a photo of him or something? Maybe I can keep an eye out."

She does have a point. I wonder if I have any old photos in the attic. Most are destroyed, I didn't want to leave any trace of Clive in my life. My old phones have been chucked away, too. But I do have an old laptop that I uploaded most of my photos onto.

"I will have a look," I tell her. "And let you know." For now, I describe Clive to her. She listens attentively.

Suzy says, "Maybe a night out is just what you need. Sure you'll enjoy yourself."

"I will, apart from having to meet Joanne again."

"Well," Suzy grins. "You're younger, better-looking and that dress will turn every man's head tonight."

I roll my eyes and grin. "Thanks, Suzy, but that's way over the top."

*****

Evening arrives, and I can't say I don't feel a tinge of excitement and anticipation as I get ready. I have been looking at the photos of Mandarin Oriental on Google and boy, does it look plush. I really hope the evening goes well and without any mishap. I don't want any shenanigans, but if Joanne kicks off about the kids, then I'm not going to keep quiet. I doubt she will, however.

Jeremy pokes his head in. He looks handsome in his dinner jacket, and he is patting down his necktie. "Looking gorgeous, gorgeous." He smiles.

Things still aren't right between us, but I know both of us will keep the act up for tonight, and sort things out after. He's just come back from work and we haven't had a chance to talk.

It's 6.30 and the babysitter arrives. I can hear Jeremy speaking to her as I add the finishing touches to my outfit. She's Jenny, an A level student whom that both myself and Eva have used in the past. I run down the stairs to greet her. Molly is chatting to her already and showing her the jigsaw puzzle that she's made. Jenny is at Crofton High, and she wants to study medicine, so both Eva and myself think she'll be a good influence on the girls. It's sweet that Molly kind of looks up to Jenny already.

I give her instructions about sleep time, and how to lock up the front and back. She has my number already, and Eva's as well in case of an emergency.

Our Uber has arrived, and after a flurry of kisses, both of us leave Molly and lock the door. Jenny has a key and is under strict instructions not to open for anyone unless it's us. I have checked and rechecked all the windows upstairs. I've also spent some time from the upstairs bedroom windows, lights off, staring out at the black, foreboding expanse of the park. Straining my eyes, searching in the shadows of the trees, for any shape that detaches itself from the morass of darkness.

I saw nothing. No moving bodies, save the wildly swinging branches of the trees, buffeted by winds. No lights. I don't know what I will do if these things suddenly appear. Call the police maybe. Part of me has thought long and hard about taking Molly up to Yorkshire and leaving her there for a few days while I sort out the situation with Clive. But I don't want to let Molly out of my sight. It's hard enough going for an evening out, unable to keep my eyes on her.

When the doors of the cab shut, I say to the driver, "Can we drive around this block once please?"

He shrugs. Jeremy looks at me questioningly.

"Just to make sure," I say lamely.

"Make sure of what, Em? There's no one hiding in the bushes?" His voice is low so the driver can't hear, but I can sense the exasperation behind it.

I'm looking out the window at the park entrance as the car drives past it. The turnstiles at the entrance are barely visible, but there's no one standing there. In this cold and windy night there shouldn't be any park visitors. The rest of the street is empty, triangular halos of yellow light illuminating the street at regular intervals.

Jeremy says, "Em, you have to stop this."

I turn towards him, unhappy that I have to defend myself. "You saw him staring at our house last night," I hiss.

"And before I could ask him anything, he had gone. That man could've been there for any reason."

"So you think I'm making up everything I said?"

"No, I didn't say that."

The back of a cab seems an odd place to have an argument. But we are having one, and part of me knows that he has a point. I've never been fond of the night. Too much darkness where eyes can hide, watching me. Daylight shows what I'm familiar with, and that familiarity brings me comfort. Night is alien, strange, another world where shadows hide forms that are invisible.

I freak out easily at night. I don't like the sounds I hear when I lie in bed, awake. Jeremy's gentle, and sometimes not so gentle, snoring, and Molly's soft breathing is fine. But there's always other sounds.

My nerves are raw and exposed, and I feel jumpy. I clench my fists into my lap. This is not how I wanted the evening to start.

"I called the police," Jeremy says. "Today, from work."

I'm sitting away from him, closer to my window. We are driving over Putney Bridge, and lights twinkle on the rippling waters of the Thames.

"What did they say?" I appreciate that he is taking this seriously.

"They took a statement off me, and said they would be in touch."

"You told them everything?"

He looks over at me. "Yes. Everything you told me. Isn't that what you wanted?"

"Yes," I say in a small voice. I hark back to my last interview with Ingram, outside Steve Ponting's burnt art gallery. I told her I didn't know who might be impersonating my husband. Now that story will have to change.

The cops already think I might have something to do with the abduction of Suzy's baby. That much was obvious when they grilled me afterwards.

Now they are certain to dig deeper, see what else I'm hiding. The windows of the taxi seem to constrict, and I can feel the space getting smaller, suffocating me. I'm in a prison of my own making, but I don't have the keys to get out.

CHAPTER 32

When we arrive, I am more than happy to get out of the cab. The cold night breeze brings the scent of rain and diesel fumes, but it's refreshing. There's a line of cabs parking up, and Jeremy opens the door for me, and I take his hand and step out.

There's a red carpet under an awning, with white marble steps leading up to the hotel. As I look up at the huge red-brick building, I momentarily forget all my worries. Right opposite the swanky department store Harvey Nichols, the Mandarin Oriental seems to take up an entire block. The first two floors are white, but the rest of the building is red-brick, lit up brilliantly, and they dazzle my eyes.

Jeremy takes my hand and we go up the stairs as liveried doormen salute and open the door for us. The huge doors swing open and...wow. We step into a gilded, baroque-style reception where the walls are brown marble, with columns etched into them. The floor is patterned black and white marble, and so is the staircase. Chandeliers hang down low from the ceiling. I feel like I have stepped back in history and arrived at some French palace. Women in white wigs and men in tights will appear any minute, fanning their faces with Chinese fans.

We go up the stairs to the reception where a bank of men and women wearing expensive suits face us. We are directed to a private function room. The chintz and gold-plated alcoves, and tops of columns, are eye-catching, as are the huge flower arrangements in vases the size of my kitchen table.

Jeremy's firm must be doing well to hire out this place. I tell him that and he grins.

"Don't forget we are part of a larger group. They have offices all over the south-west. There's going to be quite a few people here tonight."

"Oh good." I relax, safer in the knowledge that in a crowd I might be able to avoid Joanne if necessary. But I don't know anyone, and while I don't want to be stuck to Jeremy all night, it seems I have little choice.

The private function room has a partition. In the first section, which is big enough to hold a hundred people, men with dinner jackets and women in fine dresses mingle with flutes of Prosecco. I feel a little self-aware with my Topshop knee-length black dress. But it hugs my figure well, and with the black heels I am almost as tall as Jeremy.

A waiter comes around and we get our drinks. The doors at the middle of the room are tall and wide and through them I can catch a glimpse of the dining area with tables arranged. Jeremy meets someone he knows and introduces me.

I smile vacantly, and say, "Hello" to the man and his wife. They are both older than us.

The woman, whose long, cream dress and stunning diamond necklace are gorgeous, says to me, "You look stunning, Mrs Mansell."

"Thank you," I say politely. "You do as well."

I feel someone brush past behind me and turn to apologise. The woman says sorry as well and suddenly I am face to face with Joanne Burton-Smyth. She is dressed to the nines. Her hair is done up in a bob at the back. The V-neck red dress must have cost an arm and a leg, and it does make her bulges obvious. Recognition turns to surprise, then to pursed-lipped politeness. She knew I was coming, obviously.

"Hello, Emma," she says in a flat, civil tone. I am surprised that she even speaks to me. I wouldn't have, if she didn't.

"Hello, Joanne," I say, in the same cold, frosty voice as hers.

She twitches her lips and moves on, and I breathe out. She joins a group that her husband is speaking to and I look away to stand next to Jeremy, shielding myself from them. The waiter passes me by and, although I don't see his face, something about his posture looks familiar. He walks around, offering drinks, and then disappears through the double doors that are the entrance to the bar.

I excuse myself to go to the loo and check my phone. No calls which is good news. I text Jenny and she calls me back. Molly is fine and we have a brief chat, and I kiss her goodnight. I step out of the loos to find the place more crowded than before. Music is louder, Katy Perry soft pop floats down from invisible speakers in the ceiling.

I have another glass of Prosecco. It's helping with my nerves as usual, but I need to be careful I don't have too much. Dinner is announced, and we move towards the partition doors in the middle. The tables are covered in white cloth, with bows tied around the chairs with silk. We sit down at our table and I glance at the cards with names on them. The Burton-Smyths are seated at our table. I flop on my seat and take a pull on my Prosecco. Of course they would be. Tim is friends with Jeremy.

Jeremy touches my arm and I am introduced to yet more people I will never see again. I flash the same smile and have banal conversation about the weather and how nice the place is. From the corner of my eye, I see the waiter I had seen before. This time, I can see his profile as he hurries from one table to another.

My heart lurches and I can't breathe. That short-cropped blond hair, those muscular shoulders, I would recognise them anywhere. He actually glances to the side and I know it's Clive. He is so fit for his age, he mixes easily with the other waiters who are young. I don't know if he catches my eye, but I get the impression he is rushing past my table because he doesn't want me to identify him.

I excuse myself and stand up. My hands are freezing cold, and it's hard to swallow. I drain the Prosecco glass and walk quickly in the direction he went. People are standing around their tables, chatting and I dodge past them. There are sets of doors in the far wall, with round looking holes like you see in restaurant kitchen doors.

I leave the main floor and head for the doors. Waiters are rushing past me, and some of them give me a quick, puzzled glance. I'm not sure which door Clive has gone through. There are three of them. They keep getting banged open as waiters move in and out.

I feel self-conscious as the only guest out here. But there's no time for that. Palpitations are running against my ribs, the drum roll of my heart loud in my ears. Clive being here can't be an accident. He must be watching us 24/7. The thought makes me want to vomit.

I stride with purpose to the door nearest to me, and stand up on tiptoe to look through the round glass panel. It's busy inside, with rows of white-hatted chefs putting plates of food on stainless steel shelves. Waiters come up to them with pieces of paper, match them, then take the food away. I crane my neck from side to side, but I can't see Clive.

"Excuse me, ma'am," a voice says behind me.

I turn to find a young female waiter looking at me strangely. "Do you need any help, ma'am?"

"No. I just thought I recognised one of the waiters." I decide to be honest with her. I need some help to track Clive down.

She looks flustered. "Who do you mean?"

"An older man. Short, blond hair. Muscular build. In his forties."

The girl narrows her eyes and I can see she's trying to think. I look at the table behind me. Everyone is sitting down now. Our table is close to the left edge of where I'm standing, and I can see Jeremy looking around. He's searching for me, and any minute now his eyes will fall on me standing here.

I look at the girl in desperation. "Can I go inside?"

"No, ma'am, I'm sorry but you're not allowed. Wait here, and I will get the catering manager."

She goes inside, and the doors swing open and shut. I look in through again. This time, I actually open the door and stick my head in. I swivel my head side to side. The place is a hive of activity. Bodies rush past one another, balancing trays held above their heads.

Then I see him. He is facing me, but his head is down, and he hasn't seen me. His swarthy, tanned face is still square-jawed, handsome as the last time. His attention is focused on the drinks tray in front of him. He reaches inside his pocket and takes out a small vial. He looks around himself quickly, then empties the content of the vial into a red wine glass. It's a white powder. He puts the vial back into his pocket.

He looks up and I shrink backwards as fast as I can. My back slams against the wall and I take deep breaths. I look at our table, and my heart sinks when I see Jeremy standing up. I sink down against the wall, feeling foolish.

The door bangs open, and it would have hit me if I wasn't crouching. A figure strides out. It's Clive, and he is holding the tray with drinks in his left hand. I can see the glass of red wine into which he just poured the white stuff.

Jeremy turns and sees Clive striding towards him. He is heading straight for our table.

CHAPTER 33

An electric charge shoots through my spine. I straighten quickly. I know what's going to happen now. That glass of red wine is for Jeremy. He loves having it with his food. I walk up to the table rapidly. I can see Clive's plan with crystal clarity. There's poison in that glass of red wine. If he drinks it, and dies, then the suspicion will naturally fall on me. I am sitting next to him, and I'm already in trouble with the police.

Clive is serving the drinks, and he looks up as I approach. Our eyes meet and his lips curl. His dark eyes glint and flash at me, like he's sending me an invisible message. I ignore him. My eyes fall on the glasses on the table. The red wine glass is right in front of Jeremy. I am the only one standing, apart from Clive. Joanne is sitting opposite me, with her husband next to her. They both give me a look. My face feels like it's on fire. Wide-eyed, I scan the rest of the table. Tim and a couple of the other men have glasses as well, and I count another three red wine glasses.

Jeremy turns and sees me. He exclaims, "Darling! Where have you been?" I note the look in his eyes as he catches my flushed appearance.

"Will there be any more drinks for the table?" Clive, the waiter, is leaning forward. Suave and polite. The women are staring at him, frank admiration on their faces.

"That's fine for now," Tim says, and Clive smiles. He looks at me directly, holding my eyes briefly. His smile vanishes and a vicious sneer flashes across his face. It lasts only a second, but I know what he's telling me.

Don't tell anyone you saw me.

He moves away swiftly. I watch spellbound, as Jeremy reaches for his glass. I sit down close to him, unable to tear my eyes away from the blood-red glass of wine he's holding.

I cannot let him drink that. I know it's poisoned.

Images flash through my mind. Jeremy drinks it. Then he vomits, passes out, gets taken to hospital where he's pronounced dead.

I am left the grieving widow. Then Clive comes back in my life. I see him again. This time from behind the screen of a prison meeting chamber…

No, no, no! What the hell is wrong with me? What am I thinking?

He is controlling this, laughing behind my back. Like he controlled my life ten years ago.

"I propose a toast," Tim is saying. He lifts his glass of wine high in the air. "To the success of Sheldrake and Partners."

Everyone toasts apart from me. My Prosecco glass remains untouched. Jeremy is holding the glass and in slow motion he brings it closer to his lips. I watch hypnotised as the rim of the glass touches his lips.

Why am I not doing anything? I feel frozen solid, a block of ice incapable of moving.

Then suddenly, like a spring uncoiled, I move. I turn to Jeremy, cover my mouth with my hand, and lurch towards him like I'm going to vomit. Only I don't. I slap the bottom of the wine glass he holds, lifting it up in the air. Wine spurts up from the glass in an arch, a liquid crimson, poisoned rainbow. The wine falls with a splash on the dress of the woman sitting next to Jeremy. It splatters over her naked V-neck and ruins her dress, and she screams, tries to stand up, pushing her chair back.

I fall over Jeremy, and in the process, lift up his plate of food that slides over my dress, and falls on his lap. There is pandemonium at our table, with screams and shouts, and the thudding of footsteps tells me people are rushing towards us.

"Emma! Em, will you sit up? What's the matter…?" I feel Jeremy's strong hands curl around my shoulders and he's straightening me.

I resist as long as I can, and then sit up with a red face. My eyes are closed and I am sweating. I lean against Jeremy, pretending to be ill. But I look at the table for his wine glass. It's on its side, all the wine drained from it. It's also cracked. Red stains cover the white tablecloth. When I look closer, I can see a white residue at the bottom of the glass. Then I close my eyes again.

"She's sick, passed out…" someone is saying.

"Yes, it's my wife." Jeremy's voice. "I think I need to take her outside."

I open my eyes slowly, and find a few faces peering down at me. They all look relieved that I'm back. I am still reclining against Jeremy. I get off him and sit down on the chair. He kneels by my feet. His face is a mixture of concern and confusion.

"Are you alright, Emma?" he asks.

"Yes." I touch my forehead. "I think I fainted. Can we go, please? I don't feel well at all."

We say our goodbyes to the puzzled and strained faces around the table. Jeremy has a tight, fixed expression on his face, his lips set tightly in a thin line. I know he's angry. The waiters have arrived, hovering around us. They change the tablecloth and have to set the table from scratch again. The guests stand to one side. I look around for Clive, but he's nowhere to be seen.

Eventually we leave. A cab is waiting for us, and I am glad to sink into the back seat. My dress is a mess, and I've been to the loo to clean up. So has Jeremy, but he got off lightly, I think.

Very lightly.

He holds my hand, and his tone is comforting. "Shall we go to the hospital?"

I shake my head. I will tell him eventually about the whole thing, but for now I just want to get back home.

Jenny is surprised to see us back so early. I explain that I wasn't feeling well and pay her. She leaves. Jeremy goes upstairs to change, and so do I. Molly is fast asleep on her bed, and I tuck her sheets in and check the lock on her windows once again.

When I come back down, Jeremy is looking inside the fridge. He pulls out a pizza and prepares to pop it in the oven. Then he straightens and looks at me carefully.

"You're not..." He leaves the sentence unfinished. There is a gleam in his eyes, an excitement. I shake my head, feeling crestfallen as I watch the light die in his eyes.

He shrugs. "Just wondered, that's all."

I fold my arms around him, and briefly, he hugs me back. I inhale his scent, still the fragrance of the aftershave he put on before leaving. Then he detaches himself.

"Then what was that? Have you got a bug or something?"

He needs to know. "He was there, Jeremy. My ex-boyfriend. I saw him put a white powder in your drink."

Jeremy's eyebrows shoot up. "So you did all of that because you thought I was getting poisoned?"

"Not thought, Jeremy. I *saw* it with my own eyes."

There's an expression of incredulity on his face. I might as well have slapped him. "Are you serious?"

"Yes," I nod unhappily. I go on to tell him what had happened. Jeremy gets up and starts pacing.

"This is getting out of hand. This guy's mad."

I say nothing. Jeremy says, "This was bad. I'll have a lot of explaining to do when I see them tomorrow."

"Is that what you are bothered about?" I can't keep the anger out of my voice.

"I…we looked like fools in front of them, Emma. Surely you can see that." He's annoyed, too. "I had a lot of networking to do. Many of our clients were there and meeting them was kind of the whole point of the dinner."

"Well, I'm sorry I saved your life, Jeremy. No need to thank me. None at all. Why don't you go back there and meet your clients?"

I storm off, and stalk upstairs in a huff. I sit on our bed, holding my head in my hands. I feel like a knitted garment whose threads are unravelling one by one. My mind is shredded to bits, and I don't know how long I can live like this. The edge is getting closer, and all I can see is a looming black hole, ready to suck me in.

I close my eyes and lie down, not bothering to change. One question runs around in my mind like a rat in a toolbox.

What will he try next?

CHAPTER 34

Morning light flutters in through the gaps in the curtains. The rays are weak and paltry, like me, the sun seems not able to muster up enough strength to rise today.

I am awake but my eyes are closed. The alarm hasn't gone off as yet which means it's not 6.45 am. Jeremy is getting ready, I can hear him in the bathroom. His electric razor is on. I follow the sound of his footsteps as he goes into his study, where he keeps his clothes as well.

Normally we save this time in the morning for something else. Lately, on my part at least, there's not been any desire.

I get up and pad into the bathroom. Molly is up soon, and I know she will come downstairs where I'm making my coffee. Jeremy is there, too. He appraises me as he sips his tea. The steam rises from the cup, obscuring his face.

"How are you feeling?" he asks. It's the kind of loaded question I don't want to answer. Not sure what I'm supposed to say. I feel great? I feel crap? It's more the last one, definitely.

"I don't know," I say in a sullen voice, and move towards the kettle. I fill it up and boil it. I sense Jeremy behind me. I don't turn around.

"I wanted to say thanks for last night. If I had drunk that wine, I don't know what would have happened."

My bad mood melts immediately. At least he believes me, and he doesn't think it was for nothing. I turn around and fold myself against him. He isn't warm, though. He gives me a perfunctory pat around the shoulders, then says he has to get ready.

Molly is down, and reminds me I need to brush her hair today. I give her breakfast and we go upstairs. She wants her hair down in plaits but there's no time. We finish up breakfast and I check all the doors and windows again. Everything's locked.

Traffic is heavy and I have to park farther out than usual. As we walk in, I see Suzy with her daughter Lisa, and baby in a pram. She greets me with a knowing smile.

"Tell all. Was last night good?"

My face must have told half the story because her expression changed. "What's the matter?"

I tell her the best I can. She shakes her head. "Are you sure it was your ex-boyfriend? I can't remember his name."

"Clive. Yes, I'm dead sure it was him. He knows where I'm going, everything." I can't avoid craning my head up and taking a look around. Only school mums and children, with some dads. I can't help watching them closely.

"It's alright," Suzy says. She's been watching me, and her face is lined with worry. "He won't come here, I'm sure."

We are close to the school gates and I say, "Let's talk about it later, OK?" Suzy nods, and gives my hand a squeeze.

As Molly goes in, I see Miss Laker come out from the crowd of girls pushing to get inside. I have now grown used to the harassed yet patient look on her face, like she is used to being pulled in a hundred different directions, and able to go in none. I stand and wait as she comes over to me.

"Can we have a quick chat in our office please?"

Eva has arrived as well, a bit later than usual. She walks Lottie to the door of her classroom and then comes back. I am still speaking to Miss Laker.

"What for?" I ask, feeling almost as tired of this as I suspect she is getting.

She smiles resignedly without saying anything. Eva glances at me and says, "Surely you must know who's responsible for bullying Henrietta by now?"

Miss Laker turns to her sharply. "I'm not allowed to speak about another child in this manner." She reverts to me. "Please." Her tone is pleading. I take pity on her.

Eva doesn't seem happy with Miss Laker and is glaring at her. I tell her to wait for me.

"Oh don't you worry," Eva says. "I'll be here alright. To see what new rubbish *Mrs BS* has come up with." She says the name with emphasis and I can't help but smile.

Miss Laker shuts the office door before she sits down opposite me at the desk. There's no one else in here today. She looks at me apologetically.

"Henrietta has been hurt again," she says. I take a deep breath. I know what's coming, and I really don't want to hear it. Not again.

"Mrs Burton-Smyth is..." Miss Laker hesitates, her eyes downcast. I frown, as she is normally a direct person.

"What is it?"

Miss Laker makes her mind up and it all comes out. "She wants Molly to stop attending this school. She is convinced that it's your daughter who is causing the injuries to Henrietta. So she's taking out a petition against Molly, and it's being circulated from tomorrow to all the school parents."

"What?!" I can't believe myself. I can feel myself heating up, and there's a space clearing inside my head, becoming light, airy.

Miss Laker swallows. "Look, I don't agree with her. She sits on the governing board for the school, but the other governors don't like what she's doing either."

I scrape my chair back and stand up. Lights are flashing on and off in my eyes. Red, blue and yellow. I can feel a migraine coming on. Blood trickles through my veins, thin as rain, burning like acid. I turn rage-cleared eyes on Miss Laker.

"Where is she?" My voice is calm, measured.

"Who?" Miss Laker is standing up as well and there is a scared look on her face.

"Mrs BS," I say, spitting the initials out.

"She's just in a meeting with the head teacher and..."

I turn on my heels and stride out of the office. I know where the head teacher's office is. I come out of the doors and cross the courtyard. Miss Laker is running after me. Eva sees me and rushes over, and there's two of them now, trailing after me as I stalk my way to the head teacher's office.

Across the courtyard there's a covered entrance that leads to the offices. As we approach, with myself in the lead, the door opens. Joanne and Tim Burton-Smyth step out. She's dressed for work again, and holds a sheaf of papers in her hand. Her face pales when she sees me. I walk right up to her.

"Can I see those?" I say, pointing at the pieces of paper. She tries to move them, but I snatch, and pull, ripping some of the sheets. I stare at the remnant of one in my hand. The heading says: "Petition Against Molly Dixon, Year 4".

I glower at her. "What the hell are you playing at?"

"Enough is enough," she says in her snooty way. "Your behaviour at the party last night was deplorable. And guess what we learnt. Molly isn't Jeremy's child, is she? Do we even know who the father is?"

Something snaps and breaks inside my brain. I shout something but I don't know what comes out of my mouth. Then I have grabbed her face in my hands, and digging my nails in, I shove her as hard as I can. Joanne screams, and her back hits the door. The papers go flying from her hand.

I jump on her, but someone else grabs me. It's Tim, and he's much stronger than me. His arms pin me down, and he drags me off. I kick at Joanne's prostrate form but don't make contact. My legs are still scything in the air. Neither Miss Laker nor Eva move a muscle to help Joanne. She scoots back and slowly gets up, holding her face.

"Calm down," Tim whispers in my ear. I can feel his whiskers brushing against my cheeks. His breath is hot on my neck and his voice is wrought with iron.

I slow down. Tim lets me go. I shake free, then whirl round to face him. His green eyes are wary, hard, watching my movements.

Eva runs towards me. She stands next to me, and faces Tim. I say to him, "Tell your wife not to come close to my daughter, ever again."

Tim spreads his arms. "That's what she says about yours."

"And do you believe her?" My throat is raspy, my voice breaking. Rage makes me quiver, and I'll beat up Tim if necessary.

His face says it all. No, he doesn't, and its only his neurotic wife who's making him do this.

"Do you have any witnesses? Has anyone come forward to say they have seen Molly do anything?" I shout at him. A couple of the teachers are crossing the courtyard. They stop to listen. The schoolyard is quiet as the girls are inside, in their lessons.

"Even your own daughter didn't say her name last time. And they play together!"

Joanne has stood up now. From behind me she says, "I will sue you."

I turn on her. "And I'll sue you back for defamation and harassment. You want that?"

Tim says quietly, "Mrs Mansell, why don't you come and see me tomorrow? I'm sure we can settle this amicably."

"You must be joking," I say. I stalk off, Eva running with me to keep up.

CHAPTER 35

There are moments in life that feel like rips. A deep gash, destined to last. As I walk out of the school, this feels like one of those. I might have made a bad situation worse. But Joanne was asking for it, wasn't she? Whatever happens now, at least she knows that she overstepped the mark. She might be going crazy because her daughter is being bullied, but she has no right to drive everyone else around her crazy as well.

Why doesn't her daughter speak out and say who it is? The teachers have kept a close enough eye on Molly to be satisfied. And I know Molly isn't a lying type of child.

I can't think of who could be doing it, but it's weird that Hen doesn't say the name, and the child responsible is very discreet. That is disturbing. Is this child used to violence? Does she see it at her home? I don't like this chain of thought.

I tell Eva what I'm thinking, and Suzy is standing outside the gates, speaking to someone on the phone. She hangs up when she sees us, and from our expressions she knows immediately something is happening.

"Coffee," Eva says. "Let's head for Starbucks."

We agree. Coffee and cake is definitely called for, and even baby Margaret agrees, gurgling from the pram, and throwing one of her toys out of it.

As I inhale the steam of my cappuccino, I can't get over what just happened. Part of me feels ashamed. The other part still wants to bury Joanne BS underground. Well, at least that nickname for her will stick.

Eva says, "I think you should go and see the husband. He sounds sensible."

I'm inclined to agree with Eva. Tim seemed unruffled, and I might have unleashed more havoc if he hadn't restrained me.

"What if he wants me to meet me alone?" I ask. "That's not safe, is it?"

"I could come with you," Eva offers. It's sweet of her, but I shake my head.

"No. If he calls, then I go alone. He could well clam up if I come with someone." I'm actually intrigued now. What does he want to say? Tim knows I am Jeremy's wife, so I doubt he would try anything underhand. I need to get this straight with Jeremy before I go, if I do go. I will make it clear to Tim that Jeremy knows where I am, as do my friends.

Eva nods. "You do have a point there. If he wants to discuss something confidential, then me being there might work against you. But be prepared his wife might be present as well."

Suzy says, "I think so, too. Maybe they suspect another child or family, and want to chat with you about it first."

"He said, we can settle this amicably," I say to them. "What do you think he meant?"

Suzy says, "She's on the board of governors of the school. If she goes through with what she planned for Molly, then it makes her look vindictive. Maybe reduces her stature."

"Or maybe they want to pressure me into a confession. See if I behave differently out of school and without children."

Eva shrugs. "Either way, you won't know till you attend."

She has a point. My phone beeps, and I freeze. Will this be another warning from Clive? Gingerly, I remove the phone from my handbag. It's a message from Jeremy. I sigh in relief.

Informed police about last night. They want to speak to you. Inspector Rockford.

I excuse myself from my friends and call Jeremy. He answers and I tell him about what just happened. He listens with a stony silence. Of course, he's not pleased. But when I repeat what Joanne had said, he agrees she was out of line. Way out of line. I tell him that I might see Tim to discuss this. Jeremy isn't happy about that, but he can't really say no. It's my decision, concerning my daughter.

We are walking back to our cars when my phone rings again. It's a number I don't recognise. I reply.

"This is Tim Burton-Smyth," a man's voice says.

"I know who you are," I say.

He pauses for a while, then says, "This has gone far enough, don't you think?"

"You're telling me? It's not me who's taking out a petition to ban your daughter from school!" My tone is bitter, and I'm struggling to keep my voice down.

"I suggest we meet, and discuss this like rational adults."

"Meet with who?" I ask.

"Just you and me," he says and leaves it at that. I think about it. There won't be any witnesses. Can I trust this man? What if he tries to intimidate me? Guess I can always leave.

"I want to meet in a public place," I say. "Somewhere neutral."

He sighs. "That won't be a problem. I'm living in a hotel at the moment."

His tone has changed, and I sense a softer note, more downbeat. I lean against my car. The others are driving off, and I wave goodbye to them. They know who's calling. Eva makes a sign at her ear, to give her a call. Then they're gone. Tim is talking again.

"Is that OK with you?"

I am curious about his choice of meeting place. Obviously I will only see him in the hotel lobby. But still, why is he living in a hotel? I ask him.

The pause stretches on for a bit longer this time, and he clears this throat. "Let's just say Joanne and myself are having some problems of late. Nothing to do with Hen's bullying," he adds quickly. "Both of us want the best for her."

Several things click into place as I hear his words. From the beginning he has been the silent partner. I guess they've been keeping up appearances in public. I understand now why he wants to meet in private.

"I'm sorry about you and…your wife." I don't want to say her name.

"Don't be. It's been going on for a while."

"I can meet you in the hotel lobby for half an hour," I say.

"Please, that would be great. I just want the best for Hen, you know."

"Sure," I say, but part of me is also wondering what good speaking to him will do, when he doesn't even live with his wife anymore. I doubt she's going to listen to him. But it might give me more insight into their family life. There could be a different reason why that child is so scared to speak about her bully's name.

I wonder what happens inside their home. They are wealthy, well-to-do, but obviously things aren't right. In the end, no one knows what happens behind closed doors. Has Henrietta been watching her parents argue? Or is there something more twisted going on? I shudder to myself.

I'm certainly going to ask Tim when I see him. And if I get the slightest inclination something untoward is happening to Hen *at home,* then I'm calling social services.

All of which makes me wonder what sort of a woman Joanne really is.

Now that I've agreed to meet him, I'm also more worried. Was this the right thing to do? What do I know about Tim, really? He could be spinning a yarn about him and Joanne. I think of his patient eyes, and then get a jolt. From the beginning, he has looked at me with what I now think is silent appreciation. I'm not being big headed about this. He's stared at me like he wants to communicate something. Does Tim want to meet me in the hotel for something other than Henrietta's well being? Well, if he does, I will meet him at the hotel lobby, and get it out of him. And if he does know the name of the school bully, but for some reason can't share it with his wife or the teachers, then it gets Molly off the hook.

Either way, I need to see him. I just have to be careful.

CHAPTER 36

Tim is staying at a hotel in Kingston, and after taking the train from Wimbledon, I arrive at the station in half an hour.

The hotel is an end-terrace building that has been converted. Steps lead up to a door above which a sign says "Eros Hotel". It's one in a chain of several hotels on the block. This isn't a nice part of Kingston, and the hotels look seedy. Paint flakes off their walls, the signboards are tatty and the rickety windows are single-glazed.

I climb the stairs and push open the front door. A Fawlty Towers-style entrance acts as reception, and a short, chubby man is sitting behind the desk. He lifts his balding head in my direction when he hears the doorbell chime as I walk in. He stares at me as I approach the desk.

"Can I help?" he grunts in a thick voice. There's nasal hair sprouting from his nostrils, and his white shirt has stains on it. I dislike him immediately.

"I'm here to see Mr Timothy Burton-Smyth." His posh name sounds a bit incongruous in a place like this.

The man flicks over some pages and rests a fat finger on a line.

"Ah yes," he snorts. He glances up at me. "He asked you to go up to his room."

I frown. "There must be some mistake. I said clearly that I would only meet him in the lobby."

"This is the lobby, Miss."

Great. I look behind me and see two armchairs on either side of a tall potted plant. The man is leering at me, leaning on the desk. Even if there was more space here, I don't think I would want this idiot listening to our conversation.

"You don't have any other rooms here? A canteen maybe?"

He shakes his round head. Something doesn't make sense to me. Why would Tim agree to meet in the lobby when he knew what the state of the lobby was?

Well, I don't have to go inside his room. I can knock on the door and wait for him to come out. Then maybe we can go for a coffee.

"Can you not call him to say I'm here?"

The stupid man actually rolls his eyes. So much for customer service. He lifts up the phone and listens on the receiver for a while. Then he hangs up and looks at me with a half smile.

"He ain't answering."

"Where is his room?" I ask, controlling my temper.

"Up the stairs on the first floor. Third door on your right. Number 4."

Without a word to him I head towards the staircase. The carpet is dark brown with a paisley pattern, and threadbare. The steps creak as I go up them. A phone rings somewhere, its muffled sound constant through the walls. Then it stops and silence seeps in again. Something stiffens in my gut. This isnt right. I didn't agree to go up to Tim's room when I spoke to him. While I don't think he will hurt me, he might not be alone. Inwardly, I curse myself. I had to come alone and now I'm in a situation of my own making. I could just go down the stairs and get out of here...but then I won't get a chance to speak to him.

Something else occurs to me. What if something has happened to Tim? Is that why he's not answering the phone? If the police are involved again...I take out my phone, and flip open the camera. Then I press record on the video as I go up the stairs. This way, at least I can show anyone what I found. If something happens to me, the phone will have a record that I can try and send to Jeremy or Eva.

A door leads onto the first floor hallway. I push it and enter. The hallway is empty and surprisingly wide. I walk to number 4.

I knock on the door. There's no answer. I knock again, three times, harder. Still nothing. I wait for a while, debating what to do.

"Tim," I say in the end, raising my voice. "Are you there?"

No answer. I could go back down and tell the manager. He would have a spare key. But I'm here now. The door has spy keyhole and if Tim was standing on the other side, he could see me.

I push the door, and to my surprise, a latch clicks and the door falls open. When Tim had shut the door the latch might have got stuck. The door opens soundlessly. I stare at the narrow space that leads into the room. The curtains are drawn at the far end, making it dark.

There's a sideboard with a TV on it, I can make that much out. The end of a bed also juts out. A pair of jeans hangs from a chair next to the curtains. There's an old, musty smell in the room like it's not been open for a while. Then I smell something else. Not sure what it is, but it makes my nose crinkle. I keep the phone raised, recording everything on the camera.

"Tim?"

He has to be in here, or why would he ask me to come up? I don't get an answer again, and the door is open, so I take a tentative step inside. What looks like the bathroom door is open, and I catch a brief glimpse of myself in the mirror. The light in the bathroom is off, but I nudge the door open with my toe. It's empty.

I creep along the wall, and then come to a sudden stop. A man is lying on the bed, naked from the waist up. The face is bearded and I recognise it as Tim's. He is lying across the bed, with both arms above his head. His hands fall over, and there his eyes are open, cold and dead. There's a deep cut in his neck, a jagged line that has cut through muscles and tissue, and dark blood has seeped out, blackening the bedsheet.

Tim is dead.

The scream is locked inside my throat. A strangled whisper emerges. My breath comes in fast jerks. I move my eyes around but don't see a weapon. Tim has his shoes on, and part of me thinks he was getting undressed when...

I move closer, careful not to touch anything. I lean over him, and say his name once again. There is no response, and his pupils are dilated, fixed.

Shaking, with breath clawing at my throat, I run out of the room. I don't know how I stagger down the stairs without falling. The manager looks up with a frown as I almost collapse on the landing, but somehow keep my balance.

"He's dead!" I shout, finally finding my voice. "Call the police!"

I sit down. I can't form a thought in my head. There's a snowstorm of voices, images, faces that come and vanish like a film that's been fast-forwarded. The blur won't settle, it makes me dizzy, like my brain is spinning around in a washing machine.

Gasping, I cover my eyes and lower my head into my lap. I need to do something. As if from a distance, I can hear the manager shouting on the phone.

"Dead man…Eros Hotel…Chelsea Embankment."

I need to call or speak to someone. The manager's called the police already. Jeremy. He's a lawyer. He'll know what to do in this situation. I ring him, but it goes on voicemail. I call again, then leave a message and send him a text as well. I also send him the video I have recorded.

The time is 12 noon. I can hear sirens, getting louder. The police will be here and want to question me. Will I get off in time for school pick-up?

I call Eva, and send her the video as well. She doesn't answer but calls me back immediately.

"Tim…he's dead." I blurt out when she answers. I speak fast, telling her what I found. She hasn't checked the video I sent her as yet.

"What? My God, are you OK?"

"Yes, the police will be here soon. Eva, can you please do me a favour and pick up Molly, in case I don't get out of here in the next couple of hours?"

"Of course, no problem. I'll keep her with me and give her dinner, she can eat with Lottie. Then just come and pick her up."

"Only if you're sure," I say. "Hopefully I'll get out of here in time."

"Just take it easy. Don't panic. Leave Molly with me."

I hang up, feeling better that Molly will be in safe hands. The phone rings again, caller ID unknown. It must be Jeremy calling from work. I answer.

"Hello?"

"Looks bad, doesn't it, cupcake?"

I feel like shotguns have blown my knees off. I sit down heavily on the chair again. There is no mistaking that gravelly voice. It makes my skin crawl.

"I made it easy for you at the Mandarin Oriental. All you had to do was let him drink that wine."

I can't speak. Words screech inside me, but I can't get them out.

"But you didn't want the easy way out, did you? Now you have to suffer."

"Clive, you can't do this. This is…"

With a click the phone goes dead.

CHAPTER 37

The police arrive in the form of three uniformed officers. Two of them go upstairs, while one squats at my feet. The manager feels a bit sorry for me, I think, and he's made me a cup of tea.

As I'm speaking to the police, my phone rings again. It's Jeremy's number this time.

"Emma, what the hell happened?" His voice is high-pitched, and he's obviously read my text.

"Tim's dead," I whisper, and am mortified to find my eyes getting wet. I sniff and wipe them away. "I walked into his room and his…his throat had been slashed. I sent you a video. Have you seen it?"

Jeremy is speechless on the other end. Finally he says, "Give me the address. I'm coming over."

"No, look, the police are here. I'll see you when I get back home."

He won't take no for an answer. Truth is, I would like him here. I need support and his law skills could come in useful.

The officer asks me some more questions. His two colleagues come downstairs with gloomy looks on their faces.

"This is now a crime scene," one of them says. "Ma'am, would you like to come to the police station to give a formal statement?"

"I have a video to show you, about what I found upstairs." I take out my phone and they're interested, hunching forward to see it.

"We need to take this back to the station ma'am. We can give you a lift?"

I guess I don't have a choice. I send a text to Jeremy telling him where I'll be. He texts back saying he's on the train and will see me there.

I feel numb as I get into the police squad car. For the second time in one week, I am again in front of the desk sergeant of Wimbledon Police Station. He raises his eyebrows and smiles because I think he recognises me. I don't feel like smiling. I am told to take a seat and I sit down, feeling cold suddenly.

I fold my arms tightly across my chest.

A door opens to one side, and the tall, elegant form of Charles Rockford steps out. He is dressed in a sharply pressed suit, and as he walks towards me, I have to admit he is easy on the eye. He stands in front of me, and nods politely.

"Mrs Mansell, we keep meeting in unfortunate circumstances."

"Yes," I say, not knowing what sort of response is suitable for the occasion.

"Please come in and give us a statement," he says, standing back. I get up, and behind me I hear the sliding doors open.

"Emma." I look behind, and my heart floods with relief when I see Jeremy. He hugs me and I hold him tightly before letting go.

"I'm her husband," Jeremy explains to Rockford. "And also her lawyer."

"Oh yes. I spoke to you." They shake hands.

Rockford raises an eyebrow. "It's unusual that you choose to be your wife's legal representation."

"But there is nothing in the CPS that makes it illegal," Jeremy says. I only know that CPS stands for Crown Prosecution Service, England's judicial system.

"I would like to be present while she gives her statement," Jeremy says.

"This way, please," Rockford indicates.

"Can I speak to my client before we go in, please?"

"You have the interview room to yourself for five minutes before we enter," Rockford says.

When we are alone in the interview room, Jeremy leans over to me. "Tell me exactly what happened."

I tell him word for word, going over what he knows already.

"Who was present when you attacked Joanne?"

"Eva, Suzy and Tim. Then we had an argument, and two teachers heard that as well."

Jeremy writes this down in his notebook. I ask him, "Have you seen the video?"

"Yes," he nods, and his eyes clear with a suppressed smile. "Good thinking about gathering evidence. We have the time as well from the video."

Rockford comes in with Ingram. She gives me a hard, flinty look. I stare back at her, but I know I'm on slippery ground. The last time we met, outside Steve's burnt art gallery, I lied to her. I'm sure Rockford has updated her by now.

They sit down opposite me and start the tape.

"I understand that you and Joanne Burton-Smyth have a history?" Rockford asks.

Before I can say anything Jeremy interrupts. "I don't see how that has any bearing with this case."

"It has every bearing, Mr Mansell. Your wife was involved in a violent altercation with the deceased's wife just before he was discovered dead. By your wife, I might add."

"Are you saying there is a connection?" Jeremy says.

Rockford looks annoyed. He points to me. "She's here to give a statement. If she can't do it, then it's best not to waste valuable police time."

"She is here to describe the incident, not talk about hypothetical issues."

I want to get out of here as soon as I can, not hear these two argue about nothing. I raise my hand.

"Can I just tell you what happened?" I glance at all of them, and they shut up. Rockford nods.

I tell them what happened from my time at arriving at the hotel, to going into the room. I don't mention the phone call I got from Clive.

Both of the detectives make notes. Then Rockford folds his arms and fixes me with a gaze.

"It's all very coincidental, don't you think?"

"What is?" I ask.

"Let's start from the beginning. The missing baby. You found her, by yourself, in the park behind your house. No witnesses."

"I didn't know Suzy Elliot then. I had nothing to do with her."

"So you say." Before I can say anything Rockford continues. "But you did know Steve Ponting. His gallery burnt down, and you said you didn't know the person who impersonated your husband."

Both Jeremy and I are quiet. Rockford is on a roll. "Therefore your statement was false. Because apparently, an ex-boyfriend is trying to harass you. It was he who acted as your husband and cancelled your exhibition. Apparently it was also he who stood opposite your house. But when your husband went out there wasn't anyone there. And now you also claim that this person spiked your husband's drink when you went to the hotel in Central London."

Rockford checks his notes. "Kensington Police got back to us. The sample in your husband's glass was not found as the table had been cleared, unfortunately. However, we did find evidence of cocaine when we arrived at the crime scene eventually. A common recreational drug." He looked up at us. "Do you or your husband take recreational drugs?"

Jeremy sits forward, his face tight, jaw flexed. "What is the point of all this?"

"The point, Mr Mansell, is that this fictitious person is being blamed for burning down the art gallery, impersonating you and then spiking your drink as well. I am sure he will be blamed for Mr Burton-Smyth's tragic death as well. But no one has seen him. He doesn't exist. All we have is your wife's assertion that it's him."

I can't help but feel shaken. "Are you saying I made all this up?"

"No. But we need proof and evidence."

"You have her phone," Jeremy says. "Didn't you see the texts? And there will be CCTV images if you choose to look in the right places."

"Anyone could have sent those. And I believe the numbers were different PAYG phones. They can't be traced."

I can't believe this is happening. Are they trying to say all of this is my fault? That I made up Clive Connery to deflect blame from myself?

Jeremy has had enough. In a grating voice he says, "Are you going to charge my client?"

Rockford and Ingram look at each other. Jeremy says, "I have to say, any charge of homicide against my client will be laughed out of court. She called the police on discovering the body. There is no motive and she didn't have the means to commit the murder."

The detectives are listening to him. Jeremy says, "If you are not going to charge her, then can I assume we are free to go?"

The question hangs in the air, and I hold my breath. Time seems to stop, coalescing into a solid drop of tension on the table. I could reach out and touch it.

Then Rockford lowers his head and shuffles his feet. "No charge at the moment. But we have a homicide on our hands now, and already the wife has been in touch."

Inwardly, I groan. Joanne will be on the warpath now, and she will slam down anyone in her way.

"Therefore you will hear from us soon, and we will need you for additional questioning," Rockford says.

CHAPTER 38

I don't know what to feel or think when we come out of the station. Jeremy is calling a cab. He finishes the call and we sit down on a bench to wait. I haven't eaten anything all day but I don't feel hungry. I look at my watch and its almost two pm. I call Eva once more to ensure she will pick up Molly. She tells me not to worry. I'll go straight to her house from here.

When I hang up Jeremy turns to me. His eyes are deep-set, hollows under them. There is a haunted look in them.

"Emma, I need you to be completely honest with me on this. Forget about the law. This is you and me, and as your husband, you know I'll back you all the way."

My heart skips a beat as I hear his words. He is breathing heavily. "The senior partner at our firm is dead, and both of us knew him personally. I still have to work in that firm, but I don't know how."

He clutches his head in his hands and my heart fills with anguish for him. I can now see how far this trail of destruction is going to spread. Then I think of Clive and I tremble with rage. He has calculated this with cold-hearted precision. He is out to destroy everything Jeremy and I have.

Jeremy says, "I need to know. Did you have anything to do with Tim's murder?"

I feel awful, but I keep my voice firm. "No, Jeremy. I promise you, I had nothing to do with this." After a pause, I say, "He called after it happened. While I was waiting for you."

His head jerks up. "Who called?"

"Clive. He said from now it's going to get worse."

Jeremy hangs his head once again. "Oh Jesus."

*****

By the time I get to Eva's house, it's almost three pm. I ring the doorbell of her nice, semi-detached house and hear the dog starting to bark. Eva lives on the slopes of Copse Hill, where the larger houses can fetch multimillion price tags.

Eva answers the door, her face bright pink and smiling. The smile fades when she looks at me. I step inside and she hugs me. I'm emotional again but I hold it back.

"Where's Molly?" I ask.

"Upstairs playing with Lottie."

I hear little steps running down as we speak. Molly appears on the landing above, her eyes large and shining.

"Mummy!" she squeals. She runs down and jumps into my arms. I hold her so tight I feel she's going to merge into me. She doesn't mind and hugs me back tighter.

"Are you OK, Mummy?" she asks.

I smooth her hair back. "Yes, darling, all OK. Shall we go home now?"

Eva is my friend, but I don't want to overstay my welcome. She won't hear any of it. "No, stay. Let them play and you come in for a drink."

My protestations are feeble. I could do with a drink. We wander into Eva's large, open-plan kitchen, the floor made of polished cream Italian gloss tiles and the counters of black granite.

She reaches inside a cabinet that's actually a door to a chilled wine fridge. She pulls out a bottle of Sauvignon and pours us both a glass.

We don't speak for a while. In all honesty I'm still getting over the shock. Eva buzzes past me, laying tables for dinner. Then she sits down on one of the bar stools.

"The police aren't blaming you, are they?"

"Oh yes, they are," I say bitterly. "They haven't seen Clive as yet so they think he doesn't exist. Apparently I'm making all this up. Can you believe it?"

Eva says nothing, shaking her head. I hear a thump from upstairs, heavy enough to jar the glasses on the counter. Then there's a rush of little feet. Eva and I look at each other, and I put my hand up.

"I'll go and check," I say. I go up the stairs, feeling the soft carpet swallow my footsteps. The landing is wide and then the stairs break to go in two directions. The sound came from the left, which is where the bedrooms and studies are, and just above the kitchen below.

The first door on the left is a study and I peer in to find a bookcase toppled over on its face. Before I go in, I decide to check on the girls. I can hear them from Lottie's bedroom and I knock on the door and go inside. The room is big and full of Lottie's toys. There's a kiddies' bed and a sofa set as well. The girls are on the floor and from their faces I can tell they've been up to mischief. They start to giggle as soon as they see me.

"Who made that noise?" I ask in mock sternness.

"We were playing hide-and-seek," Lottie says.

"Yes and the bookcase fell over when I was hiding behind it." Molly makes a face.

"You shouldn't be playing in the study, girls. And, you could've got hurt."

They say sorry and go back to their blocks of Lego on the floor. I debate whether I should go in the study, then realise that as Molly made the mess, I should clear it up.

The study is large enough to be a bedroom but from the dust in it I can tell it's not used much. There's a leather top table to one side with a chair. Papers are strewn over the desk with some folders. The free-standing bookcase is on the floor and books have spilled out of it. It's not too heavy and I can lift it up. I stand it back against the wall and begin to stack the books on it. Most of the books are paperbacks with some family albums as well. As I lift one album up a stack of photos fall out of it.

I grab the photos and open one of the album pages to put them in when my hand stills. I frown and look closer at the photos. I can make out a much younger Eva, wearing a bikini. She's on a beach, with her arms around a man's shoulder. Somehow, the man looks familiar.

I look at the next photo and this one is a close-up. Nausea suddenly hurtles up my throat. My eyes dim and I think I'm going to fall. I kneel down and hold my forehead. My vision clears and I blink several times to clear the muzzy feeling in my head. It doesn't go but I can see again.

The close-up photo is of Eva and Clive. It's clearly taken on the same beach. Their faces are tanned, smiling, happy. Cheeks pressed against one another. With numb fingers I move to the next one. Both of them again, this time in a kiss. After that, in the water, splashing. Then inside a house, and she's sitting on his lap. There's no date on the photos. They fall from my hands, landing on the carpet like grenades.

There's an unbearable pressure inside me. Bursting to break out like water from a dam, ripping me in two.

The photos show Clive as I remember him ten years ago. When it all happened. All that time, him and Eva...

Through a mist, I sense someone standing at the door. My eyes shake from side to side as I look up. I can't focus. There's a ringing in my head, like an alarm gone berserk.

"What are you doing, Emma?" It's Eva's voice, and it seems to be coming from a distance. Dislocated, floating, like it doesn't belong to her body. I rub my eyes and focus. I'm still kneeling on the floor as Eva steps inside. I stand up and stumble backwards. My back hits the cabinet behind me. Eva is coming towards me and I have nowhere to go. Her eyes fall on the photos on the floor. She bends down and picks one of them up. It seems to be happening in slow motion.

She looks up at me. "You weren't supposed to find these, Em." Her voice is heavy, dull like it's drugged, or is it my hearing?

In the back of my mind, synapses are clicking, nerves firing as things fall into place. Eva told me about Suzy's missing baby. She knew I was heading back to the park to put posters up. She knew about my solo exhibition and what it meant to me.

When I told her about Clive, she encouraged me to contact him. Tim Burton-Smyth...it was Eva who told me to see him.

All this time, it's been her. I can't control the sudden shakes that have come over me. I feel cold, and I'm trembling like a bare boughed tree in a winter wind. I turn my wide, pulsatile eyes to her, feeling they will pop.

"You...you did this to me?"

CHAPTER 39

Eva shakes her head, her eyes full of remorse. But she seems puzzled by my question. "Did what to you?"

I stare at her uncomprehendingly. "You and Clive…"

I can't complete the sentence. Eva shakes her head, her eyes full of shame. She must be one hell of an actor. I've never seen this side of her. "It was just a fling," she says. "It was never meant to last."

I hear voices, they pierce the confusion in my mind. It's the children, and they're coming out of their room. I suddenly see the whole plot. Her plan to keep Molly while Clive went to murder Tim. They must think I'm some sort of fool, playing along with their games.

I brush past her, and she lets me go. "Molly!" I shout. She's on the hallway, just outside Lottie's bedroom. I grab her and start to pull her down the stairs.

"Mummy, what are you doing?!" she screams. I'm pulling on her hand so I bend down and take her on my lap. She puts her legs around my waist and I run down the stairs. I can hear Eva running behind me.

"Emma, wait!" Eva shouts.

Wait. Yeah, right. So you can run off with my child. I pick up my handbag and open the door. I took a cab down here. I'm on foot but I can run, and get as far as possible from here. Eva is running down the driveway as I get out on the road.

"Emma!" she shouts again. I'm afraid she's going to come after me. If she gets into her car I'm done for. A cold fear grips me when I think of Clive. He could be around, and if she calls him…I'm running as hard as I can, down the hill, gasping.

"Mummy, we're not going to fall, are we?" Molly says.

"No," I gasp. I keep looking at the road, trying to flag a cab down. There's none. I can see the bus station up ahead. There are some people waiting and that helps. Surely Eva or Clive won't try anything here. My legs feel like they're going to slide loose from my hips. Sweat pours down my face. I put Molly on the ground. She's strong from her gymnastics and can outrun me any day, bless her. Together we make a dash for the bus station. Both of us are exhausted by the time we reach it.

It's only then that I notice Molly doesn't have her schoolbag. We left it at Eva's house. I feel like kicking myself but there's not much I can do. I can never go back there. I keep an eye out for her 4x4. Luckily the massive car doesn't make an appearance. After what seems like the longest wait, finally, the bus approaches. Its only when we are on it, upstairs, with my arm around Molly, that I allow myself to think.

What the hell just happened?

Eva, my best friend from when we were teenagers. Clive and her were sleeping together behind my back? How long for?

The questions come and go, twisting together like loops of spaghetti. I don't even know if I want the answers. And now, she's playing me in a dangerous and reckless game. Clive and she are still together. And Simon? I guess cheating on her husband is nothing new to Eva. If she could do it to her best friend, she can do it to her husband.

But why is she helping Clive? To take our money and run away, to start a new life? She could take Simon's money. *She probably will, I think, and they're just greedy.* Clive knows he can blackmail me over Molly so they will try to destroy me as well.

I feel like a fool. No wonder Clive was always one step ahead. No wonder he knew about the dinner at the Mandarin Oriental. And where Tim was staying.

I trusted her with everything. Now I'm paying the price.

The bus gets near our stop and we get off.

"What happened at Lottie's house, Mummy?" Molly asks. I'm holding her hand firmly as we walk back home.

"I'll tell you later, honey," I say. I can't stop Molly playing with Lottie at school. Neither can I stop bumping into Eva at school. But I have to do something, or I will go insane.

We get back inside the house and I disable the alarm. It's finally quiet, and

I guess there are perks of living behind a park. Fewer neighbours mean less noise. I am still a mess, and I think I will be for a while. Before I start making dinner for Molly, I pull out the bottle of gin and drink from it, neat. Then I pour half a glass and mix it with some tonic water.

They can't keep this up for too long, I think to myself. This is ludicrous. Sooner or later the cops will realise I've been speaking the truth. If they start an investigation into the waiter at the hotel, on Tim's murder, they will know I wasn't making things up. Instead of treating me like a suspect, they'll go after him. I can see the problem, however.

For every situation, it's my word against theirs. I don't have a single witness. I could have spiked my husband's drink and then changed my mind. I could have slit Tim's throat and then called the police. I could have stolen, then given Suzy's baby back.

I could be the psycho bitch. Not Eva.

How well did I know Eva, really? After all these years? Bitter bile rises in my throat again and I swallow it with some gin.

The faint sound of a key turns in the lock. I'm at the door in a flash. It's Jeremy, and I heave a sigh of relief.

CHAPTER 40

I open the door, and a sullen-looking Jeremy comes in. He nods at me wearily, but his eyes are evasive. He puts his briefcase down with a thud, and hangs his coat up. Normally, he smells of his aftershave but today there is whiff of stale sweat and cigarettes. I know he smokes occasionally: after some drinks or when he's stressed. Seems as if he's had a tough day.

He avoids me, and troops into the kitchen with his shoulders slumped. Molly is upstairs, playing on her laptop. He pours himself a drink then sits down at the dining table.

"Is there anything to eat?" he asks, taking a sip of his red wine.

I haven't had time to cook since we got back, and frankly, haven't been in the mood. But I put some Brie to melt in the oven, and cut some slices of crusty bread and arrange them on top of the toaster. We can eat that with some apricot conserve. Jeremy is rubbing his eyes, he looks shattered.

I sit opposite him as the food gets done. "How did it go?" I ask, dreading the answer.

He looks at me with bloodshot eyes. "Bad. There was an emergency meeting of all the partners. I had to explain it. Why it was you who found him, about Joanne's chip on the shoulder about Molly. But." He says nothing more but stares at me.

"But what?"

"No one knew about him and his secretary, Teresa."

"Is that who he was with?"

Jeremy leans his head back. "Yes. No one in the office knew a thing. Turns out, he opened up to you only." He looks at me now. "Wonder why that was."

"I met him outside his workplace. And I did ask him why we were meeting in a hotel, I did find that odd."

Jeremy nods as if he understands my logic. I say, "How long has it been going on for?"

He shrugs. "Months. Years, who knows. He obviously had a very unhappy marriage." Our eyes meet for a second, and it's like sandpaper rubbing against our skins. He looks away quickly, but I don't, and it hurts me.

"What about Joanne?" I ask. I haven't heard anything from the school as yet, and from tomorrow it's the February half-term. When I think of her, I do feel sympathy. Maybe I should reach out to her. Put this matter with Molly aside once and for all. Then again, after Eva, I am now scared of what I might find.

"The police said they've been to her house. They have spoken to her. She's shocked obviously."

I wonder what she thinks about me meeting her husband. Come to think of it, I'm surprised she's not beating down my door. Maybe she realises her life isn't as perfect as she thought it was. I can't help feeling we are in the same predicament, just different degrees.

I remove the Brie from the oven, and put it on a plate with the bread. I bring it to the table. We dip the bread in the molten cheese and spoon some of the apricot on top. I have a bite of one and then stop. I haven't eaten lunch but I'm not hungry. My insides are a mess like my head. I don't eat all day then stuff my face late at night. It makes me sick and last night I vomited. I don't want to think about it too much.

Jeremy munches and downs his red wine. It can't wait any longer. He has to know what happened today after we left the police station.

"Something happened at Eva's house." My voice catches and he stares at me. When he sees the expression on my face he puts down the piece of bread slowly.

"What is it?"

"I found some old photos in her study upstairs. She was sleeping with Clive, behind my back. All those years ago. The photos made it obvious." After a pause I continue. "Now, I think she's behind all this. She's been helping Clive all along. That's why he knows about everything. How else would he know about our dinner at Mandarin Oriental? I told her, and she told him."

I look at Jeremy for pity, sympathy, understanding. Something. Instead, his eyes are blank, and he keeps blinking. He pushes off from the table and stands up suddenly, like there's a fire under his seat. He goes to the window and put his hands on his waist.

"I don't know if I can deal with this anymore."

I can understand where he's coming from. At the same time, I have to hold myself together, and we need each other's support.

"I'm sorry," I say and find the words have dried up inside me.

"It's just frustrating," Jeremy says. "Everywhere I turn, this guy's present."

He turns around to face me. "I have been told to take a voluntary leave of absence from my job. Because of *your* involvement in this whole mess."

His words hit me like a slap in the face. I am stunned, rooted to the spot like someone's driven nails into my feet.

I crumple and break inside, reduced to sawdust and powder. But somehow, I stand straight and hold my face together. I swallow hard, feeling a lump in my throat.

"You think I'm making all this up? These are all lies?"

The frown on his face clears, and he drops his hands from his hips. He comes closer to me. I can see the stress in the corners of his eyes. "I'm sorry, Em, I didn't mean it like that. I know you're not lying. But our lives are falling apart as a result of this shit."

He sinks down to the chair, holding his head in his hands. "I'm just so tired and fed up of all this. I had a nice career, and now it's in ruins. We were going to move into that house, start a family…"

"We can't have a family," I say flatly. "No more than what we have already."

The cold finality in my voice makes him raise his head. There is a quietness suddenly, as if the air has been sucked out of the room. Our breaths are shrink-wrapped into silence. Movement is minimised to the contraction, dilation of eyeballs.

"What do you mean?" Jeremy asks slowly. Very softly. Like he's afraid to go there. So am I.

"I can't have any more children."

"We talked about this. We can try…"

"No. You don't understand."

I tell him. As clearly as possible.

CHAPTER 41

Eight years ago
St George's Hospital, South-West London

When I came to, it was evening. The lights were dimmed in my room, and darkness was falling across the windows that looked out onto the city's skyline. Lights were starting to glow, yellow squares in the windows opposite and around.

My lips were dry. I tried to move and realised I had tubes stuck in my arm. I felt weak, so light that a gust of wind would blow me down. I lifted my head, and some numbers began flashing on a screen above my head. I looked at the squiggly lines on the screen, they made no sense to me.

I heard the door squeak open. The light was turned up, and a few people came inside. A nurse, followed by a doctor. The nurse checked my pulse, leaning over me.

I tried to speak but my lips would barely move. The nurse pressed some buttons on the screen and the beeping stopped. The doctor gazed at me, a frown on his face.

"Miss Dixon, can you hear me?"

I nodded. A look of relief appeared on his face. He turned to the nurse. "She's going to be OK. Can I have a fluids chart and arterial blood gas again please."

The nurse went off, and the doctor looked at me with the kind of expression a man has for his children.

"You've been through a lot, Miss Dixon. I'm just glad that I can speak to you finally. For a while, it was touch and go." He shook his head from side to side. "How do you feel?"

"Water," I managed to croak out. He rushed off, an embarrassed look on his face. He came back with a cup of water and helped me sit up to drink it.

157

I winced with pain as I tried to change position. My lower belly seemed to be on fire, but also felt strange and tight.

I looked up at the doctor. I was dreading his answer, but I had to ask him anyway. "What happened to me?"

His face was grave when he looked at me. "It's a miracle you are still alive. When the ambulance crew got in, they found you passed out on the floor. You were blue-lighted in, and we had to take you straight to theatre."

"Theatre?"

"Yes. You had a lot of internal bleeding, Miss Dixon." A look passed over his face, and he turned his eyes away from me briefly.

My head was spinning again, but I pressed him. "Tell me what happened."

"You had a complete miscarriage. I am sorry."

I had suspected as much, but the words still hit me like a hammer in the chest. My heart crumbled and broke like it had been made of powder. I felt tears trickle down the side of my eyes.

The doctor said, "I found your partner's number in your purse. Is he the man called Clive Connery? Do you want me to call him?"

"No," I whispered.

"Are you sure you don't want me to call someone? A friend maybe?" the doctor said. He looked like an Indian man, his name badge said Dr Raja. His voice was soothing, soft, but there was something else in it as well. I looked up at him, and found his expression more morbid than before. Breath caught in my chest.

"What is it?" I asked.

He took a deep breath. "There is no easy way to say this, Miss Dixon. Like I said, you had a miscarriage, and a prolonged bleed. I am afraid the bleeding wasn't just due to the miscarriage."

I was staring at him, spellbound. He continued, holding my eyes. "You also ruptured a blood vessel. It's called the uterine artery, and it's the main artery of the womb. When you are pregnant, that artery carried almost a quarter of the blood that pumps out of your heart."

He swallowed, his eyes getting duller. "The bleeding was so heavy that you were in danger of dying. We had to make a decision. The miscarriage had already happened and the womb was empty."

My mouth opened slightly, my chest felt empty. The meaning behind his words began to sink in, like blood soaking into dry earth.

Dr Raja took a deep breath again. "We tried everything we could. But the blood was filling your womb, and try as we might, we couldn't find the uterine artery. So we had to…" He looked away briefly, then focused on me again. "We had to carry out a hysterectomy."

My fingers were claws on the bedsheet, my knuckles bone-white. "No," I whispered.

"I am very sorry…"

"NO!" I shouted. "No, no! I…me…" I looked down at my belly, and started to pull off the bedsheets. I had to see for myself.

He tried to restrain me. "Be careful, don't pull out the stitches." He craned his head back and shouted. "Nurse! Help!"

Running feet approached. By that time, I had shoved off the sheets, and lifted up the gown that covered me. A horrible, ugly scar stretched across my lower belly, the staples on my skin shining like evil teeth. My tummy was swollen, red. It looked ghastly, alien, like it didn't belong to me.

Panic closed my throat. I wanted to jump out of the bed, run out of there. I never wanted to see these people again.

Clive…maybe Clive…No, even the thought of his face burned my face with rage. That bastard had done this to me. This was all his fault.

I became aware hands were holding my arms, pinning them down to the bed.

"10mg diazepam, now!" I heard Dr Rajah shout. "Hurry, before she takes the IV line out!"

The nurse from before was pushing my shoulders back. Tears blurred my eyes again, and I shouted once more, my voice hoarse.

"Why? Why…?"

I felt cold liquid surge up one of my veins, then the lights dimmed in my eyes again.

CHAPTER 42

Eight years ago

White light. White sky.

Sounds muffled like horses running on a sea beach, hooves pounding on sand.

Whispers. My swollen eyelids opened painfully. Jagged shards of photos burned my retina and I winced, squeezing my eyes shut. I moved my head from side to side, did the same with hands and toes.

I was here. I was alive. I wasn't sure how much of me was still left, but I was still here. I let my eyes get used to the light, then opened them. I was in a different room. It was cold and clinical. I wasn't on my own anymore, more beds were visible around me. I could see the person on the next bed, an elderly woman with a breathing tube sticking out of her mouth. Her chest rose up and down, and she was sleeping. I tried to sit up, and I heard the beeping alarm again. The sounds was annoying and I wanted to slap the screen just to shut it up.

A different nurse appeared, bustling in blue. Her name tag said, 'Linda, ITU Matron'.

"How are you, my love?" She turned the alarm off and checked my vitals. In all honesty, I was feeling a lot better. I remembered everything, it came back to me in slow, painful waves. The sheer physical drudgery wasn't there anymore. My bones didn't ache. My tummy still felt sore, and my head still hurt, but I felt stronger. Guess I had needed that sleep.

"How long was I out for?" I asked Linda.

"Two days, my love. You've really been through the mill, haven't you?" Her eyes were sympathetic, but I felt slightly irritated. Was nothing personal around here? Did everyone know my business?

Two days seemed like a long time to be asleep. But it had left me feeling better.

Linda got the message, and looked away. "Doctor will be here soon," she said, before bustling away.

I yawned and stretched. The IV lines had been removed from my arms, but I could feel a urinary catheter, which I wanted to get rid of without delay. I needed to get moving. A cloud of despondence came over me.

Clive…our flat. I had been here for three days at least. I wondered if he had tried to get in touch, or if he still cared. I looked around for my belongings. I needed to phone Dad and Eva. A movement caught my eyes and I looked up to see a group of white coats moving towards me. Dr Raja was leading the way, and with him was a lady doctor, short and plump, her blonde hair done up in a bob.

Dr Raja beamed at me. "Good to see you up, Miss Dixon. How are you feeling?"

I shrugged. What did he want me to say? I felt like shit, and I knew I didn't look any better. My hair was straggly, sticky. I wanted to have a bath for a whole year.

He gestured to the short woman. "This is Miss Beveridge. She is the gynaecology consultant who assisted us in the operation."

She stuck her podgy hand out, and I shook it. I couldn't help but stare at the fingers that had roamed around my insides, chopping and cutting. A shiver ran through me.

When she spoke, her tone was crisp, businesslike. "I am sorry for what happened." I glanced at her. Her steely blue eyes didn't look sorry at all. But there was a hint of something else. Empathy perhaps. Understanding. I looked down at my hands, a pain suddenly gripping my chest.

"Miss Dixon." She leaned forward, her blue suit straining against the rails of the bed. "Do you have any questions for me?"

I sniffed, and nodded. "What did you have to remove?"

"The uterus, as well as the tubes. I left the ovaries in there. Which means you will still ovulate and release an egg, but it will never be fertilised, and you will not have periods."

Reality was sinking in fast. This was the new me. Emma Dixon on the outside, warts and all. Inside, scooped out, hollowed. I felt strangely empty, like a drum.

I swallowed back the bitterness. "So I can never have children?"

Miss Beveridge who, despite her title, wore a wedding ring, didn't reply till I looked up at her. Then she nodded slowly, her gaze now softer, like she was supporting me as I gently fell to the ground.

"As you have no womb left, you cannot have children. Your tubes were also swollen with fluid. They were blocked, essentially, and we had to remove them. With the womb, the cervix came as well." For the first time, I caught a note of hesitation in her voice. "You shouldn't be going through this alone. Where is your partner?"

CHAPTER 43

Present day

Jeremy is standing stiff, his eyes sunk deep in their sockets, breathing heavily. I see his mind trying to make sense of my words. Then his face changes into disbelief. It breaks my heart.

Now I know there's no going back. My past has caught up with me, finally. It has to be this way. I have avoided this moment for so many years. So many near misses, half-attempts. Like the filament of a hurricane that destroys everything, this truth has swirled around us. Invisible, ever present. I have tried to grab it and it escaped with a whisper. Or maybe I wasn't really trying. I was fooling myself, playing happy family.

But now it has landed, right here, between us, in the middle of the room. Tonight, there will be no escape.

My eyes sting, and futile saline drops bubble over the surface.

Jeremy can't tear his eyes off me. "Is this true?" he asks in a hoarse whisper.

My silence is answer enough, and my sorrow is actually for him, for us. Not for me. My heart was broken a long time ago, and that part of me will never come together.

It killed my mother, when she found out. She never said it aloud, but I saw it in her eyes. Now it's killing us. And there's nothing I can do about it.

Jeremy is still staring at me, and I know I owe him an explanation.

"I never lied to you, Jeremy," I say in a strong voice. "I might not have explained everything to you, but I didn't give you false hopes."

I feel everything trembling around me, the timber slats of the floor, the walls of the house. The hurricane is sucking up my world, everything solid is turning to motes of dust.

He gets up and walks towards me. There is anger in his face, but also regret.

"And I'm not lying about Clive and Eva…"

"Shut up, Emma. Just shut up." His chest heaves up and down. "I never want to hear those two names again." He looks at me like he's seeing me for the first time. "Do I even know who you are, Emma?"

The pain hits me hard, like I've been hit by the point of a spear in the chest. "Don't say that, Jeremy, please. I love you, I always have. You have to believe me."

"Love? If you loved me then why couldn't you be straight with me from the start?" His eyes are turning red like mine.

"Because of this. Because I thought this would happen," I wipe my eyes. "You would react in this way. But I told you, didn't I?" Desperately, I search for some confirmation in his eyes, some fragment of hope that he sees it my way, that he understands. But his dark pupils are like a blank slate.

"You told me nothing. And now, this whole mess is being dumped on me." He turns away, then starts to leave the kitchen.

I run after him and hold his hand. He shakes it free. Without looking at me, he says, "I need some time away from you. We need to take a break."

Pain twists inside me, a steel vortex. "Don't say that. I need you, Jeremy. Now, more than ever."

He stares at me then, and opens his mouth to say something. But he doesn't say it. He turns around and walks away. I want to run after him, but I know it won't do any good.

But he comes back himself. "I'll move my stuff out tomorrow morning. You two can stay here. I'll carry on paying rent till you find somewhere to live."

"Where will you go?" I ask.

"I have to stay in contact with the office, so not far. Maybe a BnB for a week, I don't know."

This time, I hear him walking up the steps. I lie down on the sofa, and curl myself up into a tight ball.

If this is what Clive and Eva wanted to do to me, then they've succeeded.

CHAPTER 44

Eight years ago

I had been in hospital for a week when they allowed me to leave. I hadn't spoken to anyone, and didn't want to. The aching emptiness I felt couldn't be put into words. Nothing could help me.

I was shaking when I got back to the flat. Light had been snuffed out of the evening sky, and summer was giving way to autumn, a bony coldness in the air, stripping leaves off branches. I put the key in the lock, and stumbled in. The flat was dark, cold and empty. I trudged upstairs and lay down on the bed, still fully clothed. I curled up into a ball, trying not to think.

I never wanted to see Clive again. It was over, and I had been blind to the signs for so long. He had changed, turned into a vicious, cold monster. I didn't know him anymore. Had I really known him? No, of course not. He was a stone-hearted, evil man.

I wasn't sure how long I had spent lying, half-asleep, half awake. I daydreamt about going for dawn walks with my dad in the farm. I would help him to get the sheep out of the corral and into the stream at the bottom of the hill. Once they had grazed and fed, Pixie, Dad, and myself would put the sheep back into their pen again. In between, Dad would show me to how to use the telescope on the rifle. How to slide the breech back, load a bullet in the magazine, and push the safety catch. The wolves came occasionally, and larger cats. It was rare, but Dad always said it was best to be prepared.

I remembered the feeling of the rifle in my hand, heavy and solid. It was a pain to lift it to my shoulder, never mind sight through the telescope. But I slowly got used to it. When I helped Dad lift the bales of hay and clear the barn, as a reward, he would take me to the hills and we would practise shooting. He brought me an airgun, which was ridiculously light after handling his Remington breech action. That airgun, and the pony I got for my ninth birthday, were my favourite possessions.

I must have fallen asleep, but I woke up when I heard the front door close. It was pitch black dark, and I sat upright in bed. I could hear sounds downstairs.

"Clive!" I called out. There was no answer. Lights had come on, and I could hear him rummaging around downstairs. I gritted my teeth, and went down the stairs.

I met him in the hallway, as he was pulling out the suitcases. He looked at me and narrowed his eyes.

"Have you been sleeping?"

It was eight o'clock, I could see the clock on the wall. I stared at Clive. How could I once have been in love with this man? His face was still handsome, and he had a week's stubble on his cheeks. But his eyes were cold and calculating. He hadn't even bothered apologising for his awful behaviour.

I looked at him and shook my head slowly. "What happened to you, Clive?"

He sneered at me. "Happened to me? Look at yourself in the mirror. Who dragged you out of the rubbish bin?"

Anger flared inside me, running through my veins like lava. I stepped up to him. "Do you care about me anymore, Clive? Do you know what just happened to me?"

He must have seen something in my eyes, the hurt and indignation. His face changed as his eyes flickered all over me. "What?"

"I had a miscarriage."

He frowned, thinking. I wonder if he actually knew what it meant. I decided to spell it out for him. "I lost the baby."

He put the suitcases down, and ran a hand through his wavy, blond hair. It used to be smoothly gelled back always, but now it was long and unkempt, falling over his eyes.

"And that's not all," I said, my voice trembling. I told him everything. He was the first person I had told. I still didn't have the strength to tell Dad. I needed to speak to Eva. She was the only one I wanted near me right now.

"Jeez, I'm sorry," Clive said, not looking at me.

I balled my fists and bared my teeth. "Sorry. Sorry? Is that all you can say?"

He looked at me with a strange expression. "What do you want me to say? It's not like it's my fault, is it?"

I breathed out, trying to channel my anger into something. I wanted to scream at him, and rip his eyeballs out, but what good would that do? He was an insensitive, callous bastard, and stupid, idiotic me hadn't seen that to begin with.

What a fool I had been.

"When you pushed and hit me, you caused the internal bleeding that led to all this. So yes, this is all your fault!" I shouted at the top of my voice.

"What the hell are you talking about?" he snarled, curling his lips upward.

"You need to treat yourself, Clive. You're sick, and you need help. You bastard."

"You've lost your marbles, you really have." The anger was back in his face. He picked up the suitcases. "Get the fuck out of my way, you stupid bitch."

With a scream, I flung myself on him. I clawed his face, pulled his hair, punched him. He showed a physical ability like he knew what to do in these situations. Calmly, he sidestepped, parrying my blows. He kicked my legs and I folded. He grabbed my hair and turned me around, pressing my face against the wall.

Standing behind me, he twisted my elbows till I thought the pain would make me pass out. I fought back, but he was too strong.

"Don't push your luck, cupcake," he whispered, tightening his grip on my neck. "All I have to do is squeeze harder, and your shoulder will dislocate. Then I'm going to chop you into smaller pieces. No one's ever gonna find out. Do you understand?"

There was a cold finality in his voice that made by blood freeze into ice.

CHAPTER 45

Eight years ago

I retched on the floor, nauseated, angry, frustrated. I felt for my stitches, they were all intact. If I had a gun in my hands I would have shot him. I put a hand on the wall, and straightened up painfully. He had walked out with the suitcases, and I could hear him getting into the car. The trunk slammed down and the key turned in the ignition, but the car wouldn't start.

An idea came to me. I had to follow him, see what this "merchandise" really was. Battling the ache in my body, I went out of the back door, and got my bike. I put a coat and helmet on. I was outside by the time the BMW's engine had come to life, and I watched from the porch as he pulled out. There was traffic, and he would have to stop and start. I started to cycle after him, staying back so he wouldn't recognise me.

The cycling actually made me feel better. Clive twisted in and out of backroads, and I kept up with him, not losing sight. We had left Putney behind, and entered a seedier part of town. No parks or green spaces here, just rows of grimy terraced houses, with the occasional tall council block.

The BMW stopped outside a row of houses that had seen better days. This was Mitcham, in South London, an area that can be dangerous. And Clive had just driven into the worst part of it. I stopped far behind him, and got off my bike, crouching behind a car. I stayed out of the street lamp and hoped no one would see me.

I saw the overturned rubbish bins, and an empty shopping trolley in front of the decaying front lawn of a house. A burnt car, with its wheel missing, was parked opposite me. The night was close and humid, and I smelt danger in the air.

Clive got out of the BMW and looked around as I ducked. He opened the trunk and took out both of the suitcases. Then he wheeled them up to one of the houses. He pressed on the doorbell and waited. When the door opened and he was let in, I got up and walked towards the house.

The buildings were in various shades of disrepair. I walked past the rusting hulks of a washing machine and dishwasher. Keeping my head, I noted the number on the door. I wheeled my cycle past it quickly, heart beating fast. I couldn't exactly go inside. Clive was dangerous, I knew that now. In truth, looking back now, what did I know of him? Everything he had told me about his life could have been just fabrications.

But there was one thing he couldn't make up. The only thing that gave him some sort of humanity. His mother. I would get up early tomorrow and do two things. See Rita Connery, and take the new contract for the agency business that I had signed when I had given Clive my trust fund money, and see a lawyer.

*****

I went back to the apartment that night. I didn't want Clive anywhere near me, but I had nowhere else to go. Eva had a job outside London, and she travelled often. I texted and called her, but she didn't answer. She could be travelling. My dad was two hundred miles away, up north in Yorkshire.

I went to the kitchen, and took out one of the long kitchen knives. I had watched Dad butcher a sheep once, and while it had been disgusting, I remembered him wrapping black tape around the handle. "So it doesn't slip when the hand gets sweaty," he had told me. I did the same now, using duct tape. When I had finished putting two layers on, the knife felt firmer in my hand.

It sounded odd, but I felt safer with the knife in my hands. I went upstairs and locked the bedroom door.

I put the knife under my pillow. In front of the locked door, I put a chair, inclined to the handle. I lay down, one hand under the pillow. The night was full of sounds, and I could hear the cars rushing past on the road. I didn't know when I had fallen asleep.

*****

Light was dancing across my eyelids. Scarred memories of my mind, bruised and scorched, suddenly came back to me, and I sat upright in bed. The door was shut, and the chair was leaning against the door still.

I got dressed quickly. I hadn't been to work for almost a week, so I called in but no one picked up the phone. I spoke to my solicitors, who were also solicitors for the business, and made an appointment to see them later in the afternoon.

I rang Rita as well, but she didn't pick up the phone. No surprise there, I thought, she might be sleeping, or not have the phone next to her. I hoped she hadn't passed away. Rita was a sweet woman, and she was the only one who could help me now. Maybe she could talk some sense into her son. I felt nauseated when I thought I had just handed over my trust fund money to Clive without any reservation. I should have spoken to Rita's doctor, and arranged to forward the money to her directly. But in any case, I could still get the money back by asking the solicitors to dissolve my share of the agency business.

CHAPTER 46

Present day

I hardly sleep that night, tossing and turning. I drank more G and T before going to bed. It lulled me to sleep which didn't last long. Jeremy slept in the guest room on the sofa. I must have passed out in the early hours, because I come to when Molly is pushing me. I scramble to sit up on the bed, bleary-eyed.

"Mummy, I'm hungry," Molly whines. Oh God. I feel like a terrible mother. My head is thumping and sounds are magnified in my ears. I get out and take Molly downstairs, still in my pyjamas. She has brushed and dressed herself, bless her. I fix her milk and cereals, then sort myself out. As I splash water on my face, I can see the dark shadows under my eyes, the pimples and marks next to them. Memories of last night float back. The cold light of day hides nothing.

I get ready as Molly comes into the bedroom. I brush her hair, and there's no time for anything but a ponytail today. She's not happy. It's the last day before half-term and many of her friends will have bobs and plaits.

At school I am dreading seeing Eva, but I don't see any sign of her, or Lottie. Suzy is there, and she comes over, but I'm not in any mood for talking. Only Eva knows what happened yesterday.

"Are you OK?" Suzy asks after a while. Molly has gone inside with the others. We walk out of the school gates, Suzy pushing the pram. Haltingly, I tell her what happened to Tim. I don't tell her what I found out about Eva. I don't know if I can tell anyone, right now.

I say goodbye to Suzy, who is understandably disturbed. I tell her I'll be in touch over the half-term, which is only a week. When I get into the car, I make my mind up about something. I should see Joanne. We might not have seen eye-to-eye over the last few weeks, but she is grieving. I know she's

171

thinking about why I went to see her husband, and I need to set that straight.

I ring Suzy, who knows Joanne's address. I drive up into the village, where the big detached houses are. Both cars are in the drive. I walk down the gravel drive, after parking behind them. I have to wait for a while after I ring the doorbell. A woman answers the door, who must be the maid.

"Is Joanne home?" I ask. I can hear the TV on in some distant part of the living room. It sounds like a cartoon, and Henrietta must be at home, I think. I can't blame Joanne for keeping her off school today.

"Stay here please," the maid says. She moves away, and in the hallway behind her I see a shadow fall on the expensive glossy tiles. Then Joanne appears. She doesn't look good. There's no make-up on her face, and the stains on her cheeks, and puffy eyes are plain to see. Her hair is breaking free, falling over her face.

She says nothing when she sees me. I guess there is nothing to say. After a while she says, "You better come in."

We sit in the large, open-plan kitchen. It's bigger than the entire ground floor of my house. A large number of concertina doors are closed at the moment, but through them I can see downhill. The trees give way to the golf course and lake, then the tennis stadium, and further away, the skyline of the city.

"Tea or coffee?" Joanne asks.

"Coffee please," I say. She brings two steaming mugs over to us. We pull up bar stools and sit down on the long, L-shaped kitchen counter. White granite with flecks of stone.

Neither of us touch the coffee. The smoke curls between us. I say, "I'm sorry about what happened that day in school. I didn't want to hurt you."

"Don't worry," she says. "I was out of order as well."

I nod. She sighs heavily. In a tired voice she asks, "He called you, didn't he?"

"Yes. Said he wanted to talk about Molly. I didn't know he was living in a hotel."

"Yeah." She offers no other explanation and I don't ask.

"I want you to know I wasn't sure about it. I wanted to meet him in the lobby, but when I got there, the place was shabby and weird. There was no lobby, just two chairs."

Joanne grimaced, then lowered her head. "It's where he went to..." She doesn't finish her sentence. I can imagine what she was going to say.

Joanne examines her nails. "We've not had sex for more than a year."

I don't say anything. She says, "What did you see when you went up to his room?"

"Not sure if it's good for you to know," I say.

She looks at me directly, and for the first time, I see regret haunting her eyes. "He was my husband."

"Yes, he was. Not anymore."

"Just tell me. Please."

I guess she needs to know for the sake of closure. I find this difficult, especially when her face crumples and she lowers it. I stop but she tells me to carry on.

When I've finished, she says, "And you don't know who did it?"

"No." That's a white lie. I have a strong hunch who did it, but I don't know for sure. "The police are looking," I say.

She shakes her head slowly. "The type of place where he was, anything could have happened."

We are quiet for a while, each nursing our own pain. I say, for no reason, "Jeremy and I are going through a break as well. As you can imagine, Tim was his senior partner. There's been some fallout at work. It's all getting on top of him."

"Oh. I'm sorry."

I hold her eyes and see that she means it.

"What're you going to do?" she asks me. I have thought of this already, and I see no reason not to tell her.

"I'm going to live with my dad for a while. Take Molly with me. He lives outside London."

It's what I should have done to begin with, when this rubbish with Clive kicked off. I could have kept him away from Jeremy. Well, it's time to do it now. Because Clive hasn't given up. He's still around with his demonic helper Eva. And I have no doubt he'll make life hell for me again.

"Who do you think is doing this to Henrietta?" Joanne asks.

"I don't know," I answer honestly. "But I will ask around. I have been, and I'm sure the children know. But they don't tell us everything, do they?"

Her shoulders sag and a look of utter defeat comes over her face. I reach out and touch her hands.

"We'll find out. I promise," I say. Joanne has her head resting on her palm, and she just nods.

CHAPTER 47

Eight years ago

It was raining when I stepped off the bus in Putney. I walked past a park with children still playing in the light drizzle, wearing their colourful raincoats. Beyond the park, the sluggish grey waters of the Thames flowed like a muscular ribbon. I had a small umbrella in my handbag, but the rain wasn't hard enough, and I just pulled the hood of my jacket over, tucking the curls of my hair inside.

The complex of flats wasn't far from the bus stop and I was there after a brisk ten minutes' walk. I pressed on the buzzer three times, with the third time being the longest. I knew that it would take her a while to answer, so I waited. After more than ten minutes had passed I started getting impatient. The well-tended front lawn and gardens were empty. There was a row of cars in the car park. No one emerged from them. I walked to the end of the front garden. Ground-floor windows faced the front, and a couple of them didn't have curtains drawn. I tried to look through them, feeling foolish. A TV was on in one of the flats, and I could see a baby playing on the carpet, with a pair of legs jutting out from the sofa. I thought for a while, then leaned over the row of plants and hopped onto the grass verge. After five steps, I was at the window.

I rapped on the window, and waited. My hood was off, and I waved at the person inside. The baby turned and stared at me, mouth open. A woman got up from the sofa, and came closer, frowning.

I mouthed the word *Sorry*. It was a Velux window with a latch that only opened it a small angle at the top. That would be enough for me to speak to the woman. I gestured. She hesitated, turning around once to check the baby. Then she opened the window slightly, holding the lock, ready to slam it shut. I didn't blame her.

"I'm very sorry," I said, raising my voice. "But my mother-in-law lives in Flat 34 on the fourth floor. She is not answering the buzzer or her phone. She is very sick and lives alone. Would you please mind opening the door for me?"

The woman, a freckly-faced mother in her late-twenties, considered me for a while. Then she nodded.

"Press the buzzer for number ten. When I hear it, I will let you in. But please don't come to my door. I can't help you and it's time for the baby's nap soon."

"Yes, of course. Thank you so much."

I hurried back to the front door, and pressed the number ten buzzer. To my relief there was a clicking sound at the door and when I pushed it, it opened. The lift was taking an age to arrive, so I sprinted up the stairs, getting slightly out of breath by the time I reached the fourth floor.

I knocked on Rita's door. No answer. A jolt of fear ran through me. Had she died? I knocked several times, but there was no answer. I called her name loudly, and banged on the door for good measure. There was a sound behind me, and I opened the door to find a middle-aged woman standing there. She was Afro-Caribbean, and slim, with her hair done up in braids. She glared at me.

"That's quite a racket you're making there. Can I help you?"

"Yes, you might be able to. Do you know the old lady who lives here? Her name is Rita Connery and she is very sick. She's my partner's mother and I'm afraid something might have happened to her."

The woman frowned. "Old woman?"

I found her response odd. "Yes. You know, the old lady who lives here. Her name is Rita. She, well, she has cancer."

The lady shook her head from side to side. "I don't know any old lady who lives there."

A feeling of unreality was moving through me like a veil of smoke. A strange emptiness opened up at the back of my mind. I swallowed hard, and felt my heart thudding against my ribs.

"You must know…"

She shook her head again. "I can tell you, young lady, that flat has been empty for many years."

I opened my mouth, but words were frozen. The woman stepped out of her flat, observing me carefully.

"My name is Sheila. What's this all about?"

I breathed heavily. "Sheila, how long have you lived here for?"

"More than twenty years."

"Were you here two weeks ago, on Thursday afternoon?"

Sheila thought for a while. "No, I wasn't. I was out visiting my grandchildren."

"When did you get back?"

"The next morning. Why do you ask?"

"There would have been others living on this floor, right? On that day I mean."

"Yes, of course. Hang on, let me ask our neighbour." She walked down the corridor and knocked on the next door. There were five flats in total on this side of the fourth floor. When I came up the stairs, I had turned right. On my left, lay the entrance to another corridor and I assumed, another five flats.

Sheila had a quick chat with someone, then turned back to me. I saw an elderly woman poke her head past Sheila, staring at me.

Sheila said, "This is Mrs Edmonston, and she has lived here longer than me. Trust me, girl. That flat has always been empty. No one knows why."

I leaned against the wall, trying to think. Sheila asked, "Are you sure you have the right address?"

"Yes, I was here two weeks ago and that flat…" I stared at the brown door with the silver number 34 written on it. My finger was pointing at it, like it was a magic wand that could open it.

How was this possible? My mind was in pieces. I mumbled a goodbye, and walked out the double doors, heading for the staircase. My legs were shaking. I sat down on the stairs, holding my head in my hands. My breathing was fast and jerky.

Could this really be happening? Rita had the oxygen cylinder, the old photos, everything had seemed so real. So genuine.

Flashbacks cut through the confusion in my mind. Clive, looking at me with hopeful eyes. Down and depressed.

She has one month to live.

I won't be alive to see the little one.

The new drug costs twenty-five grand a year.

Over two years, that was fifty grand. Fifty grand was everything I had in my trust fund.

CHAPTER 47

Eight years ago

I rushed down the stairs of the flat, taking them two at a time. I burst out of the front door, fumbling with my phone as I ran. I called Clive, but it went to answerphone. I wanted to call the police, actually, I *had* to call the police, but it would have to wait. The taxi pulled up at the pavement after I paced like a caged animal for five minutes. I gave the driver directions for the Connery estate agents office on the high street. It took a while to get through the traffic and I took that time to dial 999.

"Do you want fire, ambulance or police?" a bored voice asked on the other end.

"Police please."

The line connected almost immediately. "Please tell me exactly what has happened," said another calm, male voice at the other end.

"I have been swindled out of money. All my savings. My partner has done a massive fraud…" I was trying to speak slowly, but I knew my voice was high-pitched.

The voice cut through. "Are you in danger right now?"

"What?"

He repeated the question.

I said, "Yes, I mean no. I am the victim of a huge fraud. I need the police to arrest someone."

"Are you at the scene of crime?"

This guy just wasn't getting the urgency of the situation. I wondered what he would do if he had just been tricked out of his inheritance.

"No, I'm not."

"Then you have to go to the nearest police station and file a crime report."

"I know that," I snapped, and turned the phone off. So much for help

179

from the police. I would have to involve them a bit later. My phone rang again, and I picked it up. It was my solicitor. I had put the phone to my ear when the cab parked. I paid him quickly, told the solicitor I would call him back and got out of the cab.

In front of me there was the usual parade of high street shops. Connery's estate agency was next to a charity shop, and I hurried towards it. Abruptly, I came to a standstill. The charity shop was open, but the windows of the estate agency were boarded up. The door was shut. The sign on the top still said the name, with the neon sign that stuck out sideways. My hands and feet felt cold. It was hard to breathe all of a sudden. My brain was trying to process what my eyes were seeing.

I stood in front of one of the boarded-up windows. The brown grill steel-cased boards covered most of the front, including the door. To the right there was a chip shop from where we used to get our lunches. It was open. I walked in, my head a mess. I didn't know what to say, feel or think.

The chip shop owner was frying fish, wearing a white apron with batter stains all over it. He knew me, and smiled. I couldn't remember his name.

"Our agency office," I pointed, feeling stupid. "What happened to it?"

He frowned, and folded his arms on top of the counter. "Thought you'd know, seeing you work there. They closed up shop one week ago. I didn't hear much. Saw some guys come in a van one day and board the place up." He looked at me quizzically. "Didn't you know?"

"I've been on leave. Just got back."

He raised his eyebrows. I thanked him, and walked out, calling my solicitor's bypass number. Mr Dempsey answered immediately, like he was waiting for my call.

"Did you know the office is shut down?" I started, angry and confused.

He was quiet for a while. When he spoke, his voice was very low. "Miss Dixon, I suggest you come to my office asap."

After twenty minutes, I was sitting in the renovated Edwardian building's ground-floor office. Dempsey and Sons had been doing business from these premises for the last hundred years. I was shown straight into his office.

"What's going on?" I asked, not sitting down.

Mr Dempsey was tall, thin with sunken cheeks. His white hair only grew on the sides and back. He had a defeated look on his face. My heart sank as I looked at him. He tapped the desk. I saw he had my folder out, the one that contained my contract with Clive. My share of the business in exchange of my trust fund.

In an apologetic voice Mr Dempsey said, "I am afraid the business has no assets left, Miss Dixon."

The feeling of unreality was spreading through me like a cloud again. I had difficulty speaking.

"What do you mean?"

"I mean there is nothing to sell to raise money. I am afraid your share, and any share, of the business is useless."

*****

I had nowhere else to go but back to the flat. I tried to think about what had happened to my life. I had nothing left – my heart, my body, my money – all of it had been ripped out. And all of it by one man. One man who had preyed on me, and destroyed me, systematically. It only occurred to me then how devious his plans had been.

I had to go the police. There was no other choice. Once I told them everything they might even know who he really was. He probably had a history, and a different identity. Then I stopped. Clive had taken the suitcases to that house in Mitcham. What if he was living there now? He thought I wouldn't be able to track him down.

But I had. I didn't want to go the police empty handed. I would find out exactly what he was upto first.

CHAPTER 48

Present day

I try Dad on the mobile, but on the farm reception can be patchy. Askrigg, where he lives up north, is in the Yorkshire Dales. It's a National Park, and very beautiful. Life in the farm was hard, however. I used to help Dad a lot, with Mum and a couple of farmhands. I miss those simple days.

I ring the landline, and he answers after a while. His voice is still booming and loud, and it fills me with warmth and reassurance to hear it.

"Hey up, our kid!" he shouts in his Yorkshire accent. "Forgotten about your old man, have ya?"

"No, Dad." I say quietly. I pause and he doesn't speak. Then I tell him everything. I sit down, and can't stop the tears as the words pour out of me.

"Oh, Emma. My poor lass," he laments. Then his voice hardens. "Where is that fecking bastard now, eh? Give him a taste of his own medicine, I can."

"I don't know and I don't care."

"How's Molly?"

"She's fine. Can we come and stay with you for a while, Dad?"

"What you asking for, you silly muppet? It's your house, ain't it?" Dad's always had a way with words. I haven't spoken to him for a good few weeks, and even the sound of his voice makes me want to cry.

After I've spoken to Dad, I buy the tickets on internet. They cost a bomb as I'm buying them at short notice, but I don't care. I put it on the joint credit card I have with Jeremy. I have to collect the tickets from King's Cross. We need to leave as soon as I've picked up Molly. It's an early finish at school today, at 1 pm. I'm glad and all of a sudden I'm really looking forward to spending time at home with Dad.

There is a crowd at the gates, and the children are out in the playground, running around. I see Suzy, and we pick the children up and walk back. I still haven't seen Eva today, or Lottie. Neither has Suzy. I tell her about seeing Joanne. She doesn't know about Jeremy or Eva. She asks me what I'm doing over the holiday week and I wonder what to tell her. In the end I opt for the truth.

"Something has happened between Eva and me," I say. "I can't tell you what it is, but she's betrayed me. In a very bad way." I don't elaborate. Suzy's eyes widen, and I can tell she wants to press, but I just say, "Please. I'll tell you later."

Suzy says, "OK. But I know something bad is going on. Look, Emma, without you, I wouldn't have my whole family now." She smiles and nudges the pram. "So, if I can help in any way. Even if it means having Molly for a few hours." She looks at Molly and smiles. Molly slides closer to me, and I put an arm around her.

"Thank you, Suzy," I say, meaning it. Then I tell her where I'm going. It's good to have someone who knows, in case I need to call her about the house or something else.

"Up north? Great, sure you'll have a wonderful time. Relax and get everything out of your system."

I know I'm being paranoid but I ask her anyway. "Will you keep an eye on the house? It's going to be empty for the week."

"You have an alarm, don't you?"

I say yes.

She says, "I'll drive by every now and then. A week will fly by." Suzy says again, "Remember if you need me, just ask. I really don't mind." Margaret kicked the side of the pram and sneezed.

"Thank you, Suzy. I better go. Don't want to miss the train."

"Are we really going to see Granddad, Mummy?" Molly asks, a trace of excitement in her voice. I told her when she came out of her classroom.

"Yes."

"Yippee." She skips on the road ahead of me and I run after her. There's a busy junction outside their school. As I grab Molly's hand again, my phone buzzes. I pick it up to find Eva calling me. I don't answer. When I'm getting in the car, it buzzes again. I feel like throwing it out of the window.

*****

The journey up north is uneventful, apart from Eva trying to ring me again. I steadfastly ignore all her calls. I do ring Jeremy and tell him what we're doing. The rolling blue and green hills and deep valleys or dales, as we call them here, appear soon. I'd forgotten how nice it was, even in the cold of February. When I was young we used to play in the hills. We knew where the caves were, and played hide-and-seek in the summer till sundown.

This area is now a tourist spot, but the tourists don't come in the winter. It's in July and August that the queues of cars begin. Kind of spoils the beauty of the place, in my opinion, but it also helps the farmers earn a living by letting out their homes as hotels or BnBs.

Dad never did, though. "The Dixon farm isn't a hotel," he always said. We had enough livestock, and a limestone quarry at the edge of our land. Farming isn't easy in the Dales. The hill uplands are covered by moors, and not much grows there. It's in the Dales that we have the hay meadows and drystone-walled fields. In summer the meadows are lush with growth, and all the wading birds fly down from the moorlands. The birds are red green and blue, and flutter like brushstrokes against the yellow meadows.

The journey takes a while. We get off at Skipton and have to take another slow train to finally reach Askrigg. The village is big, and served well by roads, but it is remote. Rain falls steadily from a leaden-grey sky as we approach.

Dad is waiting for us at the station. He's not hard to spot in his burly sheepskin jacket, ruddy complexion and white, bushy beard. The platform is more or less empty, only two more passengers alight with us. Molly shrieks and runs towards and he picks her up and swings her round. He envelops me in a hug, and I smell the familiar odours of hay, livestock and diesel from the tractor carts.

Dad holds me at arm's length. His eyes are blue and they twinkle even on this drab day. "So good to see you, lassie. Missed you."

"You, too, Dad." I mean it.

He picks up my heavy suitcase and we walk out of the station. I have the hoodie of my jacket up and the rain drums against it, a soft and sibilant sound. Dad's old Range Rover is waiting, and we dump all our stuff in the back and jump in. I sit with Molly in the front as Dad drives, and answers Molly's chattering.

Grey peaks of hills merge with rain-soaked clouds that fade to white sky. Curlews and wagtails fly down, floating to a stop over puddles of wet land. From the station Dad drives through the sleepy village, past the pubs, post office and stationary shops. Then a single line of black asphalt stretches to infinity between two hills, ours being the only car on it for now. I have missed this, I know now. It's such a world away from the hustle and bustle of London.

It takes half an hour to travel the forty-odd miles to the farm. As I go down the single-lane pitched road that I remember being made, my eyes are drawn to two new outhouses before we get to the house and barnyards.

"When were they built, Dad?"

He mutters a reply without saying much. I wonder if Dad is starting to think about the tourists in summer, after all.

CHAPTER 49

Molly is shattered by 8 pm and I put her to bed in my room. She'll be sharing a room with me while we stay here. Dad has got the fire going, and the timber logs hiss and splutter as they burn. I sit down in an armchair close to it, tucking my feet inside.

"Tell me again what happened," Dad says. I do.

"That swindling swine," he grunts. "Should have buried him when he came up here all those years ago." He looks at me and his features soften. "What's happening between you and Jeremy, then?"

I shrug, feeling the pain again. Jeremy is the best thing that's happened to me and I don't want to lose him. But I might not have much say in the matter anymore. It's my fault. I should have been franker with him right from the beginning.

But there's no point in going back over this again. I need to look forward, for Molly if not for myself.

"I don't know," I say honestly. "Think some time apart will be good for both of us." I say that without meaning it. I don't want to spend time without Jeremy. We should be together, a family. I think about Joanne, having to deal with Tim's funeral now. It seems weird so much has happened in these last few days. It has torn our lives to shreds, and it's all down to one man.

Anger boils inside me again. I want to make sure that Clive Connery gets his come-uppance, but I have to trust the police to deal with him.

"Dad," I say, "do you still have the gun?"

He seems surprised. "You mean the Remington 600? My old bolt-action rifle?"

"Yes."

"Replaced it for another Remington. It's a semi-automatic."

"Can I see it?"

I can see the questions behind his eyes. "You've not held a gun for years, lassie. Why do you want to try one now?"

I shrug, keeping my face neutral. "Just because."

He takes a long look at me, then shrugs as well, as if letting go of whatever was on his mind. "Come with me," he says.

We go into the kitchen, then to a small cabinet behind the pantry, just before the back doors lead to the courtyard. Daisy, our German Collie who helps Dad herd the sheep, hovers around us, aware we're up to something.

"This is where it stays," Dad says. There's a digital keypad on the cabinet, and he pushes the buttons. "It's your mother's date of birth," he says. I nod.

The long door of the cabinet opens, and he pulls out the rifle. It's black, made of carbon with a steel barrel. It feels much lighter than the old Remington. Dad shows me how to slide the rack, and attach the 30-cartridge magazine. He locks the safety on, and I take aim at the far wall. The rifle feels good in my hands. I can carry it without my arms getting too tired.

"Can I try it out tomorrow?" I ask.

"Only when I'm around," he says firmly.

We sit around and talk for a while, but I'm shattered after our long journey as well. I say goodnight to Dad and go up to my room. Daisy trots up the stairs with me, I seem to be her new favourite owner. I tell her to go downstairs and guard the kitchen, just like I used to with Pixie. She whines for a while, and I have to go down with her. The ground floor is dark now that Dad's in bed. Wind and rain lash against the window and thunder cracks over the hills. I put Daisy in her bed of rugs and tell her to stay. She gets the message finally and obeys.

I get undressed quickly, and join my sleeping daughter in bed. The bed and house feel new. I lie awake, thinking about everything, listening to the storm outside. I don't know when I fall asleep.

*****

I feel refreshed when I wake up. Like I've had a good night's sleep for the first time in ages. I didn't drink last night, and it makes me feel good. My head feels much clearer, and I vow to myself not to drink during my stay here. Molly is bundled up into a ball of sleep, and I let her have a rest.

I come down the stairs. It's cold, despite the heating being on. Dad must have left it off overnight. There's a smell of frying bacon, and I follow it into the kitchen. Dad is cooking breakfast, and for a while, I just watch him. Vivid memories of earlier years assault me. Mum standing there, in her pink and white floral apron, bustling about as she cooked breakfast for us and the farmhands. The cooking rangers were new then, shiny and cleaned. Now they have flecks of rust, the stone counter has chipped at the edges. The wooden hooks where the pots and pans hung are getting worn.

I feel a rush of guilt. After Mum died, how much have I looked after Dad, really? I've been too busy making a life for myself down south. Dad says himself there isn't much in the Dales. All the young people go down south or into the cities for jobs. There's only so many families farming and tourism can sustain.

And the Dales are far, it's not like I can come and go in a few hours. But that sounds like an excuse. As I watch Dad, back bent with approaching arthritis and age, flipping the bacon rashers, checking the eggs, I realise I have been too wrapped up in my life. Which is also Molly's life. This farm will one day be her inheritance. Will I leave a scrapyard for her? I think of the new outhouses that look like log cabins in the forest. Maybe Dad sees the writing on the wall, and is trying to be open-minded about the tourism option. His ageing body can only do so much, even with the farmhand's help.

I walk towards him, and he turns around. "Hey up." Typical Yorkshire greeting, in his typical hearty voice.

"Morning, Dad."

"Where's our Molly, then?"

"Fast asleep."

"Will she eat this? I remember you used to be well fussy."

"Actually she likes bacon, so yes, she will."

I take a cup of coffee and go upstairs. Molly is sitting up in bed, looking a little confused. I get her ready and then go downstairs. The bell goes downstairs, and I leave Molly in the kitchen to check.

"Probably the farmhand," Dad calls out after me.

I look through the window and it's a young lad in his late-teens, with acne marks on his face. I tell him to come around the back and then lock the door shut again.

CHAPTER 50

Dad fires up the buggy, which is the same size as I remember it, like a large golf cart, diesel-powered. Molly and I hang on as it wobbles over the grounds. We leave the barn behind, and the land dips and the undulating dales come into view. Its watercolour grey now, meadows drowsy with rain and fog. The hill goes down into a gentle V that stretches for several miles before rising up again into the green and yellow shades of a hill. The drystone walls act as boundaries. Part of this land is ours. There isn't another farmhouse around for fourteen miles but then we only own ten of those. Farmers have grazing grounds around us. Above the far hills is a quarry that Dad started to dig several years ago with some friends. It used to make money but I don't know what's happened to it recently. With Molly in tow, I have no wish to go near a quarry.

We pass through the sheep field, much to Molly's delight. She gets out and strokes a woolly lamb, and I have stop her from hugging it. We leave the farmhand and Daisy to open the gates and lead the sheep downhill to the stream, where they can graze and drink. Mathew, the farmhand, waves at us as we round the corner and come up to a crop of woods.

There is a small clearing adjacent to the woods. Dad shows me again how to load and release the safety catch. I get a feel of the rifle, sighting through the viewfinder at a far tree. I'm wearing jeans, and I go down on one knee. I take my time and press the trigger midway through a breath, as Dad taught me.

The rifle is suppressed, but I have earplugs on Molly anyway, in case she gets scared. The noise is like air coming out of a cycle tyre. I miss my mark by miles, and try four times before I hit the tree. Dad takes the rifle from my hands.

"You can't be blamed, chuck. When was the last time you fired a rifle?"

"Seven, maybe eight years?"

"I reckon ten," Dad harrumphs. Then he winks at me and smiles. He stands, and with the practised ease of one used to shooting, he fires at the tree. Bark flies off as the bullet hits the target. I practise a few more times, then stop as Molly's getting bored. Dad has things to do around the farm as well, so he takes the buggy and goes further down, to open his gates to let the other farmer's animal graze. Dad gets some grazing money if their cattle come onto our land. He offers to give us a lift but I decline. Molly and I need to stretch our legs.

It feels so peaceful. Apart from the odd bleating of sheep, and the crying of a wading bird up in the moors all I can hear is the sound of our boots on the wet grass. The rain has relented thankfully but judging by the skies, it's a temporary respite.

Molly and I climb up a ledge, her smaller legs keeping up with me perfectly well. If anything, I start to get winded before she does. Molly is skinny and quick. She gets to the top of the ledge before I do. There's not much shade, and we sit on some rocks, staring at the scenery in front of us. I have the urge to take out my notebook and sketch.

But I need to keep an eye on Molly as well. Out here in the hills I don't want her to wander off. There's something about the Yorkshire Dales that's not advertised well, and most visitors don't know about it.

The Dales are home to Europe's largest underground cave system. Potholes can suddenly emerge underfoot, and rivers are swallowed up into bottomless caves. It's all limestone here, soft and crumbly, and the rivers snake down the mountains, turning into waterfalls.

I know the terrain, which is one of the reasons Dad has left me alone with Molly. If I don't call back soon he'll be out looking. I check the reception on my phone. It's working, which is a miracle.

"Sit with me, Molly," I say to her.

"I want to go up there." She points.

"No. Sit down, now."

She sulks, but sits down next to me. I pacify her by taking a photo, and then a selfie of the two of us.

I try to take a photo of the hills opposite us. There's a ride a few hundred yards away that is covered in trees. I focus on it.

As I do so, a figure emerges from the margin of the trees, and walks to the edge of the ridge. It's a man. *Must be a farmer*, I think. The man walks to a piece of rock and he can't go any further. I notice that he has turned towards me. I put the camera down hastily. The natives here don't like being photographed which is understandable.

The man is facing us, and a curious sense of dread pools inside my gut as the seconds tick away. He lifts his hand and waves at me.

"Who's that man?" Molly asks. He's too far away to identify, but something about his shape is making a hollow appear in my stomach, a familiar sick feeling growing inside it.

My phone begins to ring. Caller ID unknown. My mouth is dry as I realise the man is holding a phone to his ears. I can make out that much.

Heart hammering against my ribs, I answer.

"Hello, cupcake." The deep voice rumbles like an earthquake against my eardrum. "Fancy seeing you here."

CHAPTER 51

I am running. The slate-grey hills are slippery with rain, but I don't care. Molly is keeping up with me somehow. Breath rasps in my throat, a panicked growl waiting to be let out. Both of us are panting, small clouds of vapour collecting outside our faces. I am wearing hiking boots and Molly has grips on her wellies.

"Mummy, slow down," she says. I think of picking her up and running but she's too heavy for me. I have to slow down, for her sake.

The sleepy countryside around me now has deep pits of fear, like the potholes that can appear beneath our unwary feet. I need to get out of here. Panic is tingling my skin like fire, burning in the rain.

We slip, slide and climb up the path and finally I see the stone walls of our sheep pen. I can see the head of the farmhand.

"Mathew!" I call out, but he can't hear me. I stop, gasping. Molly sinks down at my feet. I take out my phone and check it. Damn it, only one bar of reception. I call Dad, but it goes to answerphone. He could be anywhere. All I can do is keep walking till I get to the farmhouse. The land is flatter now, gently sloping upwards. I can see the outline of the farmhouse, wood and brick against the grey sky.

I call Mathew again, and this time he hears me. With Daisy, he is walking up, but the sheep are still down at the stream. I know he will go back in a few hours to put the sheep back in their pen. He's surprised to see me running and breaks into a sprint towards us.

His face is flushed when he catches up with us. "What did you see?" The expression on my face must be awful, I think. "A wolf, or big cat?"

I try to catch my breath. Molly has done very well, but the poor thing is shattered, still resting at my feet. I don't have the strength to pull her up.

"Nothing, don't worry. Can you go back and get the buggy down here? I need to get back up to the farmhouse."

My phone rings again. It's Eva. Fear blooms inside me. I turn the phone off, wanting to throw it down the hill. Is she here as well?

Molly and I lean against the stones of the sheep pen. I am looking up and down. Molly is hugging me, and both of us are wet and shivering. A pale sun lurks behind clouds, and the silvery rain forms a luminous vale that drags across the landscape. The dales far down below are almost invisible, but the hills opposite can be seen. The ridge where I saw Clive is around the corner, and only its tip is visible.

Did he follow us to King's Cross? He would have known from the train I took where I was headed. After all he has been here before, when I brought him up to meet Dad. I curse myself for that day.

The rumble of a machine comes from above us, and Dad appears, driving the buggy, fast. He brakes to a stop and jumps out.

"What's going on, like?" he says. "You look like you've seen a ghost, lassie."

"I saw Clive, Dad. He was standing on the ridge opposite the woods. I went up, and stopped just below the moors. We sat down on the rocks. Who owns that land?"

We got into the buggy as Dad thinks. "That's old Johnson's farm. He's dead now and as far as I know it's empty."

Dad fires up the engine and we head back up, bouncing and shivering as the wet wind howls around us.

The farmhouse door is open, which is not a sight that fills me with confidence. But that's the way around here. No one locks the door. I have been locking the front door since I arrived but Dad has left it open now.

It's warm inside, and a welcome respite from the rain. I get Molly undressed and into new clothes. Then I make her a hot chocolate.

"Is something bad going to happen to us, Mummy?" Molly says after a few sips of her chocolate.

I tuck a few strands of her curly hair behind her ears. "No, darling," I say, trying to sound like I mean it.

"Did you see a wolf?"

"Something like that."

"Like what?"

"A wolf."

She gazes at me in silence for a while then sips her chocolate again. "So, you grew up on the farm, but you never saw a wolf. Is that why you got scared?"

"Yes, darling."

"Who's Clive?"

A pair of pincers grab my heart and twist it violently. I need to say something, she knows when I lie to her. "Someone I used to know. Finish your drink now, come on. What do you want for dinner?"

She makes a face. I don't blame her, the hot chocolate is probably filling her up for now.

"Not hungry," she says.

Neither am I. Food is the furthest thing from my mind. I think of the gun in the cupboard behind the kitchen, and how secure it felt in my hands. How safe *I* felt with it in my hands. Is that a weird feeling? I don't know. I can't make much sense of anything right now.

My heart races when I hear the front door rattle open. In a flash I am out of my seat and in the hallway. It's Dad. He takes off his large sheepskin jacket and shakes it dry. Raindrops scatter on the stone floor.

"Raining harder now," Dad says. "Anyone would have to be barmy to be out in this weather."

I think about Clive prowling around in the dark and I shiver. The sense of safety I felt in this place has now gone. Every door and window now looks like an entry point. I doubt I'll sleep much tonight.

My phone rings again, making me jump. I remove it slowly from my pocket, afraid to look at the screen. I sigh in relief. It's Suzy.

I go upstairs as I answer the phone. Suzy is the only friend I can speak to now. She might even know where Eva is.

"He's here," I gasp, and then tell her everything. After a pause I say, "How do you think he found me? I mean, only you and Jeremy knew where I was going."

"Have you told Jeremy about this?"

"No."

"Are you wearing headphones?"

The question throws me. "What do you mean?"

"I want you to look at something on your phone. But I might have to talk you through it. Do you know what a location tracker is?"

"You mean like the location services on the iPhone?"

"Yes, a bit like that. The location services will activate your GPS. You can share location with others if you want. But there are location trackers that you can download onto any phone which will always keep GPS activated on the phone, and the owner won't know about it, unless they check."

"OK, hold on." I run downstairs, and rummage inside my handbag till I find the white wires of the headphones. I can hear Dad and Molly in the kitchen. I recheck the front door is locked, then dash upstairs again. I hear thunder crash outside, and lightning flashes through the windows.

Suzy says, "Right, go into Privacy, and look at location services."

I do, and it's turned off. She says, "Now go down the list and see if you can find something called Third Party Software."

There are only four items there. At the bottom, I see it. My heart skips a beat.

"It's here," I say with bated breath. Without her asking me to, I click on Third Party Software. It takes me to a page where there's an app installed called Mysite. Next to the name, there's a toggle switch, with the app being turned on, showing green. At the top, where the arrow icon normally indicates that location services are turned on, is absent. I turn the third party app off as quickly as I can.

"It's off now," I say. "How did you know it was there?"

"I didn't. But a lot of what you said didn't make sense. How did Clive always know where you were? I mean, he got it down with pinpoint accuracy, right? Each time. It made me wonder if there was a tracker app on your phone. It was just a hunch, and it paid off."

"Who installed it on my phone?"

There's a pause, and we both know what we're thinking. I say it before she does. "Eva."

I grip my forehead. "Oh God. She must have had dozens of opportunities to look at my phone. But how did she know my password?"

"She didn't have to. You can install these apps without accessing the iOS software."

I look at my phone and shudder. "God knows what else is in here."

"That's exactly what I was thinking. Turn it off, and separate the battery from the phone. It will send a signal for the next five hours, but he knows where you are already."

Frustrated, I rip the battery off, and throw my phone on the bed. Wish I never had the damn thing. Could they have been listening to my calls as well? No wonder they knew everything…

"How are you coping?" Suzy asks. "Sorry, that's a stupid question."

I can feel the walls closing in again. I feel helpless in here suddenly, captive. I want to be out there, doing something. Restlessness prickles my skin. I get up and start to pace the room.

"Would it help if I came over?" Suzy asks.

I stop in my tracks. Some company would do me the world of good. There would be an extra pair of eyes to look after Molly as well.

"I can't ask you to do that."

Suzy says, "Nonsense. My mum's down here, and she will help with the girls. I really don't mind."

"Are you sure?"

"Yes, of course. I wouldn't be saying otherwise. Be a break for me as well."

"Only if you're sure. I don't want to put you out."

"Don't be silly. I'll take the train tomorrow," Suzy says.

CHAPTER 52

The wind howls and moans outside, and rain lashes against the windows. The farmhouse has four bedrooms upstairs, and I have checked each one, including the one where Dad sleeps. All the windows are secure. Downstairs is as secure as it can be, and Daisy is in the kitchen, sleeping on her rug. She will hear anyone coming in. Both the front and back doors are locked.

I do the rounds one last time and go upstairs. My room faces the back, and it's above the kitchen. The pantry and galley stretch one floor below me. The roof is triangular. I look out the window and watch the black, torrid night, the furious storm spending itself against the dales and hills. I can make out the dim outline of the barn and the animal pen. The poor sheep are huddled inside the pen tonight, and I spare them a thought.

Although its ten pm, and raining buckets, there is some light. There's a full moon up there, and its scudding between clouds like a one-eyed monster, hidden behind shadows in the sky. That's why I can see the barnyard, and the grounds around it.

I don't like it. It means anyone looking at the rear of the farmhouse can see us. I close the curtains and lean back. I tiptoe downstairs, and go to the cupboard behind the pantry. Daisy wakes up and growls, then whines when she recognises my scent.

"Shh, good girl." I pat her on the head and she lies back down, tail wagging once.

I punch in my mother's date of birth on the digital keypad, a lock clicks, and the door falls open. I take the Remington 600 out, and check the magazine is loaded. I make sure the safety's on and go back upstairs.

Molly is breathing softly. I lean the gun next to the bedside table, within easy reach. I don't get fully undressed. Unhooking my bra, I lie down in my jeans and T-shirt. My socks are on and slip-on shoes are by the bed. I close my eyes and try to relax.

That's when I hear the phone buzz. It's on the bedside table. I pick it up and catch my breath. Someone is trying to ring me, and again, its caller ID withheld. I don't want to answer, but a strange compulsion is drawing the shining screen closer to my ear.

I hold it there, and go to the window. Nothing has changed outside, it's the same view. The phone keeps buzzing, and I know if I hold it for two minutes it's going to ring out. Then what? Is it going to ring again?

I press answer. There's static and I hear something else. The sound of rain and wind. Whoever this is, he or she is standing outside.

"Can't sleep?" the deep voice says. I close my eyes, clench my teeth and swallow. A warm, rich voice that at any other time I would enjoy listening to. Now it sends shivers down my spine.

"What do you want, Clive?"

He pauses again, and I wonder if he's enjoying this, watching me squirm. It would be right up his alley.

"What's rightfully mine."

"You don't know what you're talking about."

"Don't I? Apart from the obvious, I know you want to get back with me."

I bite on my lower lip. "Clive, you are deluded, and you need help."

"It's not me that needs help."

"Stop this!" I whisper. I leave the room and come out on the landing, closing the door gently behind me. I don't want to wake Molly up.

"Leave me alone, I mean it. I'm going to police tomorrow."

He laughs. "What police? The nearest town is thirty miles away."

"I'm going to call the detectives down in London and tell them you're here."

"You do that. When they realise you left without telling them, I'm sure they'll be thrilled."

We both pause for a while. This has gone on long enough. "I'm hanging up," I say.

"You need to do something." His voice suddenly has an edge to it. "Unless you want Molly to suffer."

I feel familiar emptiness inside me, and I lean backwards, feeling the cold stone wall.

He says, "You will call Jeremy and bring him up here. Make up some sob story. You're suicidal. I don't care what the story is. When he's up here, take him for a walk near the ridge where you saw me. All you have to do is push. The fall is more than a hundred feet. It will look like an accident."

My hands are claws, digging into my thighs. "I will never do that. Ever. You hear me? Ever."

He pauses for a while, and I can hear his breathing.

"Then get ready for what's coming your way." He hangs up with a click.

CHAPTER 53

I can feel the cold, hard slab of the rock as I lie over it. The sharp points press into my skin but right now I'm oblivious to the pain. There's a sharp fall, way down below in the distance obscured by mist and rain. Hills loom all around me. I look over and panic makes me scream. But only a guttural choke comes out of my throat. Molly is hanging over the ledge, her thin, tiny arm clutching a tree branch poking out. Her feet are dangling in the air. Wind swirls around her, making her little body shake.

"Help me, Mummy!" she cries.

I'm reaching down as far as I can without falling over myself. I shout at her to reach for me, but I know she can't.

"Mummy! Mummy!"

The wind is shaking my body. I hear her call again, right in my ear.

"Mummy!!"

My eyes fly open. Frigid, cold light is suffusing the whitewashed ceiling above my head. Momentarily, the dark night is banished. My daughter's coppery curls are dangling over my face, and then she comes into sharper focus.

"Mummy, will you wake up? You keep saying my name in your sleep!" she says crossly. I sit up in bed, flinging the covers away. I'm still fully clothed. I clutch my head and rub my eyes. What an awful dream that was. I give Molly a hug, and she doesn't mind. I can see that she's put on her clothes, brushed her hair in front of my dressing table and tied her hair back in a ponytail. She's such a disciplined little girl.

"Have you brushed your teeth?"

She rolls her eyes and does her best not to flop forward in mock desperation. "Yesssss! I'm hungry."

I get up and check the time. Its 9.30. Without going to the bathroom I take her downstairs and fix her a bowl of cereal. I leave an apricot jam croissant on a plate for her then go back upstairs to get ready. I can't help glancing at the shadows under my eyes. My freckles seem to have grown darker as well, on the bridge of my nose, spreading to my upper cheeks. I look tired, hungover.

Dad's not in the house so he must have started the day's work. He gets up at six like clockwork. I have a message from Suzy that makes me happy. She's on her way, and will hire a car from Skipton, the town nearest to us, and drive down. It makes sense, as the trains are slow and prone to delays.

I call Dad and he answers. He's at the fences, downhill, opening the gates for the cattle to roam in and out. I stroll into the kitchen holding the phone. Molly hasn't started eating her croissant.

She holds the croissant up and asks, "Can't Grandpa make me the scrambled eggs and bacon again?"

Her appetite seems to have got a boost in the hilly air. "I can make it if you like. Are you sure you want some?"

She nods vigorously, so I set about to cook her a fry-up. The phone is in my pocket, and apart from Suzy's messages, it hasn't buzzed. I am on tenterhooks, waiting for it to happen. Molly plays around downstairs while I finish cooking then I call for her. When she sits down I go upstairs and bring the gun back down. I put the gun in the cupboard and lock it. As the minutes and hours pass by I find myself walking around the house, checking that everything is locked. I go outside and check the perimeter. Leaving Molly locked inside, I take the gun out, and walk to the barn. The cavernous space inside is full of hay and there used to be a horse stable here in the past. Dad got rid of it, and now the place is used to store the tractors.

I'm scared out of my wits, but I hold the gun in front of me, finger on trigger. I switch all the lights on and have a look around inside. A staircase leads upstairs, and I walk up it slowly, gun pointing up. The butt feels solid against my shoulder, but the gun itself now feels heavier. What will I do if Clive suddenly appears in front of me?

Will I have the guts to shoot him? Only time will tell.

The loft space is empty apart from old building tools. I come down the stairs, lock the barn door and hurry back into the house. I call for Molly as soon as I get in the back door and she answers from the kitchen. Relief washes over me.

I need to call the police. I have the cards of Rockford and Ingram in my purse. I call Rockford first, and he answers. I explain to him where I am, and that Clive is here as well.

"Mrs Mansell." His tone is reproachful, and cold. "I did tell you that as a suspect in the murder of Timothy Burton-Smyth, your presence will be needed for more questioning."

"It's not like I've run off to Spain, is it? This is my family home, and I've only come back for a rest. And I'm calling you to inform you of where I am."

He sighs, and I sense he knows he's not going to win this battle. I am not under arrest and they can't stop me from doing anything.

He says, "I have no jurisdiction up there, you know that. If this man is still chasing, have you tried speaking to the local police?"

"The local police is twenty miles away, and even that's a sleepy little town. Can you not liaise with them, seeing that you know about my case already?"

"Well, that's the difficulty, Mrs Mansell. I know very little about your case. You said you didn't know who impersonated your husband, and then you said it was him. And no one has seen him as yet..."

"Apart from my husband. He was standing opposite our house, and Jeremy went out to meet him, but he'd already left."

"So there was no ID. It could have been anybody."

I talk to him for a bit longer, but am still unable to make him promise me that he will contact the homicide detectives in Skipton. Frustrated, I hang up.

The rain has relented for now, spent out with the storm. It's still cloudy and cold outside, but it's a relief to have some dry weather. Dad comes in from the back, Daisy at his heels.

"You ought to get outside," Dad says. "Stretch your feet. I'll be around, don't worry. Take Molly out for a walk."

I'm still not sure about venturing outside. Especially with Molly. I know it sounds silly, but I'm not in the mood. I want to wait till Suzy gets here. As I make some breakfast for Dad, I hear the sound of a car coming up the narrow road to the farmhouse. Speak of the Devil.

I look out from the front window, and the car is a 4x4, the type that Eva used to drive. I'm worried suddenly, and watch carefully as the vehicle pulls up into the drive. Suzy alights from it, and I sigh in relief. I wouldn't put it past Eva to brazenly pop over, still keeping up the best friend façade. Suzy is definitely my closest friend now, and she's here when I need her.

She pulls out her travel bag from the boot, and we hug, on the gravel driveway.

"Gosh, it's lovely down here," Suzy says. "If you had said, I would've come up with you in the beginning!"

"Wait till it's summer. That's when it's really nice. How's Margaret?"

"Very well. Putting on weight and chugging on her milk bottle night and day."

"I really can't thank you enough for coming up."

"Oh, nonsense. A break like this will do me the world of good. I can get a whole night's sleep! You know how much of a luxury that is right now. Let Paul stay up for a night for once." She giggles.

We go inside, and I introduce Dad to Suzy. I put the kettle on as they chat. Molly comes downstairs, and stands by me, watching Suzy.

After tea and chocolate cake, which is fresh and from the village, I take Suzy upstairs. I show her the room next to mine, which always served as the guest room.

Suzy flops down on the queen-sized bed, a happy expression on her face. "Great. Feels like I've come home, too."

CHAPTER 54

The browsing, low cloud banks are settling over the hills again. Its three pm but looks like seven. The sky has gone from lead-grey to a threatening dark, and I can smell rain in the air as I lean out of the back door. I tell Suzy now would be a good time to go for a walk. She agrees.

Molly comes with us, and Dad gives us a lift in the buggy. He stops near the animal pen and goes inside, while we go for a stroll. We are warmly wrapped up, with wellies on. As yet, it hasn't rained yet despite forecasts which is a miracle. But I can feel it on its way.

We walk down close to the forest near the edge of our grounds. The perimeter fence, a drystone wall, is not for another half a mile after, but we seldom go that far. I point out the ledge where I saw Clive. There's a valley between us, a deep pit of space that I find protective. But when someone is as determined as Clive, I have a feeling I won't be safe anywhere. The thought fills me with dread, and also anger.

After a while we head back. Dad is waiting for us, and Molly rides back with him in the front, much to her delight. It's time to think about dinner, but I feel restless again, and something is biting inside me. A sense of unease is bothering me again, like danger is creeping towards the farmhouse, and I can't do anything about it.

Part of me wants to relinquish my fear, and go out there. Gun in hand if need be, and I want to walk around, keeping guard. Clive can come and get me if he wants. But I know that's a foolish idea. The rain and cold will kill me with hypothermia long before Clive finds me. The elements must be a deterrent for him as well, and I wonder what his plans are.

I talk to Suzy and it helps. It stops me from looking out the window every five seconds, or getting up to look for the source of every unusual sound. Suzy looks in the fridge while I check the freezer in the pantry, and I discover the lamb casserole that I wanted to cook tonight won't be made as there's no lamb. In fact, we are down to a supply of essentials, and I should have gone shopping today.

"Why don't the two of us go to the nearest supermarket and get some stuff?" Suzy asks.

I smile. "The Tesco is in Skipton, thirty miles away. But there is a village store in Askrigg, about ten miles away."

Dad says, "If you're going, then don't wait about. The village store and butcher's shut at five."

"Come on," Suzy says. "We can drive down in my car."

"Come on, Molly," I say.

"No," Molly says. "I wanna stay here." She's got her Harry Potter book and the iPad out on the kitchen table.

Dad says, "Don't worry, lassie. She'll be fine with me. Won't you, Mollykins?"

I hesitate. I'm not happy with having Molly out of sight. I look at Dad, and I can tell that he sees the anxiety written plainly on my face.

"Look," Dad says. "I got a gun here, and I know how to use it. Anyone comes in here that shouldn't, there's no way he's getting out on two legs. I can promise you that."

Suzy says, "We won't be gone long, will we?"

Dad says, "An hour, at the very most."

Finally, I agree. Dad's right. He's tough as a grizzly bear, and I know he'll die protecting Molly, if need be.

I give Molly a hug, then Suzy and I get in the car. The 4x4 is spacious inside, and smells of the rubber seats and petrol. Suzy drives well, which is good considering she's always been a city driver. The rain arrives as we drive down, a drizzle that falls steadily.

It's half-four by the time we get there, and the village high street, a five-store parade of shops, is almost empty. Only the two pubs, one of them a hotel as well, look busy with the lights on. We do our shopping as quickly as we can, and then haul our stuff back into the car. I buy a joint of lamb, vegetables and various other essentials, and Suzy helps me carry them back to the car.

The rain has increased steadily, and it's no longer a drizzle. Our journey back takes longer, Suzy forced to drive slower. The fat drops pelt steadily against the windscreen and the wipers swing back and forth like the restlessness inside me.

We get to the farm finally, a glow of yellow amongst the inky-dark hills, shrouded in rain. The car crunches gravel, and stops near the front door. I look at the light on the porch, and my heart jumps in my mouth. A crazy dance starts in my head. The door is open. I locked it before I left. It's only open a crack, but I can tell. Without waiting for Suzy, I jump out and run down.

"Dad!" I shout as I nudge the door. It falls open on its well-oiled hinges. "Molly!"

The silence is deafening. The hallway is well lit. I can see the sideboard against one wall, the staircase, and the lounge door. Beyond it, the kitchen lights are on, and only part of it is visible. I race inside, my palpitations drumming against my skull.

The kitchen is empty. No Molly. I race into the pantry, its empty, too. I shriek Molly's name. Then I hear a groan. It's coming from the floor. Dad is sprawled out on the grey stones, a pool of blood collecting around his head. By his feet, rests Daisy. She seems fast asleep, and if she is breathing, it's very slowly.

I rush to Dad's side, and with an effort, turn him over. His face is turning pale white, and his eyes are closed. Blood smears my hands as I cradle his head.

"Dad!" My voice breaks. I hear a sound and see Suzy. She's just poked her head inside and her eyes widen.

"Oh my God. Where's Molly?"

"I don't know," I gasp. "Please have a look upstairs." In my heart, I know the answer.

"Dad," I shake him again. He doesn't open his eyes, but his lips mumble something. I get my ears close to his face.

"Get him…not far…" Dad croaks.

"Get who, Dad?" I ask but I know the answer. Dad stops mumbling and his body sags in my hands. I take his pulse at the neck – it's fast and thready. I put his head back down, then ring 999.

I give them my details, and it takes an impossibly long time. While speaking, I dash upstairs. Suzy is looking in Dad's room, and I search mine and every other. My heart shatters when I don't find Molly. I put the phone down and sink against the wall, sobs catching at my throat.

Then I think of what Dad just said. Not far. Which means this must've just happened. He's still around. My mind races. Clive couldn't take an eight-year-old out in the cold and rain and hope to get very far. He must have transport. He was waiting for this opportunity.

I make my mind up. The ambulance is on its way. I have to leave Dad and Daisy here. The paramedics will take Daisy as well, they assured me. I need to get my daughter back.

I tell Suzy, "He's close by, I know. I'll understand if you don't want to come, it's dangerous. Just give me your keys."

She shakes her head. "No, I'm coming with you. Is the ambulance on its way?"

I nod. Then I run downstairs, and get the gun out from the cupboard. Suzy and I race back to the car. She takes the gun from my hands.

"Leave it in the back seat. You might set it off by accident. No one's going to nick it from there."

She's right. I get in the car, and the headlights illuminate nothing but incessant raindrops. She starts to drive. I'm shivering in the cold, my hands are bone-white with patches of purple.

"Have you got a torch?" I say. I have one in my jacket pocket already but we need a backup.

"Not sure," she says. "Look in the glovebox."

I open the glovebox drawer. There's a mess of papers and stuff in there. I see a lighter, and I didn't know Suzy was a smoker.

Then I see a sheet of paper, and my heart stills. In the light inside the drawer, I can read it clearly.

It's a birth certificate with my daughter's name on it.

CHAPTER 55

It only lasts a few seconds, but time seems to slow down. Images and sounds collide in my brain, jerking my mind from side to side. Like a domino chain collapsing, a chain of thoughts trigger in my head.

Suzy lost her baby. She knew where I would be when I found baby Margaret abandoned in the park. The black Nissan Micra. The shape of the driver was always small, and I now realise it must have been a woman. Suzy knew about the dinner at Mandarin Oriental, because I borrowed the shoes from her. She also knew where, and when, I was going to meet Tim Burton-Smyth.

Nausea churns in my gut and my head feels dizzy. But I can't sit here, immobile. She has planned this, down to the last detail. Even my gun is in the back seat of this big car, far out of reach. Slowly, I close the dashboard drawer door. Then I lean back in the seat, watching the beams of the headlights illuminate only the pelting sheets of rain, and nothing else.

Another thing hits me. This is the car that sits in Suzy's drive. A Volvo four by four. This isn't a rental car, it's her own car. That explains why I found Molly's birth certificate in the glove compartment.

"Find anything?" Suzy asks. She doesn't turn to look at me, but I do. Her face is lit up in a green and orange glow, making it look unnatural. Her nose is sharper in the light, and her cheekbones seem to jut out. All of a sudden, her face seems hard and craggy.

"No," I say.

My mind is a whirlpool. She's got me in the car, so the plan must be to drive me to Clive. Molly must be there as well. She's their bargaining chip. They'll use her to get me to kill Jeremy.

My only priority is to get Molly safe. Suzy knows where she is, or she wouldn't be driving down this country road so confidently. If she can get me there, should I just let her? But what if she's taking me somewhere else, where Clive is waiting for me alone?

I reject that idea. They need me to see Molly, and I need to know for certain that they have her. That's their whole game plan. There's no point in me just seeing Clive. I've already said I'm not doing what Clive proposed, so they want to show me that Molly is their captive. Even when I think of Molly being held somewhere, rage, sorrow and panic claw at my throat, scratch at my heart.

I close my eyes and try to check my breathing. My fingers curl around something metallic. My phone. I can send a message to Rockford. My phone GPS is on, after I deleted that Third Party tracker. If Rockford gets, and acts on the message, I have a faint hope of getting out of this alive with my daughter.

I sneak a look towards Suzy, but her eyes are fixed on the road. I bend my left elbow slightly, and take the phone half out of the pocket. I can see the screen, just. I tap on messages, not keeping my face down for more than a few seconds at a time. I see Rockford's name and tap on it.

Using my thumb, and trying to keep my face as straight as possible, I type: *SOS. IN DANGER. HELP*

I'm about to press send when the car lurches suddenly and my fingers slip. I don't know if I pressed the right button, and the phone has slipped down my pocket again. I don't know why Suzy suddenly swerved but it becomes clear with her next question.

"What are you doing?" This time, she looks over at me, and her eyes are black, like a shark's.

"I thought there was something pressing on me," I say lamely. She's leaning forward now, white knuckles clutching the steering wheel tightly.

"Where are we going?" I ask. I know we have gone past old Johnson's deserted farm by now. The pitch-black road is swallowed up in the darkness ahead. A thin white line separates one lane from another. I haven't seen a single car from the opposite lane so far.

In reply, I see a sick grin come across Suzy's lips, then her teeth bare. It's a feral, primitive snarl and it makes my blood go cold. In my right pocket, I can feel the torchlight. I can whip it out and hit Suzy on the head with it. But if she is driving me to where Molly is, that would be mistake.

I repeat my question. "Where are we going?"

She smiles in that way again and I decide to put my foot down. I unbuckle my seat belt and an alarm starts to ping. I jerk the door handle but she's locked it. I unwind the window and cold air blasts into my face.

"Tell me or I'll throw myself out of the car."

"Put the window back up," Suzy says calmly. The alarm continues to ping. I meant what I said. My feet are coiled, and I have a hand on the window, ready to vault over. We are going past a field, and I can roll over on the wet grass. She'll have to stop the car and come for me, which gives me an advantage in the darkness.

"Do you want to see Molly alive?" Suzy says with that infuriating calmness. Her words are hard to hear in the wind, but they chill my bones to numbness. My hand comes off the window, and I slowly raise the glass up.

"Where is my daughter? What have you done with her?!" I scream.

"Your daughter?" Suzy laughs. It's an evil, cackling sound. Her voice has an accent now, and I realise she's tried to hide it in the past. But her words sink into the pit of my stomach, sending barbs of poison inside me.

I can barely speak, but somehow the words creep out. "What do you mean?"

"She's not your daughter, Emma. You know that very well."

Her words sting. The poison is released inside me, flooding my blood with venom. "She is my daughter. What do you know?"

CHAPTER 56

Suzy doesn't reply. I keep staring at her face, maniacal in the artificial light. The car swerves again, at speed, and I am thrust against the side of the car. My back rattles the door, and I bounce back up to watch the road. A log outhouse flashes past, and the black fields start again. But up ahead, I can now see a light. The wooden slats of a fence on the sides of the road are lit up by the headlights. We have taken a sharp left and are driving uphill. The place seems familiar, but I can't put my finger on it. The rain is now a deluge, and the wipers are struggling to keep up with the cascading water.

Suzy drives up to the light source. As we get clearer, I see it's a log cabin, with a light on inside. When she parks, the door opens and a figure steps out. It's Clive, and he's holding a shotgun in his hand. He steps out into the rain, boots splashing in the mud. Thunder flickers above, fracturing the sky in a fissure of white light. Momentarily, it shows Clive's face, a satisfied smirk on his face, pointing the gun straight at me.

"Open the door, you bitch," Suzy snarls at me. I look at her, fuming. Rage is boiling inside me, and I want to scratch her face to shreds. But my priority now is to see Molly.

I step out, and the rain splatters over my face and head. I pull my hoodie up, and lift my hands in surrender.

"This way!" shouts Clive, to make his voice heard above the downpour.

They fall in behind me as I climb the steps up to the porch of the log cabin. The door is open, and it creaks as I enter. Molly is inside, and my heart twists when I see her tied to a chair.

"Mummy!"

Before I can reach for her, a strong pair of hands grab me from behind and throw me on the floor. When I look up, it's at the muzzle of a double-barrelled gun.

"Get up, slowly," Clive says. He's standing between me and Molly, with

Suzy to his side. Suzy's face is a mask of hatred. She goes to move towards me, but Clive holds her back.

"Let her go," I whisper. "For God's sake, don't hurt her."

"Until you do what I want, she stays here." He takes out a phone and throws it to me. I manage to catch it.

"It has Jeremy's number on it. Call him. Tell him you need to see him up here, right now."

I glance at the phone, then at Clive. I can only see Molly partially, but she is sobbing, and it breaks my heart. I know Jeremy will come if I call him. My eyes close for a few seconds, then open. How can I do this?

"Don't wait for too long," Clive sneers. "Or we can start on her." He takes a step backwards.

"No," I say. I need to do something, play for time. Did my text to Rockford go through?

"How did the two of you get together on this?" I ask.

Suzy cackles again. "Clive and I have always been together. Yes, he cheated on you with Eva. But you never even knew me. I was his wife, while women like Eva and you were his victims."

"Victims?"

"He got money out of you, didn't he?"

My eyes shift from Clive to Suzy. Both of them have malevolent sneers on their faces. So this is what Clive did. A conman who ripped off gullible women. Only with me, he ripped off a lot more than just my bank balance.

"Let my daughter go," I say.

"You know she's not yours." Suzy's eyes are blazing, and she steps forward. "Stop lying."

My mind goes blank for a while, then memories rage upon it like raindrops on a windscreen.

CHAPTER 57

Eight years ago

I followed Clive to the house in Mitcham, where he had taken his suitcase full of drugs. I had seen the dealers go in, then come out with small packets bulging in their pockets. When Clive left, closing the door behind him, I sneaked in by opening one of the windows at the back.

The place was a pigsty, carpets torn, rubbish bins overflowing, walls covered in graffiti.

I found the empty suitcase in one corner of a bedroom. The mattress was on the floor, and used condoms and needles littered the place. The corridor was dark, and I went into the kitchen. Mice ran around my feet, gnawing at the decomposing food on the floor. Revolted, I turned to leave. When I was at the window, to crawl out into the disused garden, I heard a sound. I froze. I heard it again.

A baby's cry.

It was soft, weak, like the little voice had hardly any strength in it.

My heart hammered against ribs. Mouth dry, I retraced my steps into the hallway. The faint cries were coming from the room with the closed door, the only door I hadn't opened in this ground-floor flat. I opened it and my hand fumbled for a light switch. When the yellow bulb came on, I gasped in shock. On a white rug, a baby lay on the floor. Its skin was wrinkled, pink, mottled. The umbilical cord had been cut, but was still attached to her. Dried blood pooled around her feet. I knelt by her. Her eyes were screwed shut, and the little mouth was opening and shutting. The fists were balled, tiny knuckles of rage shaking in the air.

Something broke and gave way inside me. Tears blurred my eyes and I wiped them away quickly.

"Shh," I whispered, and lifted up her wet body, pressing her against me gently to give her some warmth. Her breathing was fast and ragged. The rug looked clean apart from the blood so I swaddled her in it. Her snub nose rested against the nape of my neck, and the fists tucked under my chin.

Like she belonged there.

I looked around the room. Apart from some more blood on the floor, it was empty. No memento for the discarded baby. What sort of mother would leave a newborn like this? I couldn't leave the baby here. If I did, she would die, I knew that for certain.

In case the mother came back, I rummaged around till I found a piece of paper in the bedroom. I had a pen in my pocket and I scribbled out a note saying which hospital I had taken the baby to. I didn't sign my name. If the mother did come back, then she would find the note.

I managed to crawl out the window with the baby held tightly against me. A passing cab took pity on me and stopped. I directed him to the hospital.

A nurse from Accident and Emergency took us up immediately to Paediatrics. They put her in a heated plastic cot that looked like an incubator. A mask was strapped to her face, and wires were stuck with tape onto her tiny fingers. I could barely breathe as I watched.

She cried when her heel was pricked for a blood test. I was at her side instantly, stroking her. Another nurse made her a bottle-feed, and gave it to me.

"You haven't set a feeding routine yet, have you?" she asked me.

"Sorry?" I asked.

"She's not more than a day old. Have you started breastfeeding, or are you expressing into a bottle?"

"Bottle," I said after a moment's thought. I took the bottle from her. The nurse lifted the green mask, and I tried to feed her. It was amazing when her little mouth opened and she sucked the teat into her mouth. My hand shook as she gulped the milk down greedily. There wasn't much in it, and she finished it quickly. I removed the teat, but she didn't want to let it go.

"She wants more," I told the nurse.

She shook her head. "No. She's suffering from hypothermia. She needs small feeds regularly." She fixed with a steely gaze. "How did baby get so cold?"

My mouth ran dry. "I didn't have money to pay for the heating. It's sorted now, but the last two days have been bad. I'm a single mum."

"Are you coping?"

I nodded, and looked away, feeling the nurse's eyes on me.

Eventually, the doctor who had taken the blood test came back. He had a grave look on his face.

"Her arterial blood gases show hypoxia. She needs oxygen, and warmth." He pointed to the mask, from which a tube sneaked into a yellow hole in the wall. "The oxygen will be for 24 hours at least. We will check her blood gases every two hours tonight. If all is well, she can go home in two days."

"Thank you," I said, meaning it.

"What's her name?"

I looked at the doctor blankly. "What?"

"Have you given her a name? Or is it still Baby?"

Colour rose to my cheeks. What should I say? To distract myself, I put my hand over hers. What happened next was almost magical. Her tiny hand opened, and the little fist closed over my index finger. It was an incredible warm, snug feeling, like she hadn't just held my finger, but wrapped her life around mine.

Someone had left her to die. I had saved her.

Why shouldn't she have my name?

"Molly," I whispered. "Molly Dixon."

The doctor went over to a screen and tapped on the keyboard. "She wasn't born at this hospital."

"No," I heard myself saying. "She was a home birth."

"Ah." The nurse and doctor exchanged a glance, and I noticed a tension leave their bodies. I understood. Home births without midwives could lead to problems with the delivery and babies.

We stayed in the hospital for two days. Molly Dixon opened her eyes on the second day, and looked at me with wonder. I tickled her chin. She opened her mouth, thinking I was about to feed her.

After two days, we left the hospital, and I didn't go back to the miserable flat that I had shared with Clive. I got Dad to send me some money, and I took a cab straight to King's Cross Station, with a one-way ticket to Skipton, North Yorkshire.

I never heard from the biological mother.

CHAPTER 58

Present day

Suzy is staring at me with daggers in her eyes. "You're lying!" she shouts.

"No," I shout back, and grit my teeth. "She *is* my daughter."

"And what about the woman who gave birth to her?" Suzy seethes.

"How do you…?" I stop, staring at her. At the rage in her eyes. I feel dizzy, and breath leaves my chest like it's been hit by a hammer.

It can't be. Can it?

We stare at each other, Clive and Molly forgotten for a while. I see anger in her eyes but also something else. I can't read it. Regret perhaps. Or maybe even gratitude. I don't know. It flits across her face then vanishes.

"Yes," Suzy whispers. "She's mine. I gave birth to her."

The words are like a slap to my face. "You're lying."

She says, "That's why I tracked you down. Got Clive to get back on you. Luckily, your husband started making some money, and we could kill two birds with one stone. I get my daughter back, and we take your money, for the second time."

I frown at her. "You have no proof. Even if you did, are you serious? You can't just waltz back into Molly's life now, after all these years." I glance at Clive who's standing rock still, gun trained on me.

"Besides, what sort of a life are you two going to give her? She's going to end up in social care when you two get arrested after this."

Clive says, "After this we are off. Once we have Jeremy's money, you won't even hear from us again."

"Or from Molly," Suzy whispers.

"Mummy, what's going on?" Molly cries out from behind them.

"Nothing, darling, just hold on." My voice trembles as I speak.

"Enough talk," Clive says. "Either you make the phone call now or else…"

Holding the gun at me with one hand, he pulls out a knife from his trousers. He walked behind Molly, and puts the knife beside her right ear.

"Are you ready?" Clive says.

I stare at him, panic suffocating me. "She's your own daughter!" I scream.

"How do I know that?" Clive scoffs. I note the frown that spreads across Suzy's face when he says the words.

I advance towards him, but he thrusts the gun towards me, and I stop. I have made some ground, however. I calculate my chances, breathing heavily. Clive is holding a rifle that's heavy. Although he's strong, his aim will be awry. I could shuffle to the side and launch myself at him. I can see the gun barrel shaking in his hand.

Suzy says to Clive, "We weren't going to do this." They hold each other's eyes and a scowl deepens on Clive's face.

He says, "It's the only way. You know it."

"No," says Suzy, stepping towards him. "This was always going to be a threat. We can't harm the girl." She points a finger at me. "Kill her if you have to. But don't harm the girl."

Suzy looks at Molly, who's terrified, and her fear-filled eyes are moving from me to Suzy.

"Don't be scared, darling," I call out. "It's alright."

To Clive I say, "Move the knife away." He doesn't. It's a stand-off. Suzy and I on one side, and Clive on the other.

"Make the call," Clive says. "Then I don't have to do this." He rests the sharp edge of the knife above the corner of Molly's right ear. My heart is my mouth, beating so loud I can't breathe.

"No," I whisper. Clive increases pressure and from Molly's eyes I can see she feels the pain.

Suzy has seen it, too, and she moves forward. "Stop it, Clive," she snarls.

He moves the gun towards Suzy. "You're going to get it as well, you bitch," he shouts.

In that instant, when the gun has moved away from me, I launch myself towards Clive. I grab the gun, and manage to kick the chair to one side. Molly screams and she falls over. The gun goes off with a blast.

Then Clive and I are wrestling on the floor, grappling for the gun. It goes off again, and I hear a grunt. I can't look up, because the knife flashes in the light and I feel a sharp sting of pain as it pierces the skin on my shoulder.

I feel the warm trickle of blood down my arm. I shout, and bite on the hand that holds the knife. I pierce flesh and taste blood before he shouts and lets go. I kick him below the belt as I pull on the gun. It comes off in my hand. Clive is scrambling up and I shoot as best I can, semi-prone on the floor. The bullets take a chunk off the ceiling, then Clive has opened the door and crashed outside. I hear him running down the steps, and into the night.

Beside me, Molly is still tied to the chair. She's awake, thank goodness. I pull and strain at the ropes, reaching for the knife that Clive has left. Blood pours in a steady trickle down my left arm, dampening the hand, flowing onto the rope. After a while the final knot gives way. I unwind the rope from around her body and she hugs me so hard I almost topple over. We're both crying, talking, babbling in relief at the same time.

My eyes fall on the gun at my feet, and then at the puddle of blood that is creeping towards it. I let go of Molly and tell her to sit down in the corner with the chair in front of her. Holding the gun, I crawl towards Suzy.

She is lying on her back, not moving. There are two gunshot wounds on her body. One in the belly, and the other in the chest. Blood is seeping out freely from both. She opens her mouth, but only a froth bubble of blood comes out. Suzy is dying. I put the gun down, and unzip her jacket. Her chest is a mess. White fragments of fractured ribs are sticking up through her vest. The abdomen wound is deep and blood is welling out of it, unstoppable. Her face is deathly white. Her eyes flutter, and lips move again.

She's trying to tell me something. I keep a wary look at her hands, but kneel down closer to her lips.

"Th…thank you." She pauses for a while, then speaks again. "For looking after my daughter."

I ask her the question that has been on my mind for eight years. "Why did you leave her?"

Her lips move in silence for a while. I only hear one word. "Drugs…."

Then the words stop, and her jaw slacks. Her eyes become wide, staring, pupils dilated. Her chest stops rising and falling. Suzy's gone.

I close her eyes, and stare at her face in silence for a few seconds. I will never know what went on in that troubled, twisted heart of hers, but tonight, for a few seconds, she was on my side. Those few seconds might yet make all the difference.

Might, not will.

I pick up the gun and rack the slide. I can feel Molly get up and come to my side. The magazine of this rifle is small, and I count four more rounds in it. It's an old weapon. I kneel by Molly.

"Darling, can you stay here till I get back?"

"I want to come with you."

I give her my phone and show her Rockford's number. "Call this man and tell him my name, and that you are in trouble. Tell him you are near our farm, about fifteen miles north-west."

I moved Molly to one corner, and turn off the light before I open the door. Lightning flashes outside, and I see the car. Further up, it's the hills, with a path snaking up into the woods covering them.

I open the back door of the car. My rifle is gone. That means Clive has it. My blood turns to ice. He could be around anywhere.

I slam the door shut, and a bullet whistles in, shattering the glass of the window next to my face.

CHAPTER 59

I fall, and scramble under the car as more bullets hit it. I come out on the other side, and crouch over the bonnet. I can't see anything in the pitch black dark. He makes the mistake of firing again, and I see where the flash came from. He's closer than I thought. But this bullet hits the front tyre, and it explodes. He's hitting them deliberately, to make sure I can't escape.

I fire back, once only, as I have three rounds left now. Then I see him, a shadow that rises out of the wet darkness. My eyes are now more used to the dark, and I fire without hesitation. He screams, and falls over. I hear a slithering sound as he tries to move down the grass.

I have to follow. I cannot let him live. He will kill Molly if I don't get him first. I stay low and run. I go past a sign, and a flash of memory jolts me. This used to be the Netherton farm. He had two sons who went to the same school as me, and both of them left the Dales with jobs in the cities. The old man died here, in similar fashion to Mr Johnson up the road.

I came to this farm as a child. I know it well. I move forward, straining my eyes and ears. I feel, more than see, some bushes move to my right. Then Clive appears, running, dragging his left leg. I fire and miss. He's vanished again, but I know the direction in which he's headed. Further up the hill.

I set off in pursuit. My left arm feels weak from the loss of blood and the pain is intensifying. Clive moves quickly for a man with a leg wound. The trees become denser as the slope gets steeper. There's a sudden bang, and bark spits and breaks a few inches away from my face. I turn and slide down to the ground.

I give him five seconds, then I move again. I can't let him get too close, and whatever I do, I can't let him go downhill, back towards the cabin and Molly.

I climb, slipping on the rain-slickened ground. My fingers dig into the mud and I haul myself back up. The cold is worse now, too, and I am only wearing my cardigan, having left my coat wrapped around Molly. I can feel the cold seeping into my bones, making me shiver.

A rumble sounds overhead, and a loud bolt of thunder cracks across the sky. The boom is deafening and the lightning couldn't have been far away. In that flash, I see him again, a shadow slipping between the trees. Slipping and sliding, I climb up, chasing.

I get closer to where he was, and go flat on the ground, waiting. He stands up, and I fire. He's about ten feet away, and I hope I don't miss. The trigger catches, and the round doesn't come out. I press the trigger again, but the magazine is soaked in the rain. The gun is useless.

I can see Clive looking around. I freeze. But his eyes move downward, and fall on me. I'm not moving, hoping he will miss me, my shadow congealed with the darkness. Then I hear leaves move, and steps coming towards me.

I hold my breath.

The steps come closer. Desperately trying to move as little as possible, I turn the gun around, holding it like a club by the barrel.

The steps are slower, more assured. Like he's crouching because he's seen something.

"Cupcake, I can see you. Just stand up like a good girl."

I clench my teeth. He's bluffing. I've barely moved, and it's too dark. The steps get closer and now he's within touching distance. I can feel the heat of his body, hear the heavy breathing.

I can smell the bastard.

He rakes the ground with the barrel of the gun. It's a clever move. The gun will still fire, and he'll catch me as well. I need to do something or it's all over.

I roll over to my left and leap to my feet in a crouch. He sees me, but he's too late. He was bluffing, and I take him by surprise. I'm holding the gun barrel and I swing it like a tennis racquet, hitting his lower leg. He lets out a howl of anguish; I must've hit the injured one. I move forward to hit him again but I see the gun coming up. He presses the trigger, and a blast of lead fires past my back, ripping into a tree.

I hurl myself into the undergrowth, pulling on twigs, branches to pull myself up the slope. I can hear him cursing. I keep moving up, knowing he's coming after me. Suddenly, I stop.

I can hear the rain all around me, and Clive below. But there is another sound rising above all else.

The sound of running water.

CHAPTER 60

I move towards the sound. It gets louder as I get closer. But you won't hear it unless you stop and listen. Even then, you might not distinguish it from the steady patter of rain, and other sounds of the night.

I can because when we were young and played in the hills, we were wary of the potholes and deep caves that could suddenly open up under our feet. The Yorkshire Dales are infamous for their hidden caves, and a deep one is as good as a death trap.

I know the Netherton farm is close to the Inglesby hill, and the River Gimble runs through it. But there is also a network of underground caves in these limestone hills. The river stops suddenly, and literally falls into the hole.

With some effort, I need to find that hole. The sound is louder ahead of me now. I can't hear Clive anymore, which worries me. The moon plays hide-and-seek with clouds, and I see it shine on the water briefly. I slide down towards it, and start moving along the bank.

There's a boom behind me, and bark comes off a tree next to me. He's found me. I move forward, and now the sound of the rushing water dims, becomes a different sound wave. Suddenly, it sounds like water dripping down a long tunnel. Again, it's a sound that only a trained ear can hear.

I protect myself behind a tree and shout to him. "Are you afraid to face me, Clive? What sort of a man are you?"

I don't hear his reply. I step off the ground into the freezing water. The current tugs at me and I have to be strong. If I get pulled under here, then I'll fall hundreds of feet into the steep drop below us.

The river isn't wide. The water comes up to almost my waist, and panic hits me as a wave of rain-swollen water hits me on the chest. The spray spatters into my face and I stumble and almost fall over. I grit my teeth and straighten myself. Struggling, heaving, somehow I pull myself to the other side. I slump on the muddy bank, falling on my chest. I don't care that I'm soaked to the bone. Every strand of hair is sticking to my skull. I hear feet splashing on water behind me.

I turn, and see Clive stepping out into the water. He's taller, and the water comes up to his knees. He is walking across far quicker than me.

There's no strength left in my limbs. Somehow, I plant my palms flat on the ground and heave myself up. I run to my right, then stop. I wave my hands like a windmill, making myself visible.

"Hey, Clive. I'm here!" I holler at him. He is a shadow in the darkness, but I see him turn. He sees me and lifts the gun to his shoulder. I dive for the ground and the bullet passes over my head. I move to the right again, staying low this time. Branches scratch my face, pull at my hair. After ten yards, the sound of the river is almost gone. All I can hear is a gurgle, and the distant sound of it going underground like falling off a subterranean cliff.

"Clive, you're shit," I scream at him. I stand up again. He's swivelling around, jerking the gun from side to side.

"Over here," I say. He sees me. I count his steps. One, two…

He lifts the gun to his shoulders. I stand still, caught between the fear of death, and witnessing the death of my tormentor.

…three steps, and the barrel is now facing me, ten yards away. Then suddenly he lurches forward, like his foot's caught in a trap. The riverbed is like a sieve where Clive is standing. A latticework of holes big enough to swallow up a man.

I hear him scream one last time, then the sound is a long, drawn-out sound, like he's vanishing down a hole. Which he is. There's nothing where Clive was once standing. I get closer to the water, and I can now see the rifle floating towards the bank.

Relief floods over me. Clive is gone, thank God. I can now get my daughter, and get the hell out of here. I fall to my knees, panting. The rifle is close to me now, and I reach out for it. It's just out of reach, and I have to stretch. My fingers close around the middle section of the gun.

With a blood-curdling scream, Clive rears out of the water, his right hand grabbing my throat.

CHAPTER 61

Water is running off his face, and his eyes are wild, alive. His claw-like fingers scratch the skin of my throat but his hands slip. But he grips the front of my vest. With a cry, I fall down. My chest hits the ground, smashing air out of my lungs. I see stars before my eyes and the pain makes my vision dim. He's pulling me into the water, keeping steady pressure on me.

I bring my leg around, and kick him in the chest with all my might. I'm wearing heavy walking shoes, and the kick hurts him, weakening his grip. But he doesn't let go. How did he come back up? He must've got lucky, and stepped between the holes, which is a miracle. The scream might have been to fool me.

My right hand is on the rifle, and I pull it out of the water, even as I feel the brackish river water hit my face. I kick and scream, thrashing my legs against him. I know what will happen if we go into the river here. Clive might have survived once, but he won't do it a second time. Both of us will fall to a dark and rocky death.

The ferocity of my kicking takes him by surprise. His grip is loosened enough in the muddy slime for me to bring the rifle to bear. I have him at point-blank range, barrel pressing against his ribs.

I'm up to waist-level in the water, but close to the bank. I'm not going in any further. Clive feels the barrel against his ribs and as if he know what's coming next, he stops pulling me.

No goodbyes. No swearing. I press the trigger and the waterproof magazine of my father's Remington fires the round. The boom resonates deep inside Clive's chest and he is pushed back like he's falling off a cliff. I scramble up to the bank, and point the gun at him again.

I want to fire but I don't have to. I see Clive trying to stand but he falls. He slips back down further into the water, and I watch him disappear as he's sucked underneath. Only bubbles break the surface where he vanished.

Then they, too, are gone.

CHAPTER 62

My teeth are chattering as I stumble down the hill, rifle in hand. My left arm feels useless, I can't even lift it up. I have left the river behind, and the gun is strapped to my back now. It feels like a dead weight. I lurch from tree to tree. Every drop of cold rain seems to cut through my skin, freezing my blood further. In the dim distance, the cabin finally comes into view as an outline. I fall to my knees. Nausea lurches in my intestines and I vomit up the river water I swallowed. Mucus trailing from my mouth, I stand up. Somehow, I put one foot in front of the other. I fall again, and slide down in the mud. Sliding is easier, and I move a long way down. Near the bottom of the slope, I move. But I don't have the strength to stand up. I crawl the last hundred yards.

Finally, I get to the cabin just as lightning illuminates it. The car is still there, one back window smashed. I crawl up the stairs on my hands and feet. I fall across the door as my shoulders get inside.

"Molly," I cry weakly.

Immediately she responds. Her voice is quiet and scared. "Mummy?"

"Yes, it's me. Come and help, sweetheart."

I hear her scrambling to her feet. I push myself up, and crawl inside, shutting the door. At long last, there is some relief from the wind and rain.

"Mummy, you're wet," Molly says.

"I know, honey. Get me the jacket." She obeys, and I wrap the jacket around me. Then Molly hugs me, and her warmth breathes life into my wrecked bones.

"I rang the policeman," she says in my ear after a while. She's not moved.

My eyes open. "And?"

"I told the man what you asked me to. He said he's going to send help."

"Good," I sigh.

Unless another miracle happens, Clive is dead. I saw him die this time, and there's no way he's coming back. Suzy's dead body lies in front of me. This room smells of death. But I don't care. My daughter is alive and in my arms. She's always been mine, just after the day she was born. And she always will be.

As if in recognition of what I am thinking, she holds me tighter. We stay like that, so tightly wrapped in each other that we are one body, till I hear the sirens in the distance.

*****

Paramedics stream in and out of the log cabin. The wood slats shake, and the light above me is blinding. Molly has been separated from me gently, and is covered in the same shiny foil cloak that is now wrapped around me. It looks silly, but I have to say it's making me feel warmer.

A nurse looms over me, and asks to see my arm. She has seen the blood crusting on my left hand. I cry out in pain as her fingers prod and feel the wound.

"Flesh wound only," she murmurs. "You're lucky. No harm to the joint."

"Lucky me," I say through gritted teeth.

There's a uniformed policeman with a cap on who settles himself on his haunches before me. His name badge says something but I'm too tired to read it.

He takes off his cap and says, "Are you Emma Dixon?"

I nod in silence. He holds up a phone in front of me. I can see the face of an Afro-Caribbean man in a suit, and after a while I realise it's Rockford. A blonde woman with short hair and an almost triangular face appears next to him. It's Ingram. They both look at me thoughtfully. It's a video link with the London Met, I guess.

"How you holding up, Emma?" Rockford asks.

"Do you believe me now, Detectives?"

Rockford grins, even Ingram's stony lips quirk a fraction. He says, "That's been your question for us all along, hasn't it?"

"Well, do you?"

He pauses for a while in that way of his. Like he still has to think. "Yes I do. And just so you know, we traced transfers from your bank account ten years ago. The money you deposited in Clive Connery's account actually belongs to a man called Charles Red Knapp. He's a serial swindler, with multiple arrests for armed robbery and violence. Now he has a murder charge to add to the list."

I sag backwards, feeling the hard wood act as support. It's a relief to know the truth about Clive, finally. Not that my brain can process much. But there's one thing I need to know without delay.

"My father," I say weakly. "What happened to him?"

The policeman in front of me replies. "He's OK. Took a heavy blunt trauma to the back of his head. He needs scalp stitches, and is admitted at the hospital. But he's stable."

Molly asks, "Is Grandpa alright?"

It strikes me that I haven't asked Molly what happened after I left. It can wait, I think.

"He's fine, darling," I say, as the nurse pulls out a syringe.

"This will hurt just a little," she says kindly.

CHAPTER 63

Sunlight is streaming in through the tall, open windows, and it's a warm day for February. Well, it is almost the end of February I think. Easter is only four weeks away. The rain clouds have grumbled for days, and finally gone. The sky is a brushed, scrubbed blue, and the few white clouds on it are plumed sailboats.

Dad is propped up on the bed. His head is still bandaged, and he had to have a clot evacuated from his skull, but he managed alright in the end. Molly is sitting up on the bed, trying to read the newspaper to him. He's listening with a half-smile on his lips, and when he looks at me, I reciprocate.

For once, the sunlight seems to melt away the tension and anxiety of the last few days. Even Daisy is better. She was fed some meat that had a crushed diazepam pill in it, according to the vet. That knocked her out for several hours.

Suzy's body has been taken down to East London, where her family lives. Clive Connery, or Charles Red Knapp, whoever he was, was found at the bottom of the caves. He was stuck on the rocks, and dead for more than twelve hours when his heavily broken remains were discovered.

After all this, having to go back to London for Molly's school seems almost boring. But I want boring. I want dull and everyday life. For her sake, if not mine. I worry about the effect all of this will have on her. Someday soon, I'll have to ask her if she understands everything that happened. I have a feeling she'll take it well.

Eva rang several more times, and I spoke to her. I've forgiven her, but I'm not sure if we can be close friends again. Joanne has been calling as well, and in some ways, I'm looking forward to getting to know her better.

There's a knock on the door, and a nurse pokes her head in. "There's a man from London to see you. Name's Jeremy Mansell."

Jeremy and I have spoken, and he is aware of everything. But I didn't expect him to come up. Surprised, I walk out into the visitors' area. Jeremy is sitting in one of the green plastic chairs, and he's holding a bouquet of flowers. He stands up slowly when he sees me.

I walk closer to him. We look for meaning in each other's eyes, and what I see is sympathy and concern. I smile to reassure him.

Jeremy says, "Are you...?"

"Yes," I say firmly. "Both Molly and I are fine. So is Dad."

He hands me the flowers. They smell of summer and promises. He also has a box of chocolates.

"For Molly," he says with a grin. Then his face becomes serious. He coughs into his hand, then says, "While you were here and I was, you know, on my own." He stops, as if he lost his strand of thought. He looks at me. "I thought to myself. A lot, I mean. And I realised, even if we can't have children, what we have is worth keeping."

We stare at each other, our eyes probing.

"Shall we sit down?" he says. I'm glad to.

"Thing is." He looks at me, lost for words. He frowns, then makes his mind up. "I love you, and, well, I missed you too much. And Molly."

Oh dear. I am welling up, and I pinch my fingers, cross my toes, but can't stop my nose from getting red. Jeremy puts his warm hand on mine.

"I know how I acted. I'm sorry. Do forgive me."

I nod, not able to speak. I take out some tissue and sniff into it.

"Jeremy!" It's Molly, and she sprints out of the room, heading for us. Jeremy stands up, grabs her up in his arms and spins her around. I laugh, and suddenly we are together again, our bonds of love not tarnished by tainted blood, but forged in fire and adversity.

Molly stays on Jeremy's arm, and he hugs me with the other. Together, we walk towards the room where Dad is resting.

THE END

AUTHOR'S NOTE

If you enjoyed this book, would you mind leaving a review? Reviews are how new readers take a chance on a book. It will take two minutes of your time, but mean the world to me.

Mick's next psychological thriller, Don't Say It, a twisty, thrilling tale about a husband who might be a serial killer, is coming next. Watch out!

You can get advance review copies by joining my email list here:
https://www.subscribepage.com/o9e8m0
or getting in touch with me on Facebook at
https://www.facebook.com/WriterMickBose/

THANK YOU SO MUCH!